Thomas Wemyss Reid

A Memoir of John Deakin Heaton, M. D.

Thomas Wemyss Reid

A Memoir of John Deakin Heaton, M. D.

ISBN/EAN: 9783337804329

Printed in Europe, USA, Canada, Australia, Japan

Cover: Foto ©Raphael Reischuk / pixelio.de

More available books at **www.hansebooks.com**

A MEMOIR

OF

JOHN DEAKIN HEATON, M.D.

OF LEEDS

EDITED BY

T. WEMYSS REID

LONDON

LONGMANS, GREEN, AND CO.

1883

CONTENTS.

MEMOIR

OF

JOHN DEAKIN HEATON, M.D.

CHAPTER I.

INTRODUCTION.

Of the making of books there is no end, and nothing
is more certain than that a justification is needed for
each successive volume that issues from the press.
Such a justification is certain to be demanded in the
present instance. Many doubtless will ask what there
can have been in the life of a medical practitioner in
a provincial town to call for a permanent record in
the shape of a biography. Dr. Heaton, to the story
of whose life the following pages are devoted, never
achieved what the world calls fame. Though he
gained something more than respectable rank in his
profession, he made no pretensions to eminence as
a man of science. Nor did he seek distinction
in politics, in literature, or in fashionable society.
Throughout his life he was content with the lot in

which Providence had placed him, and with the faithful discharge of the duties—not always light or pleasant—which appertained to that lot. 'The daily round, the common task,' as it will be depicted in the course of this narrative, will not be found to have been an exciting or eventful one, and there will be some who will look upon it as altogether unworthy of being recorded in print. But there must be others who will see it in a different light. Dr. Heaton's life is not only the representative life of hundreds of medical men who, well fitted to achieve eminence in the highest works of their profession, have been bound by fate to the dull routine of a provincial practice. Even if this were all that could be said of the career the salient incidents of which are related in these pages, the story ought not to be an uninteresting one ; for, after all, the people of the provinces are more numerous than those of the metropolis, and, sober and monotonous as their lives may seem to those who live amid the bustle and gaiety of a capital, they are nevertheless not devoid of that interest which attaches to all human life, and, above all, to all honest human effort. Dr. Heaton, however, was not the mere physician content with the routine of his professional practice. He was one of the most active and public-spirited men in a town which has never been lacking in zeal for good works. His labours for the good of his fellow-citizens during more than forty years were unremitting; and to a large extent the story of the progress of his own life after he had attained manhood is the story of the progress of Leeds.

It will be seen as the reader advances what was the condition of Leeds about the time of Dr. Heaton's birth; and some idea will be given before the close of the narrative of its state at the time of his death. The great changes which have been effected, not merely in things material but in all that concerns the culture of the people and the enlargement of their mental and spiritual field of vision, cannot of course be attributed to any one man. It is due to the slow but steady movement of forces that existed long before any modern generation of mankind appeared upon the scene. But it is something to have been, during a life of more than threescore years, a constant and successful worker in connection with the development of the leading institutions of a great provincial town. The man who has taken a conspicuous part in the public life of a community like that of Leeds cannot have been a drone in the hive; and his achievements, though they may have been accomplished at a distance from the centres of publicity, may well be kept in remembrance by all who can honour a useful life devoted to duty and to the service of one's fellow-men.

It was not until Dr. Heaton had passed away from us that the full value of his life and character was recognised, even by those who had been most intimately associated with him in public affairs. It was only when his place among us was empty that men recognised how useful he had been, how constantly his time and his energies had been at the service of his fellow-townsmen, how difficult it would be to find any one to replace him. During life he had so steadily avoided anything savouring of ostentation, had accepted with so much quietness any reward that might chance to come in his way unsought, had shown so much equanimity when the rewards went, as they often did, to others ; had through it all preserved such an evenness of temper, such a steady, unbroken devotion to duty, that men had learned to look upon all that he did for the community as a mere matter of course. It was Dr. Heaton's *place* to labour in this and the other movement for improving the health, or the education, or the morals of the town. He was certain to do what he was asked to do, with cheerfulness and ungrudging acquiescence in the demands made upon him. So his fellow-townsmen had almost ceased to think of this patient perseverance in public labours, this resolute subservience of his own pleasure and convenience to the interests of others, as having anything remarkable about it. He was willing to work without hope of reward : and it was natural enough therefore that he should be allowed to work to the full extent of his powers.

He had his recompense in the knowledge that he had aided to no small extent in the improvement and advancement of his native town. Perhaps he himself was unaware of the degree to which the progress of Leeds in which he assisted was accompanied by progress on his own part. Yet those who knew him best, and who watched his life most closely, saw most clearly how his own character was developed by the work in which he was engaged; and how, whilst labouring with unremitting zeal for the elevation of those around him, he underwent a corresponding elevation on his own part.

When he died, with startling suddenness, his colleagues in public work first began to realise all that he had been and all that he had done in the affairs of Leeds; and they saw then that one had gone from among them who had really played a far larger part in the community to which they belonged than many whose names were more familiar to the world. It was natural then that a wish should be expressed that the facts of this useful life of patient labour should be put on record; and that the story of the man himself should be connected as closely as possible with the story of the town he loved and for which he did so much. It is with the object of gratifying this wish that the present volume has been prepared.

It deals, as has already been said, with a subject that is not exciting or eventful; but it is believed that there will be many who knew Dr. Heaton who will be glad to hear something of his public career, and to have some light thrown upon the personal character of one who by his retiring habits and natural modesty was secluded to a large extent even from those with whom in public affairs he was most constantly in contact.

It will be found that this volume avoids almost entirely the details of Dr. Heaton's domestic life. In following this course the writer has adhered most closely to what it is believed would have been Dr. Heaton's own wish. The object has been not merely to sketch the chief incidents of his career, but to say something of the many useful public works in which he was engaged from his entrance upon manhood to the very eve of his death.

CHAPTER II.

At the beginning of the present century the town of
Leeds presented a marvellous contrast in outward
appearance to the vast and busy centre of Yorkshire
industry which now bears that name. Before entering upon the narrative of the career of one who was
throughout his life closely identified with Leeds and
its progress both material and moral, a brief sketch
of the town as it existed at the beginning of the
present century will not be uninteresting—especially
to those who are acquainted with its condition to-day.

When the census was taken in 1801, the number
of inhabited houses in the town was 6,694, and the
number of residents 30,669. In other words Leeds
was less than one tenth of the size it has now attained.
Yet even in those early days it was a town famed
throughout the West Riding for the industry and
frugality of its citizens, and for the sturdy perseverance with which they devoted themselves to that
which they conceived to be their proper business.
The cloth trade was at that time the staple industry;

but it was carried on under conditions altogether different from those which now prevail. The manufacturers, as a rule, did not reside in Leeds, but in the small hamlets lying to the west of the town. They conducted their industry in the simplest fashion, and with the rudest implements. As the wayfarer walked through one of these outlying villages—many of which have since been included in the circuit of the great borough—he would hear the whir of the loom and the rattle of the shuttle as the manufacturer of these days busied himself under his own roof with the production of that which was literally ' homespun ' cloth. Twice a week the manufacturer would carry his goods by cart or pack-horse .into Leeds, and taking his stand in the Mixed or the White Cloth Hall, according to the particular branch of the trade in which he was engaged, would await the visits of the merchants who duly came round to attest the quality of his wares by ' rule of thumb,' and who were not only his sole customers, but the agents through whom the outer world received its supply of Yorkshire woollen goods. These cloth merchants were at that time the commercial aristocracy of Leeds ; for the iron trade of the town was in its infancy, the leather trade was unknown, and the only other branch of industry that had attained any importance was that of pottery—which for a few years flourished exceedingly and then suddenly died out.

A shrewd careful race of men the people who
built up the fortunes of Leeds undoubtedly were.
Perhaps their chief fault was their lack of enterprise.
From time immemorial, the tradition regarding Leeds
has been that it wanted the life and vivacity of its
smaller neighbour and rival, Bradford. The truth is
that the peculiar conditions under which the trade of
the town was carried on were not conducive to that
kind of enterprise and activity by which city life is
distinguished. The men who conducted the leading
business of the town were hardly townspeople themselves. Twice a week they came down from the hills
lying to the west of Leeds, and stood with their
goods in the Cloth Hall, as their forefathers had stood
on Leeds Bridge in bygone times. They heard the
news of the day, and bought their copies of the
' Leeds Mercury ' or the ' Leeds Intelligencer.' They
discussed the price of cloth and the prospects of the
war over their pipes and ale in one or other of the
numerous public houses that even then were to be
found in and about Briggate and Boar Lane; and
then in the early evening they set off for their homes
at Morley, Gildersome, Pudsey, Yeadon, Guiseley,
Horsforth, Ossett, or Dewsbury, and resigned themselves to their quiet country life. Such men were not
likely to exercise a very stimulating influence upon
the life of Leeds. But they gave a ' tone ' to the
place, and the tone, though peculiar and distinctive,

was not unwholesome. A contemporary writer [1]
commenting on this subject says: 'The dispersed
state of the manufacturers in villages and single
houses over the whole face of the country, is highly
favourable to their morals and happiness. They are
generally men of small capitals, and often annex a
small farm to their business; great numbers of the
rest have a field or two to support a horse and cow,
and are for the most part blessed with the comforts
without the superfluities of life.' They presented, in
fact, a quaint mixture of town and country characteristics. During five or six days of the week they
dwelt in their own little village, among trees and
fields, taking no thought of the outside world and
contenting themselves with the homely gossip of their
farmstead or hamlet. But on Tuesday and Saturday
they went down into the town, and showed the towns-
folk that they could drive as shrewd a bargain as the
sharpest of ' cits.' No one who has known Leeds for
any considerable number of years will fail to recall
the bi-weekly irruption of these rural manufacturers,
who came into the town in shoals, clad in their quaint
corduroy breeches, broad-brimmed hats, and brass-
buttoned coats of antique cut. They lingered among
us so recently as a dozen or twenty years ago; yet
so far back as the beginning of the century their

---

[1] *The Leeds Guide; including a Sketch of the Environs and Kirkstall
Abbey.* Leeds; printed for the author by Edward Baines, 1806.

influence on the town life of Leeds was beginning to decline, for the writer just quoted goes on as follows : ' But we regret to say, that this state of the manufacture is likely to be impaired, by the increasing habit of merchants concentrating in themselves the whole process of a manufactory from the raw wool to the finished piece ; and of course it must be carried on in large buildings by the joint labour of numerous workpeople, where the contaminating influence of vice spreads with fatal rapidity ; and this depravity of morals must, to consider the subject merely in the narrow view of policy, ultimately prove highly injurious to the real prosperity of the clothing district.' The change that this conscientious writer foresaw has duly happened. It would be interesting to know, supposing he could ' revisit the pale glimpses of the moon,' if he would be of the same opinion as of old regarding the inevitable consequences of that change.

But in 1801 the people in Leeds were still a long way off the days of huge mills and manufactories, worked by steam, wherein hundreds or thousands of men and women were to be congregated for many hours daily, amid all the vicious influences which the writer just quoted deplored. Happier in this respect than the people of Manchester and the great manufacturing towns of the cotton country, they were able to conduct their daily business under more healthful and wholesome conditions than those which prevailed in most of the large provincial towns of England. Thus it came to pass that Leeds was at that time distinguished by a distinct smack of rusticity in its life and in the characteristics of the community who dwelt there. They were townspeople, it is true; but they had such close and constant intercourse with those manufacturers from the West Riding villages who thronged their streets and filled their Cloth Halls twice a week, that their sympathies were almost equally divided between town and country. And so, though not so 'quick' as the people of neighbouring Bradford, they possessed in an unwonted degree, for an urban community, some of those solid and wholesome characteristics that are as a rule peculiar to village life. Dull they undoubtedly were; not given to great mental briskness or activity, nor prone to rush into dangerous mercantile speculation. But possessed, withal, with a native shrewdness that enabled them to appreciate the blessings of liberty, and that led them to sympathise with the political party to whom the cause of liberty was for the moment entrusted. They might not know so much as they ought to have done of book-learning; but they were sober godly souls for the most part; regular in their attendance at public worship, and upon the whole preferring the plebeian zeal of the chapel to the aristocratic repose of the church.

They had not at that time a single literary or educational society. The 'Circulating Library,' which still exists under the name of the Leeds Library, had then been established, it is true; but it was comparatively insignificant in its dimensions, and was housed in a room under the Rotation Office, where the local magistrates sat in turn to hear police cases. The price of a ticket for the library was in those days four guineas, the annual subscription being seven shillings and sixpence. Beyond this library there was no institution in the town that was meant for the fostering of the native intelligence. 'Under this head,' says the writer already quoted, when speaking of arts and sciences, 'we have nothing that is particularly interesting to communicate; for excepting those arts which have an immediate reference to commerce and manufacture, the town of Leeds has not been eminently disposed to foster the productions of art and genius, or to aid and encourage the researches of the philosopher. No societies of a literary or philosophical nature exist, to afford the means of concentrating and bringing before the public eye the discoveries or improvements made by individuals, and for the rational employment of the leisure of young men, who might be inspired by such an institution with a taste for literary refinement, instead of cultivating vicious habits.' To those who know Leeds now it must seem that their forefathers in 1806, when the foregoing lines were written, must have been living in the middle of the dark ages. What wonder that down to a comparatively recent period there was little sympathy with art, with literature, or with science, in a town which thus had no means of cultivating a taste for any of these things.

But if there were no literary institutions in Leeds in those days, the town was distinguished not merely by its outward observance of piety but by its genuine benevolence, as exhibited in the number of charitable institutions it maintained. Of these the General Infirmary was even then the most important, for Leeds was early astir in the good work of helping the sick. In a subsequent chapter more will be said regarding the history of this most admirable institution. All that need be said of it here is that at the beginning of this century it had secured a permanent place among the charities of Leeds, and enjoyed the support of all the chief inhabitants of the town. Howard, who visited Leeds in 1788, had pronounced the building used for the purpose of the Infirmary to be ' one of the best hospitals in the kingdom,' and, after dwelling upon the attention paid to ventilation, he added significantly, ' many are here cured of compound fractures, who would lose their limbs in the unventilated and offensive wards of some hospitals.' Next to the Infirmary the House of Recovery ranked in those days as the most important of the charitable institutions of

Leeds. It had been founded by public subscription in 1802, for the purpose of receiving patients suffering from contagious and infectious fevers. Down to the date of its establishment there was no provision worthy of the name for the poor who fell victims to one or other of the many loathsome scourges of humanity. The fever patient remained where he was, in the damp and noisome cellar or garret, surrounded by a closely packed crew of his fellow-poor. It is not wonderful that death spread rapidly in a town like Leeds when once a case of infectious fever had declared itself. But at last the House of Recovery was established, and proof was afforded that, even eighty years ago, in the dark ages of sanitary science, Leeds could boast of some inhabitants so far enlightened as to their duty to their fellows as to be capable of devising and founding an institution of this character. There will be much more to be said of the House of Recovery in the course of this narrative; and the reader will see at what a cost, not of money but of health and life, it was carried on by the devoted men who were connected with it. But no one can doubt that, ever since its establishment in 1802, it has been of the greatest benefit to the inhabitants of the town.

There was yet one other charitable institution of Leeds in the olden days that deserves notice, because it belonged to an order of charities by no means common in those days. The people of Leeds, as the reader has seen, were somewhat peculiar in their customs and characteristics. In no large town in England at the beginning of the present century was the tone of provincialism more marked and distinctive, and nowhere was there a greater suspicion of the foreigner—the foreigner being, in the eyes of a Leeds man, not necessarily one who had been born beyond the seas, but one who had lived outside the boundaries of Yorkshire. Yet along with this feeling of doubt there was a strong desire among the better class of the inhabitants to show hospitality to the unfortunate among the strangers who were found within the gates of the town ; and so, towards the close of the last century, the Strangers' Friend Society was established—chiefly, it is said, through the exertions of the old Methodists. ' The name by which this charity is known,' says the writer already quoted, ' sufficiently points out its peculiar design. The friendless and strangers who are sinking under the pressure of poverty or disease are sought out and relieved, and many who must have perished for want of prompt assistance have by the efficacious aid and exertions of the managers of this institution been restored to comfort and to usefulness.' The Society was not wealthy or powerful, or even fashionable. But it did good in its way, scores of years before Charity Organisation Associations had been thought of ; and the existence of such an institution in Leeds deserves to be noted, not merely because of the light it throws upon the methodical way in which these sturdy Yorkshire people went about the business of charity, as well as the other businesses in which they were engaged, but because of the extent to which it redeems them from the reproach that might otherwise have fairly rested upon them, of a harsh and inhospitable exclusiveness.

The outward appearance of Leeds at the beginning of the present century was strangely different from that which it now wears. The number of its inhabitants has already been stated. Some description of the town by a contemporary writer will serve to bring home to those who are acquainted with the Leeds of to-day, an idea of the immense progress which these eighty years have witnessed. The greatest length of the town at that time, from west to east, was about a mile and a half, the western extremity being Park Place, and the eastern St. Peter's Square. From north to south, it then extended barely half a mile—from the river to St. John's Church. It is hardly necessary to say that these extreme boundaries have long since been swept away, and that practically the Leeds of 1800 is to the Leeds of 1882 what the city of London is to the greater London of the Metropolitan area.

In 1806 Park Place was the elegant suburban retreat of wealthy merchants and others who, having

amassed a competency or secured an established position, no longer found it necessary to live in immediate proximity to their places of business. At that
time Park Place was described as 'a very elegant
range of buildings,' and as in front of the houses
gardens and green fields stretched all the way down
to the banks of the Aire, we can well believe the
statement that the Place furnished 'the most pleas-
ing promenade in the town.' Immediately behind it was
an unfinished square, then known as St. Paul's Square,
though long since re-named Park Square. Here houses
even more pretentious than those in the adjoining
Park Place were being erected, and the simple-minded
people of the town were beginning to wonder where a
sufficient number of persons affluent enough to dwell
in such imposing mansions, and idle enough to be able
to live at such a distance from the centre of industry,
were to be found to inhabit them. Passing from Park
Square, East Parade was duly reached, and here the
appearance of the town presented a remarkable contrast to its appearance as now seen from the same
spot. The houses on the western side of East
Parade formed one side of this vast square, the other
sides of which were formed by the Infirmary and
Coloured Cloth Hall, by the east side of Park Row,
and by the north side of South Parade. This particular area enclosed by that square is now one of the
most densely populated and closely built sites in

Leeds. But at that time all this great enclosure, within the boundaries we have named, was occupied by fields and gardens. The townsman who had wandered from his house in Briggate or Kirkgate as far as the western end of Boar Lane thus found himself in the midst of trees and flowers, and in an essentially suburban district. The Cloth Hall was then what it is to-day—to the disgrace of Leeds—but it stood practically outside the town, with fields and gentlemen's gardens on two sides of it. Near to it, occupying a site not far from the present Queen's Hotel, was an elegant house once the residence of Dr. Watson, Bishop of Bristol, the grounds of which extended to the banks of the Aire. Near Boar Lane stood the King's Mills, the existence of which was a relic of feudal times. It is strange indeed to think that so recently as the beginning of the present century, in the lifetime of men who still take an active part in the affairs of their native town, the inhabitants of Leeds were compelled to have all their corn ground at a particular mill. 'Ten thousand pounds,' says the indignant local writer, 'have been offered and been refused to redeem the town from this badge of slavery.' Without parliamentary representation, without a free corporation, and with a press which was then just beginning to struggle into a position of independence, the inhabitants of the great town of Leeds were compelled to submit as

patiently as might be to the practical grievance
which the existence of the King's Mills imposed upon
them.   To-day probably few among the residents are
aware that the familiar name Mill Hill commemorates
a system so absurd and iniquitous as that under
which their forefathers groaned.

Passing by way of Boar Lane, then the most
narrow and crooked of thoroughfares, into Briggate,
the visitor would find himself in what was then, in
the estimation of the inhabitants, a noble and spacious street.   But the Briggate of those days was
very different from the Briggate with which we are
now familiar.   From the point where it is touched
by Kirkgate down to Leeds Bridge, its breadth was
very nearly the same as it now is.   But in the parts
lying beyond Kirkgate to the north the ' noble and
spacious ' street was completely lost.   The middle of
the thoroughfare was occupied by rows of houses
and by the Moot Hall.   Behind the Moot Hall, in
a narrow and confined space, at the point where
Upperhead and Lowerhead Rows now intersect the
street, was the Cross, at which the weekly market, for
corn, butter, eggs, and poultry, was held.   Beyond
this again, by narrow lanes, St. John's Church could
be reached ; and here, as has already been said, was
the northern limit of the town.

But with the new century new signs of life were
becoming visible ; and the sleepy, steady-going town,

that had so long been content to jog on at its own pace, without paying heed to what was passing beyond its walls, began to take thought of other things and to extend its boundaries. Away to the east, near the large Methodist Meeting-house erected under the eye of John Wesley himself, St. Peter's Square had been built for the accommodation of the middle classes, who, though anxious to escape from the confined streets in the neighbourhood of the parish church, were unable to aspire to the elegance of the west end. Running parallel with Briggate, but beyond the noise and bustle of the town, a new and well-built thoroughfare, then and still known as Albion Street, had been erected. It was looked upon as the rival of Park Place itself in elegance and fashion ; and the houses were the favourite residences of professional gentlemen and merchants—all retail trading in the street being strictly forbidden.

Further away from the town to the north-west, marvellous improvements were already contemplated. A new square, Queen's Square, had been laid out, though at this time, for some reason or other, the scheme for building it hung fire. Probably prudent men, such as the inhabitants of Old Leeds undoubtedly were, could not be readily brought to approve of a plan for the erection of a number of elegant houses in the midst of what was then the open country. Beyond Queen's Square, however, a

number of houses had already been built. These
formed the present St. James's Street, and they were
—strange as it may seem—the sanatorium, the
health resort, of the Leeds invalids of eighty years
ago. The doctors sent their patients out of the town
up to lodgings in St. James's Street, in order that
they might enjoy the fine and bracing air ; and this
now shabby and decaying thoroughfare, above which
the cloud of smoke raised by the tall chimneys in the
valley ever hangs like a pall, was at the beginning
of the century the Ilkley and Harrogate combined of
the people of Leeds. One drawback there was to residence in this delightful suburb. It lay beyond the
limits of the town water supply, and the inhabitants
had therefore to be content with such water as they
could obtain from the wells on their premises. But
perhaps this was not after all so great a misfortune as
the contemporary chroniclers seem to have imagined,
for at that time the recognised source of the water
supply of Leeds was the river Aire ; not then, it is
true, reduced to the condition described so graphi-
cally by Mr. Lewis Morris in his poem called ' A
Yorkshire River,' but still polluted by the sewage
of many hamlets and towns, including the considerable town of Bradford. Not very far from St.
James's Street was ' Little Woodhouse,' an ancient
village or hamlet, described as ' a charming rural
spot,' where a considerable number of gentlemen's

seats had been built, far away from the noise and smoke of the town. Among these buildings was one now known as Claremont, of which much will be heard in these pages. But, alas! Little Woodhouse is no longer to be described as 'a charming rural spot.' It has been absorbed in the big town ; and the sound of the whistle of the locomotive, or the roar of ' the clamorous iron flail ' of the great works in the valley below, may be heard both by day and night within its dwellings.

Enough has been said to show how great is the contrast between the Leeds of to-day and that of eighty years ago. It should be added that the southern side of the town, on the right bank of the Aire, was then a fashionable quarter, containing many handsome residences—some of which are still to be seen standing amid the crowd of meaner edifices— and boasting of a larger number of private carriages than were to be found in the greater Leeds that lay on the other side of the river. Hunslet and Holbeck were still, however, little more than manufacturing villages.

Some idea of the condition of the commercial community of Leeds in those days may be gathered from the fact that no building had been appro- priated as a Post Office. Wherever the postmaster chanced to reside, there the Post Office had been fixed for the time being. Leeds, as it happened, lay apart from the Great North Road between London and Edinburgh; but it had its daily mails north and south, as well as to Manchester and Liverpool, and was as well supplied in this respect as most of the manufacturing towns of England. It had, moreover, two newspapers, representing the two different factions in politics, and both well known and widely read throughout the West Riding. There was a mean Theatre in Hunslet Lane, near Leeds Bridge, where strolling companies of actors performed during the summer months. In winter the local aristocracy —who were but poor patrons of the drama—found amusement in the assemblies, which began in October and were continued until the following spring. These assemblies were conducted in the strict fashion then in vogue, under the superintendence of a master of the ceremonies, whose function it was to decide upon the eligibility of candidates for admission to these solemn entertainments. The church was then in a state of lukewarmness. The Nonconformists had absorbed the more active spirits of the town, the Unitarians, Wesleyans, and Independents being the most powerful bodies among the Dissenters. But though Dissent was strong, and in a certain sense fashionable in Leeds in those days, it still laboured under the social and political disabilities that attached to it in the last century; and the inhabitant of Leeds who desired to be married, whatever might be his religious faith, was compelled to go to the parish church in order that the due sanction of the law might be given to his union.

Such was Leeds at the beginning of this century. Busy, but free from bustle; fairly intelligent, yet by no means intellectual; with a keen eye to business, but a warm side for old manners and customs and the duties of hospitality, its people represented the sturdy English character in its best aspect in the days before railways, and electric telegraphs, and parliamentary reform, and penny newspapers had revolutionised the age. They have been sketched, so far as their moral characteristics are concerned, with admirable power and faithfulness in the pages of Charlotte Brontë. To understand the character of the men and women of the West Riding at the beginning of the present century, indeed, one must go to 'Shirley' and 'The Professor.' The genius of a great woman has there given permanence to the salient features which then characterised the Yorkshire tradesman or merchant.

CHAPTER III.

MR. HEATON, SENIOR.

THE grandfather of the subject of our memoir was John Heaton of Ossett, who was born on September 4, 1736. He married one Mary Metcalfe, a person in a somewhat superior position in life to himself, the daughter of Urban Metcalfe, a cloth manufacturer of Hunslet; which was then, as will have been gathered from the particulars given in the preceding chapter, a small manufacturing village. It was probably the fact of his having married this Hunslet bride, who there is reason to believe was in a small way an heiress, that induced John Heaton to remove from Ossett to the spot where his wife had been born. At all events he settled in Hunslet very soon after his marriage to Mary Metcalfe in July 1765, and remained in or near Leeds for the rest of his days.

Three children were born of the marriage, the eldest being John Heaton, the father of Dr. Heaton, born July 22, 1769. The two other children were a son William, and a daughter Hannah.

'In the year 1783,' says Dr. Heaton in his

journal, ' my grandfather purchased part of the small estate in Hunslet which I now (1859) possess. His father-in-law, Urban Metcalfe, was residing on it at the time ; his name as tenant being mentioned in the conveyance. My grandfather himself afterwards resided on his own property, and his widow continued to live there after his death. He died August 1st, 1790, and was buried in the graveyard attached to the chapel at Hunslet, then a chapel-of-ease to the Leeds parish church. His will makes his widow and my father executors. He leaves his personal property to his wife, who has to pay out of it 100*l.* to his daughter Hannah, and his freehold property, consisting of this Hunslet estate, equally between his two sons, each to come into the enjoyment of his share when of the age of twenty-one. William came of age in 1794, and in the year following, 1795, the two brothers united in the purchase of an additional portion, the whole forming, as I suppose, the estate as it now stands. The two brothers continued in this joint possession up to the time of their death. William resided in the house of his parents throughout his life, carrying on a shopkeeping business, though with little success. In the latter part of his life he got into debt, of which he was relieved by my father, who also allowed him the whole of the proceeds of their joint estate for his maintenance.'

I have given this extract from the journal,
although it somewhat anticipates the course of the
narrative, because it throws a good deal of light upon
the character both of the father and grandfather, and
incidentally illustrates the strong characteristics of
Dr. Heaton himself. Here is first the shrewd, steady
young manufacturer from Ossett, who makes a match
with a woman who is considered above him in station,
but between whom and himself there were no dis-
crepancies of temper and disposition. He comes to
Leeds, the most important town of the district in
which he was born, in order 'to make his fortune';
and in a modest manner he succeeds. Before long
he can buy the little piece of property on which his
father-in-law resides, and can add to it bit by bit, so
that at his death his wife and children are not left
altogether without resources. He makes an honest
will, giving to his wife and his several children their
just dues, and then dies, leaving no other sign behind
him to recall his existence. He is the type of a class
from whom probably more great and successful
families have sprung than from any other in the
community. Unless such men were willing indeed and
able to lay the foundation of the family, often laying
it quite unperceived by their own generation, there
would be no hope for the stability of the edifice when
at last it came to be reared. Old John Heaton, the
first of the family to make Leeds his home, lived his

honest frugal life, and died, having made no noise of any kind in his own generation, but withal having accomplished the work assigned to him.

And then comes his son, the next John Heaton, who has his father's shrewdness and frugality, but added to those things a quiet and sterling benevolence of character, of which we have no record left in the case of the elder man. He too makes his way in the world, and, as the extract I have given shows, is able to be something more than just to his less fortunate brother; can give a ready ear to his appeal for help, relieving him of his debts, allowing him to live in the old family house in Hunslet, even permitting him—the younger son—to enjoy all through his life the exclusive benefit of the little patrimony which had come to them. Even if no other record of this John Heaton's life were left than that contained in the few lines I have transcribed from his son's journal, there would be enough here to commend the man to our affection and respect. Fortunately, however, other records of this really remarkable as well as worthy man are left; and it is a comparatively easy matter to picture him as he was during his busy and prosperous life in the town where he had been born.

'Fortunately,' says his son, 'for him and his children, he was not confined to the dull obscurity of what was at that time a suburban village, separ-

ated by a mile or two of country road without
habitation from the more busy town. He was apprenticed, I suppose about the customary age of
fifteen years, to Mr. John Binns, who had then the
largest business as a bookseller and stationer in the
town of Leeds, and I believe in the North of England. His business was carried on in the premises
No. 7 Briggate, subsequently purchased and long occupied by my father in the same business. My father
possessed several qualities admirably fitted for main-
taining the full efficiency of a business already well
established; but his quiet manner might not have
equally insured success had he attempted the establishment of a new concern. He was diligent, orderly,
self-denying, and of unswerving uprightness; he
possessed great transparency of character, and was
remarkably free from guile, evasiveness, or subter-
fuge of any kind. I may add that he was singularly
free from all malice or hostile feeling. I often used
to tell him that, like Moses, he was the meekest of
men. I scarcely ever saw him seriously angry, so
that it was almost impossible for any one to quarrel
with him, and, as was said with perfect truthfulness
after his death, he had not an enemy in the world.'

Young John Heaton, in addition to the admirable
moral qualities here depicted, possessed others
equally exalted. Very early in life he became the
subject of deep religious conviction. His father was

an Independent, and had regularly attended the Old White Chapel, in Hunslet Lane, Leeds, now in the occupation of a leather currier. The son shared the ecclesiastical convictions of the father; whilst his experience of personal religion made him still more zealous than his parent in the service of the denomination to which he belonged. These were the days when Dissent lay under something more than a merely social disability; and when even among Dissenters it was not so easy to be an Independent as to follow in the wake of the emotional religionists who had founded Methodism. John Heaton, however, felt that he had a reason for the faith that was in him, and all through life he clung firmly and yet gently to the body of which his father had been a member. When in course of time it became desirable that the Old White Chapel should be exchanged for a more commodious edifice in a more suitable locality, his purse and his influence were alike employed to the fullest possible extent in the promotion of the scheme: and it was in a great measure owing to his exertions that Queen Street Chapel, Leeds, was erected. There he continued to worship down to the time of his death, with one brief interval, when some difference in the church led to the withdrawal of ' a few of the older and more respectable members,' including Mr. Clapham and Mr. Heaton. ' Mr. Clapham never returned to it,' says Dr. Heaton, ' but my father was of a peculiarly

meek and forgiving disposition and was much
attached to the chapel, so he soon returned, and continued to be a most regular attendant throughout the
remainder of his life.'

Such was the character of the young man who
entered the bookseller's shop of Mr. Binns as an
apprentice about 1785, and who, having done his duty
faithfully during the time of his apprenticeship, was
promoted to the management of the shop when his
' articles ' had expired, somewhere about the year
1791. A bookseller's shop in the country in those
days was very different from any institution of the
kind at the present time. These were not the times
of clubs, news-rooms, commercial exchanges, and
philosophical or literary societies. Whilst the taverns
furnished a rendezvous for the local politicians, the
booksellers' shops were the recognised gathering-
places of those who were inclined towards literature.
It was here that the clergy met on Monday morning,
to discuss together perchance the sermons of the
previous day, more probably the last pamphlet from
London, or the contents of the new number of ' The
Gentleman's Magazine.' It was here, too, that they
found that rare article a daily newspaper, not more
than three or four days old, and giving news of events
in Paris which had happened so recently as a fortnight back. With the clergy of the Church of
England might be seen mingled a Dissenting minister

or two, whose tastes lay rather in the direction of science or literature than of theology, and who had no idea of measuring swords with their exalted episcopalian brethren on the subject of disestablishment. Of such men Leeds was not devoid, as the mention of the name of Priestley will suffice to remind my readers. The magistrates, the gentry, and even the better class of professional men and merchants were naturally attracted to the same common centre; so that, a hundred years ago, the shop of the leading bookseller of a provincial town was a place of far more importance than it can now claim to be, and supplied in a great degree the lack of those institutions which have since been established in all directions, for the promotion of social intercourse and of literary and scientific inquiry in every conceivable mode. The talk which went on from day to day in such a place, though necessarily often frivolous and trivial, was upon the whole interesting and not seldom instructive; and no young man could listen to it without getting a certain amount of enlightenment which would hardly have come to him in any other branch of business.

Perhaps it was this fact, or perhaps it may have been the actual superiority of the bookselling business in those days compared with its present state, but whatever may have been the cause, it is certain that the old-fashioned bookseller of the last century was as a rule a person of much higher intelligence and better education than can be generally found in the shopkeeper of to-day. He was expected to know something more than the outsides of the books in which he dealt, and as a rule he did so. Mr. Binns, the master to whom young Heaton had been apprenticed, was an excellent specimen of the order of man I am describing. That he had more than a merely local fame was evidenced by the fact that some time after his death Mr. John Heaton was solicited to write an account of him for publication in Nichols's 'Literary Anecdotes.' The son of a bookseller at Halifax, where he was born in the year 1744, Mr. Binns may be said to have been brought up among books. Very early in life he showed a great taste not only for literary pursuits but for music. In his eighteenth year he prepared—in happy anticipation of the more elaborate work of Dr. Grove—a 'Dictionary of Music,' which was published a few years afterwards, though the name of the author did not appear on the title-page. About 1765 he went to Leeds and started business there in a quaint little shop in Briggate. Here he remained throughout his life. What I have said as to his musical and bibliographic tastes shows that he was a man of superior attainments. Before long 'Mr. Binns's shop' had become the local centre of intellect and intelligence; and on market days those of the neighbouring gentry

who had any taste for literature or any desire to
meet with the leading spirits of the busy town
resorted to the place, and peeping into the newest
books from London or chatting over the news in the
latest journal converted the dingy little shop into the
semblance of a club. The gentle, dreamy musician
—who was himself a performer of no common
excellence on more than one instrument—did not
take much part in the discussions which related to
politics, for his tastes lay in another direction. He
was himself a Conservative, as most of his patrons
were. But he was more concerned in picking up
some rare tracts relating to the local history of the
district, or in mastering the latest news about the
performances of Handel's music, than in the discussion of the rights of the American colonists or the
speeches of Mr. Burke. His knowledge of books was
most extensive and profound ; and to him every
inhabitant of Leeds and the surrounding country
who desired to obtain any bibliographic information
resorted, seldom to be disappointed in his quest. It
was something that, in what the present generation
regards as the dark age of the eighteenth century, a
bustling manufacturing town should have contained
one such man as this. Who can tell what services
he rendered to the place where he led his useful,
unostentatious life ? It is probable that, if we could
trace the origin of some of the most imposing move-

ments which now occupy our attention, we should be led back step by step to that dingy little bookseller's shop at the bottom of Briggate, where John Binns met the eager inquirers after knowledge and fed them out of his own stores, dropping the while many a quiet hint which, like the seed that has fallen to the ground unseen, was to bring forth its fruit long after the sower himself was forgotten. At all events 'Mr. Binns's shop' is not a place of which the people of Leeds have reason to think lightly; nor ought the pleasant homely figure of the musical bookseller of that remote day to be allowed to drop entirely out of sight, in the place where his name is no longer heard.

Side by side with that figure of the cultured, learned, and gentle master, we now get a glimpse of another, that of the industrious and God-fearing assistant. From Mr. Binns young John Heaton learned much. Not only did he acquire that knowledge of books by which he in turn became distinguished in the course of his business, but he caught some of his master's gentleness of spirit and demeanour. 'My father was the meekest of men,' says John Heaton's son; and in this case the proverb 'like master like man' is strictly applicable. But the young man had still his way to make in the world, and was as yet far from the position of wealth and social influence which his employer had secured for himself. Perhaps too it would be but fair to admit that he lacked the more brilliant intellectual qualities which distinguished the latter. He had no 'gift' like that which had carried the fame of Mr. Binns far beyond local bibliographic circles. But he had, what in its way was even more valuable, sterling principles, a firm though gentle perseverance, and an absorbing desire to do his duty by all with whom he was brought in contact. So after all John Heaton was by no means badly equipped for the battle of life.

In 1794 Mr. Binns added to his business by purchasing the 'Leeds Mercury' from its former proprietor, Mr. Bowling, and conducting it in connection with a general printing business in a building on the left hand of what is now called Heaton's Court, in Briggate. This event led to several changes of importance, not only in the shop, but in the town of Leeds itself. One day in 1795 a young man, weary with a long walk across the hills from Lancashire, entered Mr. Binns's shop and asked for employment as a printer. He was referred to the little printing-office in the adjoining yard ; and there, having given evidence of his good character and ability, he was forthwith engaged. It is recorded of Edward Baines, who entered the town of Leeds and commenced the work of his life in this modest position, that he resolved on being admitted to Mr. Binns's establishment, that if he could obtain employment there he

would never seek to get another situation : and it is
not necessary that I should pause to repeat the story
of how he kept this vow. In the following year, 1796,
Mr. John Binns, whilst on a journey from London,
whither he had been on a book-buying expedition,
was attacked by serious illness at Grantham. After
several days of intense suffering he died there. His
body was brought to Leeds and interred in a vault in
the parish church, where a monument recording his
name is still to be seen. Whilst the good man lay
dying he was able to attend to his worldly affairs, and
duly made his will a day or two before his death.
In this will, whilst chiefly mindful of those who were
near to him in blood, he did not forget his faithful
shopman, and by a legacy of twenty pounds bore the
last testimony of his regard for the character of John
Heaton.

Mrs. Binns was left with her two sons to carry
on the bookselling business. Each of these two sons
in turn was placed at its head ; but in reality the
management was left almost entirely in the hands of
John Heaton. Mrs. Binns and her children continued
for some years to reside above the shop ; and being
an active capable woman she took a lively interest in
all that was passing in the business. In the printing-
office Edward Baines had now secured the leading
position, just as John Heaton held it in the bookseller's shop. Naturally, under such circumstances the

two young men became fast friends, though they must have differed much in disposition. They shared in common, it is true, the sterling principles which must form the foundation of all true character, and no widow could have been more highly favoured in those to whom she had to trust for the management of her affairs than was Mrs. Binns in having Edward Baines and John Heaton in her service. But whilst Baines was full of courage and enthusiasm, taking a lively interest in passing events, quick to note the humorous as well as the serious side of things, and bent upon making his way in the world if he could do so honestly and honourably, Heaton was shy, retiring, and grave. The atmosphere of books in which he dwelt was altogether different from that atmosphere of the printing-office in which his more brilliant fellow-workman moved. He had acquired some of the outward characteristics of the bookworm, whilst his companion, with his fine flow of animal spirits, his brightness and vigour, was the very type of the journalist. 'I always know that Edward Baines is in the shop,' said Mrs. Binns one day, ' when I hear John Heaton laugh.'

In 1801 a great change took place in the position and prospects of one of the two friends. The Liberals of Yorkshire, feeling the want of a newspaper which could represent their principles in a proper manner, determined to buy the ' Leeds Mercury,' and to

place Mr Edward Baines in charge of it. This was
accordingly done.   Mr. Baines, backed by many
influential men in Leeds and the district, became the
purchaser of the paper from Mrs. Binns, and continued to carry it on for some years in the printing-
office adjoining the bookseller's shop. John Binns,
the eldest son of the old bookseller, died in this year,
1801, and the business was transferred to his young
brother Thomas, who was, however, at that time a
youth of only seventeen years. Like his brother, he
died young; and in 1805 Mrs. Binns found herself
left without a son to whom to entrust the conduct
of the business established by her husband. In these
circumstances she took that which was undoubtedly
the wisest course open to her. Hitherto, although
she was in easy and indeed affluent circumstances, she
had continued to live in the cramped apartments
above the shop where her husband had made his
home on coming to Leeds many years before. She
now resolved to leave Leeds and make a home for
herself and her daughters in London ; and, mindful
of the faithful services of John Heaton, she bestowed
upon him the good-will of her husband's business.

It was a valuable gift, for in those days 'good-
will ' was something more than a phrase, and an
established business was not exposed to the risks
from pushing rivalries which now dog the footsteps
of even the most fortunate of tradespeople. Heaton

had, however, well deserved this much of Mrs. Binns's confidence, which was accompanied by a further proof of her approval in the shape of a gift of a gold watch-seal, engraved with his initials. The large and very valuable stock of books in the shop was bought by John Heaton, and henceforth he carried on the business on his own account—the familiar name of Binns having given place to one which was destined eventually to become even more familiar to the people of Leeds.

Two years after entering into possession of the business, and at a time when he was just beginning to gather together the wealth which he eventually accumulated, Mr. Heaton married, as his first wife, Martha Hobson. Her brother was a silk-mercer carrying on his business in the shop adjoining that which John Heaton occupied ; and after the fashion of these times he lived behind his shop, his sister living with him. This Mr. Hobson was himself subsequently a public man of some little note in Leeds, and took a considerable part in the establishment of the Gas Company. The marriage of his sister with Mr. Heaton is spoken of by the son of the latter as having been ' an affair of convenience rather than of warm affection.' Heaton was engrossed with his business throughout the day, and had no leisure in which to enjoy the pleasures of society. But he could not avoid making the acquaintance of his next-door neighbour and his sister ; and eventually he came to the conclusion that, needing some one to manage his household affairs, he could not do better than contract a union with Miss Hobson. He had, when entering into possession of the bookselling business, succeeded to the occupancy of the house in which his former employer and his family had lived so long, and there can be no doubt that he was already, as a steady and prosperous young tradesman, a very eligible suitor in the eyes of those around him. At all events nothing happened to interfere with his brief courtship of Martha Hobson, to whom he was married on June 18, 1807. Their married life was, however, of short duration. Mrs. Heaton, who had always been weakly, died less than three years after her marriage, and John Heaton, now becoming through his diligence and success in business a man of no inconsiderable wealth, was left a widower.

There had been a secret romance in the young bookseller's life, as there is in most lives. I have spoken of Mrs. Binns and the two daughters with whom she went to London in 1805, when Heaton became the purchaser of the bookselling business. These daughters were sprightly and handsome young ladies, moving in the very best circle of society in Leeds, and there is reason to suppose that John Heaton admired the younger of them afar off during many years. The difference of station which separated the heiresses—for such the daughters of Mr. Binns were—from the young tradesman was too great to be bridged over; but judging by certain letters which remain, and by memoranda discovered by his son after his death, he long cherished a great regard for one of the young ladies whom he had seen as children running about the rooms in which he had himself lived, and who continued for many years to show a sincere affection and respect for their father's old and faithful servant. The correspondence which was maintained between Mrs. Binns and her daughters on one side, and Mr. Heaton on the other, after the removal of the family to London, is in the highest degree honourable to both parties. It shows the wealthy widow and daughters cherishing a warm feeling of respect and gratitude towards their old friend. There are many invitations to the young bookseller to visit London and make the house of Mrs. Turner—the elder daughter of Mr. Binns—his home. There are little presents and messages regularly interchanged between the fashionable people in London and the simple frugal tradesman in Leeds. After his wife's death, when, apparently on the strength of his improved position in business, Mr. Heaton allowed himself to indulge in recollections of the past, when the handsome daughters of his old patron were constant visitors to the shop, there was apparently a decided disposition on the part of the younger of these ladies to reciprocate his feelings. But the little romance was never to be converted into reality, and on October 23, 1812, he received—it is to be feared with mingled feelings—the announcement of the marriage of Miss Binns to Colonel Wall of Worcester, accompanied by a portion of the bride-cake, of which he is requested to let Mr. Baines have a taste.

For a year or two after this Mr Heaton devoted himself entirely to his business, the only relaxation he allowed himself being that which he found in connection with his congenial labours as a member of the White Chapel. He continued to prosper in business; his stock increased in value, and out of his profits he was able to purchase several blocks of property in the immediate neighbourhood of his shop. But presently the need of companionship began to force itself upon the mind of the lonely, self-concentrated bookseller. Apparently he knew no one who seemed likely to suit his tastes. He had lived so long among his books that he had found no time to make acquaintance with living people. His first marriage had not been altogether a successful venture, and the little episodical romance which had preceded and followed it was now at an end.

In these circumstances he applied to his minister, the Rev. William Eccles, for advice, and eventually asked that worthy man if he knew of any one who would be suitable as a wife. It is not in this way that marriages are usually contracted in novels ; and perhaps, even when a minister of religion is the originator of such an alliance, it can hardly be classed among those which are traditionally supposed to be 'made in heaven.' But the common experience of mankind proves that unions which are contracted in this prosaic fashion are not always the most unfortunate, and that not a little of real happiness may spring from them.

Mr. Eccles did know of a family whom he could recommend to the young bookseller as being likely to furnish him with a worthy and congenial partner in life. This was the family of Mr. William Deakin, a substantial yeoman, farming a considerable piece of land, his own property, in Attercliffe and Tinsley. Mr. Deakin's wife had died some time before, and he now lived at Attercliffe in a quaint country house, built by his father some thirty years previously, where he enjoyed the companionship of several unmarried daughters. His two sons were both married, and his third daughter was the wife of the Rev. Maurice Phillips, minister of the Independent Chapel at Atter- cliffe, through whom it is probable Mr. Eccles had become acquainted with the family. Accordingly on a certain Good Friday, when shops were shut and no business was to be done, the worthy bookseller and his minister set off in a gig, ostensibly to drive from

Leeds to Masbro' College, where Mr. Eccles was supposed to have some business to transact. The precise year of this memorable expedition is not known, but it was either in 1814 or 1815. Attercliffe had to be taken on the way to Masbro', and what more natural than that the minister should call, as he passed through the village, at the house of his friend Mr. Deakin? Five daughters of the house were then living at home. As it chanced, the door was opened by Ann, the second in age, and her kindly and unaffected welcome, not only to the minister but to his companion, at once made a most favourable impression upon the latter. Nor did she suffer subsequently in his estimation when Mr. Heaton was able to compare her with her sisters. It was towards her that his heart from the first inclined. She on her part reciprocated his feelings, and after a brief courtship, during which the sober lovers met more than once at Harrogate or Leeds, good Mr. Eccles entertaining the young lady at his house, they were married on September 21, 1815.

'The courtship,' says Dr. Heaton in his diary, ' may seem somewhat brief; but the marriage was a still more summary process. My grandfather Deakin was rapidly sinking from old age and infirmity, and not expected to live long. After his death it would be inappropriate to have a marriage without the customary interval of mourning. It was determined, therefore, that the marriage should take place without delay. But my mother could not leave her father, on whom she was the chief attendant. My father, also, was so devoted to his business at this time that he could not absent himself for long, even for so interesting an occasion as his marriage. It was arranged, therefore, that my father just came over for the day; he and my mother were married in the most quiet way at the parish church at Sheffield, and he went back alone to Leeds the same evening. The marriage took place on September 21, 1815; my grandfather died a fortnight afterwards, on October 4, and as soon as was convenient after that (I believe about a fortnight after her father's death) my mother went to her husband at Leeds, accompanied by my eldest aunt, Mary. It was certainly a dreary commencement of her married life. And thus she settled down in her new home.'

By the marriage with Miss Deakin, John Heaton found himself introduced into the midst of a somewhat numerous and active family, whose habits both of mind and body must have presented a decided contrast to those of the gentle, self-secluded bookseller. The Deakin family was one of very considerable antiquity. 'I have in my possession,' says Dr. Heaton, 'a pedigree tracing in unbroken succession my grandfather's descent from the ancient family of Dakeynes of Biggin Grange and Stubbing Edge, county Derby. The pedigree commences in the fifteenth century; but the works on Heraldry refer the same family to De Akeney, who held lands in the Peak of Derbyshire in the reigns of Edward the First and Edward the Second; and the first known of whose name was some mythical hero who came into this country with William the Conqueror. Thus it would seem, with a reasonable probability, that both my father's and mother's families were originally Norman, and that the patronymic of both had the patrician prefix " De." '

What is quite certain, apart from any of the traditions of the Heralds' College, is that the Deakins or Dakeynes of Attercliffe had held the position of substantial yeomen in that part of Yorkshire for nearly a century and a half before John Heaton's first interview with his future wife. Mrs. Deakin, the mother of Mrs. Heaton, had been dead for several years previous to her daughter's marriage, and I have just told how the father's death took place immediately after the somewhat curious wedding. 'Of my grandfather and grandmother Deakin,' says Dr. Heaton, 'I of course only know what I have heard from my mother and aunts. They were excellent, simple-minded, pious people, and lived in a plain country fashion; liberally, but without show. Amongst my mother's papers found after her death was a short manuscript in her handwriting, containing a sketch of her mother's character, and a history of her last illness and death. In this she says, "My mother was one of the most active, cheerful, and industrious women in her family; kind, affectionate, and tender to her dear husband, between whom and herself there was, I believe, as tender an attachment as ever did subsist between persons who were engaged in the connubial state. It was her uniform and consistent practice to endeavour to excite in the minds of her offspring veneration and affection towards our dear father, affection, kindness, and union among us as a family of children. With these sentiments she aimed to impress our minds from our infancy; and this desire, if possible, gained strength in her later days, together with an ardent wish that each of us should be made a partaker of grace and live to the glory of God." '

The Deakins were originally members of the Church of England; but it appears that, owing to the great dissatisfaction felt at the cold and formal manner in which the services of the church were conducted at Attercliffe, Mr. Deakin, the father of Mrs. Heaton, together with some of his neighbours, established a small Independent Church there, of which Mr. Maurice Phillips, Mr. Deakin's eldest son-in-law, subsequently became the first minister.

Such was the family which John Heaton entered by marriage in the year in which the battle of

Waterloo was fought. He was at this time a prosperous, almost, indeed, a wealthy tradesman, possessing the chief bookselling business in Yorkshire, and
owning a not inconsiderable amount of house property
in Leeds. But it is worth noting, as a memorial of
the manners of the times in which he lived, the frugal
and unpretentious fashion in which he and his wife
commenced housekeeping.

He resided, as has already been told, in the house
attached to his shop and warehouses, No. 7 Briggate.
The parlour, or common sitting-room, was on the
ground floor, at the side of the shop, and looked out
upon the busy main thoroughfare of Leeds. This
little sitting-room was the last room of the kind in
Briggate. It was not converted into a shop until
after the death of Mr. Heaton ; long before which
time every other ground-floor apartment fronting
Briggate had undergone that change. Behind the
little sitting-room was the kitchen, and over these
two rooms were two bedrooms. Over the front shop
was a large apartment, which in the time of the
Binnses had been the pride of the house, and had
been a really handsome drawing-room. John Heaton,
however, had no occasion for a drawing-room, and
no desire in this matter to follow the example of his
predecessor. So the room stood empty during the
whole of his occupancy of the premises, and was used
as a play-room by his children. Behind this apart-

ment was the spare bed-room, appropriated to
visitors, whilst the whole of the upper floors, with
the exception of certain small rooms devoted to
servants, were employed for business purposes. One
large room was filled with an immense number of
second-hand books, of which Mr. Heaton had now a
very valuable stock ; another was used as a store-
room for paper. At the back of the house was a
pleasant little garden, where seventy years ago the
lilacs bloomed luxuriantly and flowers could be
reared. Though in the very centre of the town, the
home was not an unpleasant one ; and it is worth
being described, as it was undoubtedly a type of the
house of the prosperous tradesman at the beginning
of the present century. Nobody then was ashamed
of 'the shop,' and John Heaton, like thousands of
other men whose children have risen in social rank,
had duly mastered the old proverb, 'Keep to the
shop and the shop will keep to you.'

Here he brought his bride from Attercliffe in that
year 1815 ; and here he continued to plod on, doing
his duty quietly and unostentatiously both as a trader
and a citizen, whilst riches accumulated upon him,
and children were born to bear his name.

CHAPTER IV.

Two children were born to Mr. and Mrs. Heaton in the homely house in Briggate which is described in the last chapter. On November 23, 1817, a son, the subject of this memoir, was born. Mr. and Mrs. Heaton had one other child—a daughter, who still lives. The girl was named Ellen, whilst the boy was called, after his father and the family name of his mother, John Deakin Heaton.

In infancy and early childhood he was weakly; but in spite of his physical feebleness he showed great activity of mind. His earliest training was given to him by his mother, who was a woman of decidedly superior intelligence, and under her gentle direction both the brother and the sister were taught to read with ease before they were five years old. At that age the two were sent to a day-school kept by Mr. Langdon, the minister of the Baptist Church in Leeds. This school was kept in the house in which Mr. Langdon at that time lived, a commodious brick building now used as the Cloth Hall Tavern, and situated in Infirmary Street, just opposite the Coloured Cloth Hall Yard. This district of Leeds was then regarded as a fashionable suburb; King Street, which almost adjoins Infirmary Street, being looked upon as the furthest limit of the town. Gardens and detached villa residences then occupied nearly the whole of the space westward of Park Square, and the district beyond, which is now crowded with dwelling-houses and manufactories, was then the open country. Twice a day the two children walked to Mr. Langdon's school from their father's house in Briggate, their route being through the narrow and tortuous thoroughfare of Boar Lane, which underwent so great a change in 1867. At that time that which was regarded as a great public improvement was being carried on at the western end of Boar Lane. This was the erection of the Commercial Buildings—a really handsome as well as substantial edifice, and the first of those new public buildings of which Leeds has received so many during the present century. The Commercial Buildings, the erection of which Dr. Heaton had watched as a young schoolboy, had no long existence. In 1869 they were purchased by the Corporation, to permit of the widening of the west end of Boar Lane, and on that portion of the site they occupied which was not thrown into the street now stands the Royal Exchange.

'At this time,' says Dr. Heaton in his diary, ' my father's shop was a common resort for several gentlemen of leisure in the town, who spent their spare time there, looking over the books or chatting together on public and social affairs. Among those whom I remember are, Mr. Casson, the brother of Mrs. Binns, Mr. John Broadhead, Mr. Hobson, my father's brother-in-law, Captain Billam, and Mr. Jarvis Benson. Several of these gentlemen were unmarried or had no children of their own, and they paid much attention to my sister and myself, making themselves very friendly and familiar with us. Mr. Casson lived in a brick house, the back of which is in Wade Lane, off Potter's Almshouses. The front has two bow windows. It then looked upon a large piece of garden, extending over what is now Belgrave Street. The house still stands (1860), but is divided into two, and has lost nearly all its garden. To the garden and the housekeeper's part of the residence we had unrestricted admission; and accordingly the garden was our favourite playground on holiday afternoons. Mr. Casson, who was an old bachelor, was in the habit of joining in our play. Mr. Broadhead, another of the frequenters of my father's shop, was a member of the Society of Friends. He lived in Brunswick Place, and was married, though without family. He was fond of writing little books of rhymes for children, one of which, called " The Scarbro'

Guide," was printed and published by my father. I
had just before the appearance of the volume paid
my first visit to Scarbro', accompanied by my mother,
and this fact caused Mr. Broadhead to put upon the
title-page of his little volume the words, " Published
by J. D. Heaton, a little bookseller, not five years
old." Among the relics of my childhood which I
still treasure is a copy of this book, and I also
possess some of the manuscript effusions of this
forgotten Leeds worthy.

' Captain Billam was one of the Leeds notabilities
of his day. He was an old bachelor, of narrow means
but good family, being one of the Billams of Otley.
He was lame, and lived in a small cottage at Little
Woodhouse, very near to my present residence of
Claremont. His taste led him to accumulate old
prints, rare books, &c., so that he was quite at home
in my father's shop. I think that he eked out his
resources by buying unsuspected treasures of this
kind, and afterwards selling them at their full value
to the London dealers. Captain Billam was a great
promoter of the " Northern Exhibition," which
was held in Leeds in my early days, and which
was the forerunner of so many institutions of the
same kind. The exhibition consisted of a collection of paintings by living artists resident in the
north of England. It was held yearly in the
Music Hall, but was never supported as it should

have been by the public, and finally was given up
by its promoters.

'I likewise remember Mr. Eddison, a member of
the Society of Friends, who lived in a country house
with a paddock before it in Water Lane. The
approach to the house was by a small bridge crossing
the Beck. This Mr. Eddison was a relation of the
Eddisons of Gateford in Nottinghamshire, who were
old friends of my mother's family. I have a very
distinct recollection of going on a visit of a day or
two to Gateford from Attercliffe with my mother, one
of my aunts, and Ellen. This was in the year 1826, I
being then in my ninth and Ellen in her tenth year.
We spent the first night at the house of Miss Vessey,
an ancient maiden lady, the last of her name, who
resided on her own land and farmed it herself, living
in a plain rural fashion. Her house was an old one;
and it was built on the site of a still more ancient
building, which had been surrounded by a moat.
Part of this moat still remained as a pond at the back
of the house, whilst the remainder could be distinctly
traced. In front of the house were some very old
yew trees, clipped into quaint fantastic shapes. I
mention this visit because I remember how much I
was interested even then in the antiquities by which
I was surrounded. This was in fact the first occasion
on which my liking for antiquarian study showed
itself. Miss Vessey had been a schoolfellow of my

aunt Mary's, as also had been Mrs. Eddison, whom we next visited at Gateford. This lady was a widow, living on a large farm which she managed. She had a family of sons and daughters, one of whom is Edwin Eddison, the solicitor, of Leeds, another being Booth Eddison, the eminent surgeon of Nottingham. This was my first introduction to farming and country life.'

Shortly before this visit to Gateford the brother and sister were removed from the school to which they had first been sent, the latter now going to a school kept by Miss Plint, a lady well known in Leeds in her time, and the former to a school kept by the son of his first teacher, Mr. Langdon. Dr. Heaton himself admitted in after years that his progress in learning was not very rapid, and he bitterly deplored the fact that his father would not allow him to learn French.

In the year 1827 Mr. Heaton took an important step in retiring from business and removing from Briggate to a more comfortable place of residence. Thanks to his diligence, intelligence, and integrity, he had now acquired a considerable fortune, and he had done so in spite of the very heavy losses in which he had been involved by his singularly confiding nature. ' He had a habit,' says his son, ' of lending money in large sums to needy tradesmen on mere personal security—promissory notes. As he never took more than five per cent. interest for these accommodations, he could have had no desire of gain in this practice, and his losses were manifest and frequent. To my knowledge he lost many thousands of pounds, and incurred much trouble and annoyance. He became only too well known for his readiness to advance money on these convenient terms, and applications to him were numerous. They seldom met with a refusal. I believe he was led into this costly practice partly by his real desire to assist tradesmen out of what he believed to be temporary difficulties, partly by a too credulous trust in plausible representations into the truth of which he made little inquiry, and partly by a constitutional difficulty in refusing any pressing request.' Still it cannot be said that Mr. Heaton had permanently injured his fortunes by the practice which his son thus condemns. At the time of his retirement from business his stock-in-trade was valued at six thousand pounds, and his property in the town at between thirty and forty thousand pounds. As his habits were frugal he had no difficulty in living within the income furnished by the interest of this sum; and though he now gave up his business—the character of which was beginning to change under the influence of modern competition, he did not give up his life-long habits of frugality and industry, but continued to accumulate wealth as well as to dispense it, in the way I have described, among his poorer neighbours. His place of business he handed over to his nephew, John Heaton, jun., who had been his apprentice and shopman, and whom throughout his life he treated with much generosity. The house to which he and his family removed from the old residence in Briggate was in Park Square, and here Mr. Heaton remained until his death.

In 1830 the subject of our memoir first became connected with a famous Leeds institution with which in later life he was to be very closely identified. This was the Grammar School. Mr. Walker, who had been head-master of the school for several years, had died just before young Heaton entered it, and Dr. Holmes had been appointed as his successor. He had not yet, however, entered upon his duties, and the school was temporarily under the charge of Mr. Wollaston, the second master. The following account by Dr. Heaton of the course of education at the time of his admission to the school, more than half a century ago, will be of interest to all educationists.

'I was a very quiet, timid boy, and went with a heavy heart amongst all the rough strange boys at this new school. When I first made my appearance, having never learned the Eton Latin Grammar, with its "Propria quæ Maribus" and "As in Præsenti," I was put into the first or second form under Spencer, with little vulgar boys with whom I had no sentiments in common. In a few days it was found, however, that

though I had not learned the grammar there in use,
I had a fair knowledge of Latin grammar generally,
and I was accordingly at once promoted to the third
form, which was the lower of the two forms in Mr.
Wollaston's school. Here I was set to learn the
Eton Latin and Greek Grammars, the latter written
in Latin and very imperfectly understood, but at all
events committed to memory. This, with the translation of the Latin Delectus, the Analecta Græca
Minora, some passages from White's Diatessaron, and
—on Monday mornings—the Collect, Epistle, and
Gospel of the previous day, formed absolutely all that
I was at this time taught. English, writing, history,
geography, and modern foreign languages were all
neglected. Most gentlemen's sons at the Grammar
School had in addition some private tuition in these
essential parts of a liberal education. But my father
provided none of them for me; having put me to
school he had done enough, as he thought; and
during the whole time of my schooling, till I left
the Grammar School to go to Mr. Braithwaite's
surgery, the little Greek and Latin and the rudiments
of algebra and mathematics taught in the Grammar
School were all the teaching I had. Anything of the
modern languages, history, or geography which I
knew was accidentally picked up and known most
imperfectly, for I was by no means studious or fond
of learning for its own sake. The imperfection of my

education has been a serious disadvantage to me all my life since. I fancied I had a taste for drawing, and for one quarter of a year, by great importunity, I persuaded my father to allow me to have drawing lessons of old John Rhodes on the half-holiday afternoons; but my zeal was soon exhausted. I missed the play at cricket or other games with my schoolfellows, and neither I nor my father was unwilling that I should discontinue the drawing lessons at the end of the first quarter. This little bit of extra tuition was all that I received beyond the dry routine of the Grammar School system as then existing, a system which was inert and inefficient to the last degree.'

Whilst the education imparted at the Leeds Grammar School in those days was of this description, the manner in which it was imparted deserves note as being equally distinctive of the times in which young Heaton began his training for the battle of life. He was placed in Mr. Wollaston's class on the advent of Dr. Holmes as head-master, and he gives a graphic account of the experiences he now passed through. 'From all the tales I had heard from the other boys of Mr. Wollaston's severity, I looked upon him with great dread. He made free and indiscriminate use of the stick, and I came in for a pretty good share of its application—sometimes no doubt deservedly enough, at other times most unreasonably. It may be well to give an instance of one of the longest and most severe canings that I received. I was repeating a Greek verb to him. At that point I hesitated as though uncertain, but actually gave the form correctly. "What's that, fool?" said he suddenly, according to his customary form of address. I, not very familiar with my task, and frightened at his manner of addressing me, guessed something else. "Hold out your hand, fool!" and several stinging blows were speedily administered which did not particularly tend to clear my mind. "Guess again, fool!" and each time I answered incorrectly I met with another caning over my swollen and aching hands. At last he said, "Now then, *think* before you guess any more," and after some hesitation I said, "I think it is what I said at first." "To be sure it is, fool! Why could you not stick to it?" It was a common practice with him to hold our hands tight by the wrists on the table with the palms downwards, and then to hammer on the knuckles with a cane or thick end of a riding-whip which he used till it was completely destroyed. This would raise hard lumps on the knuckles which long remained, and I believe some boys' hands were permanently injured by this kind of punishment. I have seen him beat the son of Milner, the late librarian of the Subscription Library, striking him indiscriminately all over his head and body, till he seemed ready to faint.'

It appears, however, that this tyrant of the class room, like many a more important member of the detestable order of bullies, was himself the slave of another. 'His wife, the daughter of the then vicar Mr. Fawcett, had him it is said as much under control as he had his scholars. I have seen her come to him at his desk and chuck him under the chin in a familiar manner, a liberty which to us boys seemed strangely inconsistent with the awe in which we held him.'

Such were the surroundings of Dr. Heaton, and such the influences brought to bear upon him during his career at the Leeds Grammar School. In course of time he escaped from the brutal charge of Mr. Wollaston, and came under the milder sway of Dr. Holmes. But the mischief had then been done, and the youth had ceased to take any real interest in studies which were enforced upon him by the use of the cane and of language such as, nowadays, the humblest village pedagogue would be ashamed to use. Dr. Heaton himself never hesitated to admit that he learned little at school, did not care for his lessons, and was more anxious to shirk his tasks than to please his teachers. After reading the preceding account of the Leeds Grammar School as it existed fifty years ago, the reader will probably feel that it would have been surprising if the contrary had been the case. Among the friends whom the boy made during these days at school were Thomas Sheepshanks, afterwards vicar of Bilton near Harrogate; Markland, subsequently a solicitor in Leeds; and C. J. Hare, afterwards a well-known London physician, whose father at that time managed a lunatic asylum at New Wortley. To the grounds of this asylum the boys were wont to resort on half-holidays for skittles, archery, and other amusements.

In October 1834 a great change in the career of Dr. Heaton took place. His father withdrew him from the Grammar School and apprenticed him to Mr. Braithwaite, surgeon, of Leeds, to be initiated into the mysteries of the profession in which he was destined eventually to attain eminence. Those who knew Dr. Heaton in later years, and who were aware of the zeal and enthusiasm with which he pursued his calling, of the devoted attachment to it which he showed upon all occasions, and of the manner in which he regarded all who were his colleagues in that noble pursuit, will hear with not a little surprise that in his youth he had no natural bent towards medicine. In what direction his tastes did tend it is now impossible to say. He himself declared that he had no inclination for any particular calling; and in all probability he was more concerned then with his juvenile amusements than with any of the more serious affairs of life. He had, however, one very strong feeling with regard to his future calling,

and that was an intense antipathy to surgery. Great
therefore was his consternation when his father one
day summarily announced to him that he was forthwith to be placed in the surgery of Mr. Braithwaite.
The boy felt inclined to rebel against the parental
decree, but was well aware that it would be useless
to do so. His father, though ' one of the meekest of
men,' was very firm when carrying out any intention
he had formed respecting his children, and implicit
obedience was duly expected from and rendered by
the son on this occasion. It cannot be said that the
circumstances under which the young man began his
study of medicine were calculated to remove his
prejudices against the calling into which he had
been thus summarily pitchforked. Mr. Braithwaite's
practice was a large one, but at that time it lay almost
entirely among the poorer classes. Those were not
days in which luxury was studied among the young,
and Mr. Braithwaite's apprentices had to bear their
full share in the rough experiences then common
among medical students. They had to prepare the
medicines, pounding the drugs in the big mortar and
making up the mixtures in bottles; they had to post
Mr. Braithwaite's ledger, and had not only to make
out the accounts against the patients, but to deliver
them. But after all it was the kind of school in which
many of the most useful lessons of life are learned.
The boy had idled through his earlier years. No idling

was tolerated now. He had trusted to his father for everything that he needed in the way of comfort, ease, or pleasure. Now he had to fight his own battles, and look only to himself for any means of escape from the pressure of daily toil. It is not surprising that we should find that despite the seemingly unfavourable influences of the new home into which he had entered, young Heaton began to show signs of development in character which afforded hope that he would eventually become a useful and valuable member of society. He entered at the Leeds Medical School in the winter of 1835, and began to attend the lectures. The school had even then secured that great reputation which it still retains, and names of high eminence in the profession were already associated with it. For two sessions, however, the young student remained insensible to the spirit of the place, and indifferent to success. The evil influences of the Grammar School still pursued him; and he looked upon all education as a task which it was his chief duty to shirk if possible. It was not until the winter session of 1837 that a change came over his spirit. He was seized with a desire to win a prize. For learning for its own sake he still cared nothing, and was utterly indifferent as to the progress which he might make in his adopted profession. But some youthful jealousy had stirred his ambition. He had seen others gain prizes and praise, and he made up his mind that he would endeavour to emulate their course. Accordingly he plunged into a severe course of cramming, thinking of nothing but the prize he had set his heart upon winning, and devoting his whole time to work in connection with it. Anatomy was the subject to which he devoted himself, and for which he neglected all other studies. Finding that the practical process of dissection was too slow to permit him to make the progress he desired, he devoted himself wholly to books and plates, and by means of these acquired such an amount of knowledge that by the end of the session he was able to give the anatomy of almost any part of the human body from memory, ' though,' he adds, when stating this fact, ' I fear I could not have demonstrated the parts from the dissected body very efficiently.'

The end of this sudden and fierce spurt was that, to the astonishment of his friends and the delight of his parents, Dr. Heaton gained the prize in Anatomy, his chief rival in the competition being a much older man than himself. Nor was this all: for at the distribution of prizes he was specially complimented by the Council on the excellence of his answers, and at the subsequent dinner of the students which was attended by the members of the Council, he had to take the place of honour in returning thanks for the successful students. This was his first appearance as a public speaker ; and it is not surprising that he

was very nervous in discharging the honourable
duty thus imposed upon him.

His success had set a new train of ideas in motion
in his mind. The secret springs of ambition had at
last been touched; and somewhat tardily he had
awoke to a consciousness of the fact that he had not
been sent into the world merely to idle away his time.
Doubtless the fact that his father was known to be a
man of considerable and growing wealth, and that he
and his only sister were thus secure of something
more than a competence, had operated as a deterrent
to the youth in first entering upon his studies. But
even this circumstance failed to stifle his ambition
now that it had been fairly roused to life. ' I now
thought sincerely,' he tells us, ' that gaining prizes
was the first object of existence and the most important duty; and resolved that to this great task I
would devote my energies.' He adds, writing in his
mature age, words which are worth being remembered
in an age of cram : ' Of course no mistake could be
greater than this. Reading and studying, and com-
mitting to memory the facts so acquired, are doubtless important parts of education; but if they be
pursued to the neglect of observation, the exercise of
the perceptive faculties, and the practical exercise of
one's knowledge—to the neglect, also, of the reasoning faculty and original thought—the whole result
may be well nigh worthless, and may end merely in

the acquisition of the prize, not in that preparation of the mind for the serious business of life which is the true object of education. This I fear was too much my case; but I sincerely believed at the time that I was following the right course in acquiring prizes, and for this I too much neglected the dissecting room and the bedside.'

In the following summer he gained the medal in the Botanical Class, and about the same time he undertook a work which to the end of his life was a congenial one to him, by becoming secretary to the Students' Debating Society. At the close of the session he went on a brief visit to his friend C. J. Hare, who was then a student of Caius College, Cambridge. This was his first long journey from home, and it bore fruit afterwards by filling him with a desire to follow his friend to Cambridge, in order to complete his education there. However, in the meantime he continued the task of prize-winning at the Leeds School of Medicine, and he did so with a success that was truly surprising. Mr. Braithwaite's ' idle apprentice ' had suddenly been transformed into the most industrious of students, and such was his good fortune in prize-winning that there positively seemed to be no limits to the honours which were within his reach. In the winter session of 1838 he obtained the silver medals—the first prizes—both in Chemistry and in the Practice of Medicine, and the second prize in

Surgery. In the previous session, it ought to be mentioned, he had gained the second prize for Forensic Medicine under somewhat peculiar circumstances. He had not made any special preparation for the examination, and had not intended to compete. One of his fellow-students, however, who thought himself certain of winning the first prize, begged him to go into the examination merely in order to swell the number of competitors, and thus increase the glory of the prize-winner. Heaton did so without having the remotest hope of securing anything for himself, and to his own great astonishment came in second in the competition. This fact should be borne in mind when we hear his own self-accusations concerning the superficial character of the knowledge he acquired whilst studying for prizes. It is clear that he must have laid ' a good foundation ' of knowledge during the course of these severe competitive studies.

In the summer of 1839 he gained the medal in the Forensic Medicine Class, this being the fifth prize he gained out of the seven given. The two he did not gain were for Materia Medica and Surgery, and in neither of these departments did he offer himself for the competition. From the time that he gained his first medal, that for Anatomy, he was always first in every competition which he entered save in that which I have just mentioned for Forensic Medicine

in the summer of 1838, and which he entered under
such peculiar circumstances. His indenture of
apprenticeship to Mr. Braithwaite expired when he
was twenty-one years old, in 1838, but he continued
to reside with him for a few months as gratuitous
assistant. He then returned to his father's roof and
spent a short season of leisure after his hard work in
prize-winning.

The experience he had obtained under the roof of
Mr. Braithwaite had by no means removed his original
distaste for the life of a general practitioner. That
life he had discovered to be one not merely of hard
work, but in many cases of something like drudgery.
His father wished him to pursue the ordinary course
of the young surgeon, and, having obtained the necessary qualification, to begin practice among the poorest
classes, trusting to his industry and popularity for any
improvement in position. Such a scheme, however,
by no means suited the ambition of the son. His
success in the School of Medicine had fired him with
the idea of taking a higher position than that of an
ordinary family practitioner, and he resolved to aim
at becoming a consulting physician. His education,
however—sadly neglected as it had been at the
Grammar School—was not such as to fit him for this
position, and it therefore became necessary that he
should resume his studies. His father, after consulting Dr. Williamson, at that time the leading

physician in Leeds, wished him to go to University College, London ; but the young man had been fired by the wish to become a member of one of the older Universities, and, having seen something of Cambridge during his brief visit to his friend C. J. Hare, he urged his father to allow him to proceed thither in order that he might there complete his studies. After some demur Mr. Heaton consented, and the son accordingly entered at Caius College, Cambridge, in the autumn of 1839. On his way to the University he paid a brief visit to London, where he stayed with his mother's sister, Mrs. Strange, and saw as many of the sights of the town as it was possible to visit within the two or three days at his command.

Cambridge, however, did not suit him. He seems to have suffered from home-sickness during his brief sojourn there, and also to have been somewhat unwell. He was older than most of the men who were about him, and he found, after his active and laborious life in Mr. Braithwaite's surgery, that it was most distasteful to have to resume the quiet occupations of the student. Moreover, the very instinct which had made him so successful a prize-winner at Leeds impelled him to devote his whole time and attention to studies immediately connected with his adopted profession. It seemed a waste of time to be returning to the lessons which he had pored over at the Grammar School, when he now knew that it was to be the business of his life to cure disease and alleviate human suffering. Accordingly, before he had been many weeks at Cambridge he implored his father to consent to his leaving that place, and to his entering himself as a medical student at University College, London. Mr. Heaton reluctantly agreed to this sudden change in his plans, and early in 1840 he went to London and entered himself at University College.

His course there, so far as prize-winning was concerned, was as distinguished as it had been at Leeds. In his first session, it is true, he gained no particular distinction. That, however, was due to the fact that he only attended the lectures during a small portion of the term. At the close of the summer session following, he was second in the examination of the University College Class and received a silver medal; and in an examination in Botany, at Apothecaries Hall, open to all medical students, he also gained the second prize, a silver medal and a handsome gift of books. In the same month in which he gained these prizes, he passed the preliminary examination for the degree of M.B. at the University of London. Too old to enter for honours, he was only able to take a place in the first class. This was the record of his work from February to July 1840.

In the latter month he took part in an interesting public ceremonial which he thus describes: 'In July

1840 there was a deputation from the Universities of Oxford and Cambridge to the Queen, to congratulate her upon her escape from the attempt upon her life made by the pot-boy Oxford. Any member of either University was allowed to accompany the deputation. Hare being then in town, and being a member of the University of Cambridge, determined to form part of the deputation. I had only recently taken my name off the books at Cambridge in order to save further unnecessary expense there, so that I was no longer a member of the University. But being encouraged by my friend, I determined to put a bold face on, and accompany Hare, running the risk of a challenge which I was assured was not very likely to be given. I had sold my own cap and gown on leaving Cambridge, so I applied to a robe-maker's for the loan of one. There was, however, so great a demand for them on the occasion that the only gown I could borrow was that of an Oxford B.A. I boldly took this and a cap, and accompanied Hare to the Thatched House Tavern, St. James's Street, where the deputation assembled. Here I managed to escape observation, and fell into the procession, which was headed by the dons, among whom were several bishops in lawn, professors, heads of houses, &c. The procession walked to Buckingham Palace, where we were ushered up the grand staircase into the antechamber. Soon some folding doors were thrown open, and we entered the audience chamber. Here we found the Queen, seated on the throne, whilst Prince Albert, the ladies in waiting, and the various members of the Court, stood beside her. The address was duly read ; Her Majesty read a suitable reply, and then the deputation bowed and backed out of the room. The folding doors were once more closed upon us, and we were left to get out of the palace as we pleased.'

Returning to London from Leeds in October of this year 1840, he resumed his studies at University College, and in the following May went in for honours at the examinations in Medical Physiology and Comparative Anatomy. The result was that in Medicine he was first, receiving the gold medal; in Physiology he was second, receiving the silver medal, and in Physiology, after an extraordinarily close contest, he was also second, and silver medallist. Writing subsequently about these successes, he characteristically observes : ' My gaining these three prizes was thought a great distinction, and at once placed me in a position of eminence among the students. Each of the professors whose classes I had attended invited me to his house, and, after having been shy and modest almost to a fault, I now began to form conceited opinions about myself and my abilities.'

It was at the very time when he was thus gaining distinctions which gladdened the hearts of his friends and, above all, of his parents, that the first great sorrow of his life befell him.

'There were two or three days' interval between the end of the winter session and the commencement of the summer session, and for that short time I allowed myself complete rest from study. I had received a letter from my father mentioning that my mother was out of health, but that Mr. Hey had seen her and did not apprehend any danger. She had long been more or less an invalid, and this account of her state did not excite any alarm in me. I think it was on Saturday, May 1 (1841), that I went by railway to the village of Harrow-on-the-Hill for a day's excursion. The day was very fine and I greatly enjoyed my escape from the confinement of College lectures and London streets. I wandered through the country lanes, visiting the church and school buildings, and returned home fatigued, but delighted with my day's excursion. At that very time my mother was lying at the point of death, and I had been summoned to her bedside. There being no Sunday delivery in London, I did not receive the letter calling me to Leeds until Monday morning. I left London by the next train. When I drove up to the door of my father's house in Park Square on the evening of that day, the blinds were all drawn and I knew what had happened. My dear mother had died the previous day, May 2, 1841. She had been more indisposed than usual for some days, and had been feverish, but no alarm had been felt. Then she had passed into a semi-comatose state, which at last became complete coma, in which she died. I believe much of her tenderest love was bestowed upon me The last words she uttered were an inquiry for me.'

The son stayed with his bereaved father and sister for a fortnight—'and a sad and gloomy fortnight it was'—and then returned to London and resumed his studies. He became the clinical clerk of Dr. Williams, and, besides attending the Botanical Lectures and reading for them, attended Dr. Williams in his visits at the hospital, and kept daily records of all his cases. He also attended the Clinical Lectures of the same eminent professor, taking full notes of them, from which reports of the lectures were subsequently published in the 'Medical Gazette.' He competed at this time for two prizes given for Reports of Cases in the hospital; one the Fellows' Gold Medal, in competing for which it was necessary to give a brief report of all the medical cases in the hospital at the time, and full reports and commentaries on particular cases singled out for that purpose. The other prize . was a set of books given by Dr. Thompson for reports on cases under his charge. In both of these competitions he was successful, and was highly complimented by the examiners on the merit of his

reports. On the other hand he was only second in
the Botanical examination. In November of this
year he passed his M.B. examination in the first
class, and gained the gold medal in Botany, but to
his intense chagrin did not distinguish himself in
any other subject.

In February 1842 he quitted University College,
where he had worked so hard and had gained such
high distinction as a successful student. I find in
his diary a reference to the manner in which he had
lived whilst a student in London, which deserves to be
quoted, for Dr. Heaton was his own severest critic,
and would never have written the following lines if
he had not known them to be absolutely true : ‘ At
this time (1841), and for some time previously and
afterwards, I might truly be said “ to shun delights
and live laborious days.” During my time in London
I scarcely went to any entertainments or relaxed my
constant round of attending lectures and hospitals
and reading at home early and late.’ His successes
in the examination had procured him much notice
from the professors, and he was frequently asked to
their houses. I find from his diary, however, that
he declined the invitation of one of these gentlemen
on the ground that the invitation was for a Sunday.
His early training in the home of the Leeds nonconformist clearly still sufficed to guard him against
even so slight an infraction of Puritan decorum as

would have been involved in his visit to one of his tutors on the Sabbath. Among the friends with whom he was intimate whilst at University College were C. J. Hare, his old companion at Leeds, Garrod, and Parkes, who have all since attained eminence in their profession.

On leaving London he went at once to Paris, where he attended the hospitals and the School of Medicine to the end of the summer session. There is no record of the professional results he secured from this short sojourn in the French capital, and it is probable that his want of proficiency in the language hampered him in his studies. In August he returned home, much out of health, and remained in Leeds during the winter, residing with his father in Park Square. Early in 1843 he once more set off for the Continent, and made a prolonged tour through Italy. His antiquarian tastes, which had asserted themselves very early in life, were confirmed by his visit to that classic country. He made many purchases of curious relics and small works of art during his travels, but to his great vexation found that, owing to a trivial and innocent irregularity at the English Custom House when landing at Southampton in August of the same year, he was compelled to part with them all. Some he subsequently recovered by purchase, but many of the most interesting were never restored to him.

He immediately set to work on his return home
to prepare for his M.D. examination, which was to
take place in November. In October of that year
Dr. Chadwick, the well-known physician of Leeds,
resigned his office as physician to the Dispensary in
that town; and having the M.D. qualification, Mr.
Heaton offered himself as a candidate in Dr. Chadwick's place. Dr. Smart, a gentleman who had
recently settled in Leeds, was also an applicant for
the post; but after a sharp contest, Mr. Heaton was
elected by 190 votes to 66. On November 8 he
went to London for his examination. The contest
for the Dispensary appointment had necessarily interfered much with his preparation for the examination,
but he once more met with what might fairly be
called his customary success. He was placed in the
first class, received a certificate of special proficiency,
and won the gold medal for the best Commentary on a
Case in Medicine. On December 11, 1843, having then
attained the age of twenty-six, he returned to Leeds,
and forthwith began his duties at the Dispensary. He
took up his residence temporarily with his father in
Park Square, until the house No. 2 East Parade,
which Mr. Heaton had purchased for him, could be
prepared for his occupation.

CHAPTER V.

PUBLIC LIFE IN LEEDS.

In the preceding chapter we have dealt exclusively with the personal career of Dr. Heaton during his childhood and youth. We have seen him in his early days at the Leeds Grammar School or Mr. Braithwaite's surgery, like most lads of his age, careless and indifferent both with regard to his studies and his future career, thinking more of present enjoyment than of any of the more serious duties of life, and giving no promise of future reputation or usefulness. Then we have seen the curious ' new departure' which he made during the course of his studies at the Leeds Medical School, when suddenly fired with the ambition of winning prizes, and the remarkable results which followed. I need tell none who are acquainted with the course of study followed by Dr. Heaton in Leeds and the University of London that it was no small thing which he achieved when he thus carried off prize after prize in these severe competitions. He himself to the last day of his life was singularly diffident with regard to his personal abilities and acquirements. If he spoke of them at all, it was always to express regret that he had not enjoyed greater advantages in his early youth, or that he had not made better use of those advantages which he did enjoy. A few words I quoted from his diary in the preceding chapter show that he dwelt almost with scorn upon the natural elation with which as a young man he had regarded his success at college. Yet there was every reason for his being proud of his career at University College ; and when he came to Leeds to begin practice in his native town, it was with the reputation of having attained a brilliant success in his medical studies. More happily situated than many men who have afterwards attained eminence in the same profession, he was not troubled at the outset of his career by any anxiety respecting pecuniary matters. His father had purchased for and presented to him a commodious house in East Parade, then a fashionable residential street in Leeds, and he was well able to wait for practice without making any attempt to force it by methods which were repugnant to his nature. Thus young, active, well-to-do, and possessing a considerable reputation, he entered upon his life's work under the very happiest auspices ; and if he failed at once to take a commanding position among the profession in Leeds, the fact must be attributed to his own diffidence, and not to any lack of ability or opportunity.

Henceforward, in this record of his life and work, we shall have to deal with Dr. Heaton as a leading public man in a great provincial town. This, as has been intimated in the introductory remarks, is after all the aspect of his life which has most of value and interest for the general reader. In his own home he was beloved for a rare combination of gifts—gentleness, humour, affection; among the members of his profession he was respected for his solid attainments, and for that ' brilliant common sense' which he brought to the study and determination of any difficult problem. But it is not in either of these capacities that his life is best worth being studied by those who were not personally acquainted with him. It is because he was one of a class of men who are too little known to the world at large, whose work is too often ignored, and whose great though unobtrusive influence on our social life is felt but not acknowledged. The life of a provincial town presents no charms to the cultivated but superficial observer. Biography has nothing to say of the men who have had most to do with the building up of the fortunes of Birmingham and Manchester. of Live pool and Leeds. The local reputation must acquire the stamp of metropolitan approbation before it is thought worthy of notice even by the most thoughtful of social students. Thus it comes to pass that in English literature and English thought, a great and useful class of men are systematically ignored; and those who are diligent in observing and investigating the manners and customs of some tribe in the heart of Africa, or of the inhabitants of some island in the South Seas, are altogether ignorant of what is passing at their own doors, under their own eyes, in towns which, although they cannot boast of the historic glories of the great capitals of Europe, are even now superior to many of them in wealth and population, and are laying broad and deep the foundations of a future destiny which may vie in interest and importance with that of some of the most famous cities of the ancient world.

It was Dr. Heaton's lot to live in a provincial town. We have seen what his education had been. That, at least, can hardly be called provincial. He had obtained a glimpse of life at one of the old Universities; he had pursued for years a most successful course of study in the capital of the empire; he had worked for a season in Paris, and he had spent more than six months in travelling in Italy. No man of even ordinary intelligence could go through these experiences and come back to Leeds a mere provincial citizen, with no ideas that ranged beyond the narrow limits of his own town. Least of all could a man of Dr. Heaton's sterling common sense do so. So, when he returned to Leeds, it was to identify himself with the social life of the place, not with a view to his own aggrandisement or enrichment—for he never sought those political honours which are so dear to some, and never tried to obtain more than a fair return for his capital—but with a view to the elevation and improvement of the whole tone of life, the creation and extension of public institutions calculated either to relieve the physical wants of the poor and suffering, or to stimulate the intellectual faculties of those more happily situated. It is my wish to show what the life of a public-spirited man in a provincial town may be when he gives himself up with rare devotion to public work; and though such a record is seldom offered to the public, and may possibly seem tame and monotonous to some, it is one that cannot be without its value to all who are interested in the agencies by which the social life of England is being developed.

In that year, 1843, when Dr. Heaton commenced practice in Leeds, it is to be feared that the public and municipal life of the town was in a somewhat stagnant condition. Those who know it now, and who are aware of the large number of handsome public buildings and great charitable and educational institutions of which it boasts, will hardly understand how people existed in those days, near though they are to the present. There was then no Town Hall such as that which now fills the stranger with admiration: the building occupied by the Philosophical

and Literary Society had not been erected; where
Sir Gilbert Scott's great Hospital now stands, there
were open fields and a few tumble-down dwelling·
houses ; Dr. Hook's magnificent scheme for the erection of churches adequate in number to meet the
wants of the population had not been promulgated ;
and Boar Lane was a narrow, crooked, and filthy
lane, a disgrace to the town and to its local rulers.
The public buildings which did exist were few in
number, and they were for the most part by no
means imposing. The principal among them were
the parish church, then just re-erected through the
active and untiring efforts of the vicar ; East Parade
Chapel, which was opened in 1841, and which was
regarded as one of the ornaments of the town ; the
Commercial Buildings at the corner of Boar Lane,
since swept away ; and the Court House, now occupied
by the Post Office, where the local affairs of the
borough were administered. The latest addition to
these public edifices before Dr. Heaton began his
practice was a building which stood very near to his
own house—the Mechanics' Institution, in South
Parade. The friends of the institution were justly
proud at that time of the handsome and commodious
house which they had thus secured, and which presented so great a contrast to the garret in which the
members of the institution had originally met. Yet
there is almost as great a contrast between the

building in South Parade and the really stately and imposing structure in Cookridge Street, as there was between the former and the shed in which the institution had its birth.

Of public halls in which meetings could be held for the discussion of political and other questions of importance, there were then only the Music Hall in Albion Street, the Court House, and the new room of the Mechanics' Institution. Perhaps the want of such places of assembly was not so much felt as it would be at the present time, for, judging by the newspapers of forty years ago, public meetings were not then by any means so common as they are now, and when they were held—except on rare occasions of national interest—they were by no means largely attended.

And whilst the Leeds of 1843 presented this striking contrast to the Leeds of to-day, seeming to be, as it were, a poor and unembellished edition of the great town we now know, without good streets or fine public buildings, there were other differences less noticeable on the surface, but not less striking. At that time it is no exaggeration to say, the manner in which the poor of our great towns were lodged was a reproach upon our boasted civilisation. The public conscience had not been awakened or enlightened with regard to sanitary matters. Even in the dwellings of the upper and middle classes, defects which would now call for the prompt and stern interference of the authorities were then regarded as a matter of course, and were hardly perceived by the people who were their victims. And whilst this was the case in the squares and terraces where the local aristocracy lived, something infinitely worse—a state of things so terrible that it is impossible to describe it in detail—characterised the dwellings of the poor.

There are many among us who think that the manner in which, even to the present day, the working-classes are housed is not creditable to us as a nation. The long rows of ill-built cottages, fronting streets that are waiting for the attentions of the pavior, are not objects of which any of us have reason to be proud; and it is not surprising that writers like Mr. Carlyle should lose no opportunity of denouncing the cheap and nasty provision which is thus made for our labouring men. But let any who feel inclined to exalt the past in order to depreciate the present recall the state of things which existed in a town like Leeds forty years ago. Suburban districts had not then been appropriated to the poor, and they were herded together in dense masses in the heart of the town. In buildings rotten with age, reeking with filth and damp, and shut up in the narrowest and foulest of courts, far away from the free air of heaven or the light of the sun, whole colonies of the poor then dwelt. They lived, in literal truth, in the midst of filth and wretchedness such as cannot be described. The public conscience, I say, had not then been touched by their horrible condition, nor had any sense of the true interest of the community awakened the local authorities to active efforts for the mitigation of the evil. It seemed enough that a man should be willing to live in a certain place in order to prove that the place in question was fit to be a human habitation. No questions were asked about the cubic space allotted in a particular building to each resident; nobody thought of seeing if the roof was proof against rain, or the floors against damp; and as for the notion that the sewage of such a place was worthy of being attended to, the bold man who ventured to broach it would have been laughed to scorn. So when the young doctor who had been trained in the most advanced and powerful Medical School of his day began his life's work in Leeds, he found the poor herding together in all the courts and lanes running from Kirkgate and the other central portions of the town, some in cellars where the light of day never penetrated, some in garrets from which the snows and rains and winds of winter could not be excluded, many in sheds that had been erected in the darker corners of the courts, and that were without any of the ordinary provisions for human comfort, and all in the midst of filth and misery such as rivalled the horrors of the Ghetto or of the purlieus of Cologne. Naturally the public reaped the fruits of their own offending in.this matter. Fevers of the worst kind and successive visitations of cholera swept down upon the town and carried off hundreds—on one memorable occasion, thousands—of the inhabitants. Naturally, too, these epidemics revelled among such spots as those of which I have spoken, the nests of hovels where the poor were crowded together under the shadow of the noble parish church ; but their ravages were not confined to these places, and many of the wealthy, as well as some of those benevolent and pious persons whose chief mission it was to succour the victims of these recurring visitations, perished along with the ill-housed poor. Dr. Heaton, as I shall have occasion presently to tell, was himself one of those medical men who suffered greatly in health through their efforts to cope with the epidemics which were then so common in Leeds.

Such was the state of the town forty years ago. Of political activity there was no lack. Cobden and Bright were then frequent visitors to the chief city of the West Riding, and frequent speakers in the Music Hall, then the scene of most political meetings. Dr. Hook and his antagonists, Mr. (now Sir Edward) Baines and Dr. Winter Hamilton, were engaged in discussing the true theory of a system of national education and the other questions upon which Churchmen and Nonconformists were naturally divided in opinion. Public spirit ran just as high then as it does now in our great provincial towns. But it was a time when the quaint social conservatism which had given a distinctive character of its own to each great town and city throughout the country was rapidly disappearing, and when as yet its place had not been taken by that local patriotism which has since been developed so largely. People living in towns like Leeds recognised the fact that they were provincial, and made no attempt to escape from their provincialism. Though they had plenty to say about the repeal of the Corn Laws, or any other exciting political question, they had not yet realised the fact that at their own doors there was work to be done in its way not less important than that intrusted to the Imperial Parliament. To lay out wide and handsome streets, to erect imposing public buildings, to establish really efficient systems of lighting and draining, to reform the dwellings of the poor, and to sweep out of existence the vile dens in which ague, cholera, and fever constantly lurked; to provide means by which the inhabitants even of a great manufacturing town, separated by hundreds of miles from the capital and from the great seats of learning might yet acquire something of the higher culture, and be placed in sympathy with those movements of human intelligence and national feeling which did not concern

Acts of Parliament or the policy of Ministers ; and in general to elevate and enlighten a provincial community, sweetening its life and raising its aspirations, was a work to which few felt themselves to be called —a work, indeed, the very existence of which was hardly realised by the vast majority of persons.

Dr. Heaton had no taste for politics, nor did he appreciate the charms of ecclesiastical dialectics. Unlike his father, he took no interest in the Nonconformist community with which his early years had been associated ; and, as a mere boy, he left the Independents and became a regular attendant at St. Paul's Church, and when he subsequently settled in Leeds and began practice he became a seat-holder at St. George's Church, of which the Rev. William Sinclair was then the incumbent, and this church he continued to attend to the day of his death. This separation from the creed of his fathers, and his dislike for mere political conflict, shut him off to a great extent from the field in which in those days the largest amount of mental activity and public spirit was displayed. But he was not a man who could shut himself up within the narrow limits of domestic or professional life, and it was the natural consequence of the position in which he found himself, strongly attached to neither political party, that he was thrown into that branch of public work which was just beginning to assert its claims upon the thoughtful and liberal-minded inhabitants of our large provincial towns. It was to the duties of a citizen that he devoted himself very early after his establishment in practice in Leeds, and it was as the useful, laborious, and public-spirited local worker that he subsequently reached his highest reputation and his widest sphere of usefulness. It will be my duty now to show the various works for the improvement and development of Leeds, and of the inhabitants of the district in which Leeds is situated, in which he took part during his public career.

Naturally enough, during his earliest years of professional work he made that work his chief occupation. I have hinted at some of the conditions which then affected the health of the poor of Leeds. As physician to the Public Dispensary, Dr. Heaton found that he could at once obtain any amount of practice among the very poor. It was not of course remunerative labour, but it had great attractions for him. The boyish fastidiousness which had led him to turn with something like disgust from the heavy and often unpleasant duties which had belonged to him as the assistant of a general practitioner, had now yielded to the enthusiasm of his calling. He had mastered the great truth that the first thought of the physician must be for his patient, his last thought for himself; and that no work, however menial or heavy it may be, which is undertaken for

the purpose of relieving human pain and misery,
ought to be obnoxious to one who has devoted himself to the medical profession. Accordingly we find
that, during these early years of his practice in Leeds,
he was more at home among the squalid residences
of the poor or in the consulting rooms of the Dispensary than in his own house in East Parade.
Taking a real and deep interest in his work, he
busied himself during his scanty leisure in preparing
reports upon the most interesting cases which came
under his care, for publication in the 'Medical
Gazette.'

That leisure must have been scant indeed during
the first year of his practice in Leeds. Early in 1844
he was offered a lectureship in the Medical School, of
which he was now justly regarded as one of the
most distinguished pupils. The offer was made to
him on the usual condition of his purchasing a share
in the School and becoming a member of the Council.
The particular lectureship he was asked to undertake
was one for which he was peculiarly qualified by his
own studies—that of Botany. He eagerly accepted
the offer, and at once set about the preparation of his
lectures, the delivery of which was to commence in
May. Before the summer session of the School was
at an end he was asked to undertake a new and very
onerous duty in connection with it. Dr. Duncan had
resigned the lectureship on Materia Medica, and the

Council had come to the conclusion that there was at
the time no one in Leeds eligible to succeed him as a
member of the Council. They accordingly requested
Dr. Pyemont Smith and Dr. Heaton to undertake the
lectures on Materia Medica between them, in addition
to their other duties. Thus the young doctor, whose
work though unremunerative was already pressing
heavily upon him, found himself saddled during this
year with the preparation of fifty additional lectures.
It may be mentioned that in preparing the lectures
on Botany he found that he had himself to provide
both plants and diagrams for their illustration—a
duty which added not a little both to the expense
and the laboriousness of his task.

That his zeal for professional work was not
damped by any of these things is proved by the fact
that in 1846 he successfully applied for the post of
physician to the House of Recovery, an admirable
institution designed for the relief of the victims of
fever and other infectious complaints. Such a post
was not without its serious perils, as Dr. Heaton was
himself before long to experience. In 1847 he had
suffered considerably in his health in consequence of
a poisoned wound caused whilst dissecting a tortoise.
In October of that year he was still suffering from
this wound. He was at the same time very busily
engaged, both in preparing an article for the 'British
Quarterly Review,' to which he had become a con-

tributor, and in arranging for some chemical lectures
in the Medical School, which he had undertaken to
give in an emergency occasioned by the resignation
of Mr. West. Leeds was just then subject to one of
the periodical outbreaks of fever due to the culpable
negligence of the local authorities and the general
ignorance which at that time prevailed regarding the
laws of health. It was of course one of the duties of
the physician to the House of Recovery to be in the
very thick of an epidemic of this kind, whenever it
occurred. It is a part of the physician's lot which
scarcely attracts the observation of the outer world.
Men and women seem to suppose that ' the doctor '
has a charmed life, or that he possesses some potent
protective against infection which is hidden from the
rest of mankind. How sadly they are mistaken in
their ideas upon the subject could be shown by
countless widows and orphans who have been bereaved, because the head of the household, a medical
man, has nobly set at naught the fear of danger to
himself, and has gone down into the thick of the
battle against disease, in order to rescue the victim of
some horrible malady. We are a long way as yet
from the time when heroism of this kind will be
recognised as being equal in degree to the more showy
exploits of the battle-field ; and when we hear that a
doctor has succumbed to disease contracted in the
course of his professional labours, we shrug our

shoulders and pass on with an easy phrase of
compassion.

Dr. Heaton was laid low by the fever in this
month of October 1847. It was a part of the price
he had to pay for the honour of being physician
to the House of Recovery. He did not die ; but the
attack was a most severe one, and for many days his
life was in the most serious jeopardy. Happily he
recovered rapidly when once amendment had commenced, and by the close of the year, after a brief
visit during his convalescence to Scarbro', he was
once more able to resume his practice.

Some little time before this illness Dr. Heaton
had entered upon a new field of social usefulness, one
in which he was destined to labour to the end of his
days. This was in connection with the Philosophical
and Literary Society of Leeds. The story of that
society is a very interesting one. It had its origin in
a letter published by the present Sir Edward Baines,
then a very young man, in the 'Leeds Mercury,' in
the year 1818. The seed thus sown by the hand of
a boy did not fall upon stony soil. The idea which
he propounded was taken up by persons of influence
and reputation in the town ; a meeting was held, and
in 1819 it was resolved to found a society for promoting philosophical and literary studies among the
inhabitants of Leeds. At that time very few of our
large provincial towns possessed institutions of this

kind. Newcastle, more highly favoured than most
places, had its Literary and Philosophical Society, a
still flourishing and most admirable institution ; but
in those towns which had grown with the development of local manufactures, and which were not
either the capitals of counties or the seats of very
ancient and important industries, the local bookseller's shop or the tavern parlour was still the only
place of meeting for kindred spirits interested in
literature, science, or politics.

In Leeds the proposal to establish a first-class
institution, which should not only include the leading features of the model society at Newcastle but
should possess other and novel attractions, met with
general favour.   Among those who attended the preliminary meeting at the Court House, held on December 11, 1818, for the purpose of establishing the
society, were not only the elder Mr. Heaton's old
fellow-workman, Mr. Baines, and his son, the present
Sir Edward Baines, but most of those who had been
familiar figures in the bookseller's shop in Briggate.
Mr. Gott, Mr. Marshall, Mr. Tottie, Mr. William Hey,
Mr. John Bischoff, Mr. John Atkinson, and a host of
other 'Leeds worthies' of their day, took part in the
proceedings, and great unanimity and public spirit
characterising the meeting, it was found an easy
matter to take the necessary steps for forming the
society.   Money was freely subscribed by the

wealthier citizens of the town ; a site at the junction of Bond Street and Park Row—still occupied by the institution—was purchased, and a commodious edifice erected. This it need hardly be said was by no means identical with the building which is now so familiar to the inhabitants of Leeds. Though it commenced its operations under singularly favourable auspices, the beginning of the Philosophical and Literary Society was modest in comparison with the development it has since attained. Yet, such as it was, even then it had a high place among institutions of this kind throughout the country, and accomplished a most useful work among the great community whose leading citizens had reared it.

The history of the Philosophical and Literary Society of Leeds cannot be written in full in these pages. If it were possible to tell its story here, the reader would find that it was one of singular interest and value. For more than sixty years it has been a little torch of culture, burning in the midst of the darkness of provincial philistinism. Dense indeed was that darkness when this torch was first lighted, and striking was the contrast between the intellec‑ tual atmosphere of the institution and that which prevailed outside the limits of its influence. How great that influence has been can only be known to those who have been familiar with its work during many years, and who have seen how it has stimu‑

lated the minds of thousands, and developed the taste for science and literature—for it is notable that science very quickly took the place of philosophy in the scope of the institution—among those who but for its existence would hardly have felt an interest in these things.

Dr. Heaton had become a member of the society immediately after his return from London; and he found time, in spite of the heavy pressure of his professional labours, not only to take an active interest in the lectures given before the members, but himself to become one of the lecturers of the institution. It was probably in recognition of what he had thus done that in 1845 he was elected a member of the Council. From that time forward he did not cease to take a most active and powerful part in its management. As it grew it prospered and strengthened, and about the year 1860 it became necessary to provide a new building for the use of the members. It was then that the present very convenient edifice was erected. The valuable library and museum were then for the first time suitably housed, and a lecture hall in which the members could assemble without inconvenience was provided. In all these works for the benefit of the society, as well as in the task of managing the institution, and taking charge of the library and the valuable specimens in the museum, Dr. Heaton for more than thirty years took a leading part. Thus the first enlargement of his field of labour beyond the limits of his own profession was in this decidedly useful and beneficial direction.

The social life of a provincial town forty years ago presented a great contrast to that which now exists. I have spoken of provincial residents as being at that time not ashamed of being provincial. In nothing was this more clearly shown than in their customary domestic habits. The wealthy manufacturer or merchant, who, having secured a fortune equal to that of many noblemen, found himself returned to Parliament by his fellow-townsmen, did not forthwith imitate as far as might be the manners and customs of the rich and fashionable in London. When he was in London, it is true, attending Parliament, he lived as other people did in the great metropolis: dined late, attended balls and concerts, and generally lived in the style to which society is now universally accustomed. But when he returned to his home in the suburbs of a provincial town, even though that home might be a sumptuously appointed mansion, he made no attempt to introduce the manners and customs of the capital.

Forty years ago the ordinary dinner hour of the upper classes in a town like Leeds was two o'clock, or perchance, if a particular family had a strong inclination towards the pomps and vanities of life,

it might be an hour later. The time at which one
ordinarily dines may seem a very trivial matter, and
yet nothing is more certain than that it influences
the whole current of social life. A dinner at mid-
day or in the early afternoon is not a meal to which
it is possible to invite friends for ordinary social
enjoyment. It comes, not at the close of the day's
business but in the middle of it, and consequently
busy men—and in provincial towns most men are
busy—cannot afford to interchange hospitalities at
such a time. It followed from this state of things
that forty years ago there were no such banquetings
as are now one of the commonest features of social
life in our big manufacturing towns. The age of
entrées, of French cooks, of champagne, and of hired
waiters had not set in, and dinner was still the plain
substantial meal which was known to our ancestors
in the last century. But the early dinner hour
afforded society one great advantage which it lacks
under the more artificial mode of life now prevailing.
It gave us all the long evening of which such admirable use may be made for purposes of enjoyment
or instruction. Tea at six or half-past six o'clock was
the customary meal for which invitations were issued;
then came three or four hours for pleasant talk or
amusement. Everybody was in the best of possible
humours for occupation of this kind. Nobody had
been made drowsy or listless by partaking of a heavy

meal and of a variety of wines, more or less pure ; there was no separation of the sexes at the very time when mutual conversation ought to be most enjoyable to both ; and it need hardly be said that, in provincial towns at least, there was not then the faintest suspicion that a time would come when tobacco would compete not unsuccessfully with the fair sex for the attention of the gentlemen. At the close of the evening thus pleasantly spent, came a meal which gave completeness to the entertainment—supper. It was the custom in Leeds in those days, in the houses of the fashionable, to serve this meal about ten o'clock at a buffet. It was not a heavy meal, and though I am aware of the horror in which the present generation professes to hold the very idea of supper, I am prepared to maintain that a light meal of two courses under this name at ten o'clock is not necessarily more injurious to the digestion than a heavy meal of ten or twelve courses, under the name of dinner, at eight or nine o'clock.

It was one of the most fortunate results of the custom then prevailing in Leeds of having early dinners, that social gatherings at the houses of friends were then both more numerous and more largely attended than is now the case. A set dinner of sixteen or twenty covers is always a formidable undertaking for any save the wealthy and those who happen to be at the head of exceptionally large establishments. But the mistress of even a modest home, or the master of a comparatively poor establishment, can without too much trouble or expense entertain a score of persons in the fashion I have described. Consequently, between 1840 and 1855 social gatherings of this kind were very common in Leeds, and were marked·by many interesting features. Dr. Heaton was from the first a prominent figure in these ' evenings at home ' in the houses of the leading inhabitants, and I find under the date of 1848 a passage in his diary which is interesting, not only because it shows the manner in which in some cases the evenings thus engaged were occupied, but because of the mention it makes of a name that has since become illustrious.

' This spring "The Glow-worm " was commenced. It was a manuscript monthly periodical of which Miss Forrest, the lady housekeeper of Mr. (afterwards Sir Peter) Fairbairn, was the editress, and to which a party of amateur writers were the contributors. Its most valuable part was the illustrations, of which many of singular beauty were furnished by Messrs. Bateman and Corson, two architects who had lately commenced business in partnership in Leeds, and who were pupils of Mr. Owen Jones. Other artists also contributed illustrations, especially Mr. Millais, who was at that time an unknown young man who had been brought to Leeds by Messrs. Bateman and

Corson to design some decorations for the house of Mr. Atkinson of Little Woodhouse, which they were employed in restoring. "The Glow-worm" existed for just a year, and then died a natural death. The work remained in the hands of Miss Forrest, the editress. On her death in 1858 she left it to me by her will; and I have since had the loose sheets bound up into a handsome volume, which is valuable to me not only because of my own share in its production, but because of the many beautiful illustrations which it contains.'

The year 1849, which thus saw the extinction of 'The Glow-worm,' witnessed the birth of another modest instrument for the intellectual improvement of Leeds, which still lives and flourishes. This was the Conversation Club, which was founded in June of that year. The club is so essentially private in its character that I feel almost bound to apologise to my fellow-members for alluding to it in these pages; and yet the work that it has accomplished in its unpretending way, and the good that it has done not only to its members but to the outer world, is so great that I may venture to make some reference to it. It was, moreover, one of the social spheres in which for more than forty years Dr. Heaton found his chief delight. One of the original members of the club, he continued to be the most regular attendant at its meetings for the remainder of his life, and a very

few weeks before his death he entertained its members
at his house. The club consists of twelve members,
and it holds its meetings monthly, the meeting being
held in rotation at the houses of the different members,
so that each member entertains the club once a year.
In its original days, true to that state of provincial
society which I have just depicted, the rule of the
club was that members should first partake of tea,
then engage in conversation, and sup together before
separating. A good many years ago this plan was
abandoned in favour of the modern fashion of dining,
and it is now after dinner that the conversation takes
place. The great feature of the club is that it *is*
conversation, and not debating or lecturing, which
it is designed to promote. By a very ingenious plan,
matters are so arranged that no particular member
can know beforehand what will be the subject for
discussion at any meeting, and the evil of set orations
or debating society dialectics is thus avoided. The
members aim at talking together as friends casually
assembled round a hospitable fireside might be expected to do, and they have a pious horror of the
formalities of the discussion forum. Dr. Heaton, I
have said, was one of the most regular attendants at
these gatherings during more than thirty years, and
his plain common sense, vigorous downright utter-
ances upon all the questions submitted to the club,
and businesslike faculty of reaching the kernel of

any subject by the shortest possible road, made him one of our most valuable members. Among his colleagues were such men as Sir Edward Baines— who to this day is regular in his attendance at the meetings—the Bishops of Hereford and Ely, Sir Peter Fairbairn, Mr. Kitson, Mr. Thomas Wilson, and the late Rev. J. H. McCheane. All manner of subjects are discussed, and, as various shades of opinion both political and theological are represented in the club, the result of the conversations is to bring about among those who take part in them a much clearer idea of the views of those from whom they happen to differ than it is usually possible to obtain in the polite world.

The club has not, however, had for its sole object the amusement or instruction of a dozen Leeds gentlemen. Containing, as it always has done in its number, some of the leading and most active members of the community, it has aimed at dealing with practical questions in a practical manner, and more than one important local movement has had its birth in the pleasant evening conversations of the club. Among these must be mentioned the Leeds Improvement Society and the Educational Council. Regarding the former Dr. Heaton writes: 'On January 27, 1851, I was at a meeting of the Conversation Club, at which a new society, called the Leeds Improvement Society, was constituted, I being made honorary

secretary. The object was to suggest and promote
architectural and other public improvements in the
town. The society was maintained by subscriptions,
and existed for two or three years, during which time
I was involved in a great deal of trouble and labour
in connection with it. We had public lectures on
practical subjects, such as the consumption of smoke
in furnaces, the best construction of roads, &c. The
society had, however, no executive authority. It
could only make suggestions on the matters with
which it dealt, and was constantly in danger of coming
into collision with the Town Council and other local
public bodies. In spite of this drawback, however,
it did some good, though I am not prepared to say
that it was commensurate with the trouble and
expenditure which had to be incurred in carrying out
its operations. It obtained the widening of at least
one of the streets of the town ; in consequence of the
energy it showed in bringing the subject of the
smoke nuisance prominently before the public, it
forced upon the Town Council the appointment of a
Smoke Inspector ; and, by constant objections to the
lavish use of cinders in the construction of the roads,
it led to the adoption of a better mode of making
them. The more active members of the society
gradually fell off, however, discouraged by the small
results we were able to obtain, and I and Mr. Thomas
Wilson, the treasurer, were left alone. Even the

paid secretary resigned discouraged ; and the society finally died a natural death, leaving behind it about 50*l.* in money, which is now (1861) lying at Beckett's Bank, waiting for some object on which it can properly be bestowed.'

The result of this particular effort was not very encouraging, but it deserves to be noted in connection with what has been said in the earlier portion of this chapter regarding the state of feeling in provincial towns forty years ago. Within the first decade after Dr. Heaton's settlement in practice in Leeds, we see not a few agencies established for the social and intellectual improvement of the inhabitants of the town. Some of these agencies are still in full operation among us; others, like the Improvement Society, after doing a certain amount of work, fell into a state of suspended animation, in which one or two of them still remain, but from which others, after a slumber of several years' duration, were roused to renewed activity. In every case, however, they show the gradual awakening and development of public opinion with regard to questions concerning which our fathers had never thought of troubling themselves. They had been content to go on like their fathers before them. The idea of Conversation Clubs, of amateur magazines, of popular scientific lectures, had never occurred to them. Nor had they troubled themselves about the narrowness of the streets through which they moved, or the smoke-laden atmosphere which they were compelled to breathe. Gradually, however, in great part through the agency of modest institutions like the Leeds Conversation Club, and through the energetic and self-denying labours of men like Dr. Heaton, public opinion on these questions began to be formed, and efforts like those which I have described were made.

CHAPTER VI.

MARRIAGE AND FAMILY LIFE.

IT was about the year 1848, when Dr. Heaton was first beginning the public career of which I have spoken in the preceding chapter, that he made the acquaintance of Miss Fanny Heaton, the lady to whom he was subsequently united in marriage; and who, though bearing the same surname as himself, was only distantly, if at all, related to him. It is obviously impossible in these pages to dwell at any length upon the story of an engagement between two persons one of whom is still living. One would like to print Dr. Heaton's own account of his courtship, because of the light which it throws upon his personal character —a light which reflects nothing but honour upon him—but for many reasons that is out of the question. What may be said is, however, that from the first moment of his meeting with Miss Heaton, he was greatly attracted by her, and that before their acquaintance had lasted more than a few weeks he had resolved to win her as his wife. To his resolution he adhered firmly in spite of difficulties and discouragements which were of more than ordinary gravity. The tenacity of his nature was in nothing shown more clearly than in this pursuit of a wife, whose friends, for some reason not clearly explained, did not approve of the connection. For two years, from 1848 to 1850, nothing occupied so large a share of his thoughts as his intended marriage, and the obstacles which threatened to prevent it. Those obstacles were at length happily removed, and on April 3, 1850, he and Miss Heaton were married by the Rev. William Sinclair at the parish church of St. George's. Dr. Heaton's sister Ellen, and the bride's sister Marian, were the bridesmaids, whilst Mr. Aldam Heaton and Mr. (now Sir Andrew) Fairbairn acted as groomsmen.

The young couple proceeded immediately after the marriage to the Continent for that trip up the Rhine which in those days was the traditional marriage tour. During their absence a vacancy occurred in the medical staff of the Leeds Infirmary by the resignation of Dr. Hopper, one of the physicians. Dr. Heaton had anticipated this event, and before leaving on his marriage journey had prepared printed circulars addressed to the trustees of the Infirmary, in which he made application for the post. The circulars were positively addressed by him before he left home, so that when the vacancy actually occurred all that was to be done was to post them. He was elected without opposition to the office of physician to the Infirmary, which he continued to fill until his death.

On returning home with his wife, he at once threw himself with, if possible, increased ardour into the work of his profession. He was now physician to both of the chief medical charities of the town, as well as to the House of Recovery. At the Dispensary, indeed, he had to do the work of two physicians ; whilst to add to his labours, during this year 1850, he had to contend with another severe fever epidemic which filled the House of Recovery, and had to deliver, during the summer, daily lectures at the Medical School on Botany and Materia Medica. In the autumn of the same year he wrote two articles for the ' British Quarterly Review,' one upon ' Apparitions ' and the other upon 'Microscopes.' In addition, he lectured twice before the members of the Mechanics' Institution upon Botany, and then, as if all these employments were not sufficient to occupy him, he voluntarily undertook in September the whole of the physician's work at the Dispensary, Dr. Ronayne, who had hitherto shared the duties with him, having resigned. These facts show what his life was at the time of his marriage. His private practice, though it must have been an object of importance to the young husband to secure some addition to his income, was made subordinate to his public work ; and for many hours of every day he laboured gratuitously among the poor, whilst the evenings were devoted to honorary labours like those in connection with the lectures of which I have spoken.

In January 1851 a child was born. 'On the 31st March,' says the young father, with natural pride, 'the decennial census was taken, and our baby's name was added to the list of the population.' Nothing of special interest occurs in the record of Dr. Heaton's private life during the next year. In 1852 he mentions a meeting with Mrs. Kemble the actress at the house of Mr. Fairbairn, and speaks, not certainly in terms of approbation, of her 'bold, haughty, and overbearing manners.' The entertainment of friends in the house at East Parade, visits to London and to Lincoln, the death of Mr. William Heaton, Dr. Heaton's uncle, and the birth of a second daughter, fill up the story until we reach the month of July 1852, when we come to the following passage in Dr. Heaton's narrative :—

'We had only just come well out of this great trouble '—the serious illness of Mrs. Heaton—' when another very sad event cast a gloom over our little circle, and caused a considerable change in our circumstances, besides giving me much anxious occupation for a lengthened term. Ellen and my father had gone to Harrogate for about a fortnight, as was my

father's custom during the summer, on the 12th of
July, immediately on the appearance of some decided
improvement in Fanny's state. My father seemed
hale and in his usual health, and there was no
apparent reason to apprehend any danger to him.
Between two and three o'clock on Friday morning,
July 23, I was awakened by a ring at the door bell,
and a groom on horseback from Harrogate presented
to me a note from Dr. Kennion informing me of my
father's sudden death. I went to Harrogate by the
first train, reaching the house about seven o'clock.
There I found Ellen in great distress. My father had
been going about as usual the previous day, but his
breathing, which was always oppressed, had been
worse than usual owing to his having taken cold.
He did not, however, go to bed till his usual time on
the evening of Thursday the 22nd. The recumbent
posture seems to have aggravated his symptoms,
for his breathing was so bad that some one hearing
it sent Ellen to him. She found him livid and almost
insensible. He died shortly after midnight, on his
eighty-third birthday, having, I believe, been unable
to say anything from the time when he was first found
ill in bed. Thus both my father and my mother died
whilst I was absent and unable to give any assistance.'

Death, when it overtakes a good man at such an
age as that which Mr. Heaton had attained, cannot be
regarded as an evil, and the swift and almost pain-

less fall of the final blow in this case hardly left anything to be desired. It was true that the good man
had died not in his own home, but in an inn, among
strangers. Yet with that happy power of looking
only at the brighter side in connection with the fate
of the departed which is one of the compensations
the mourner usually enjoys, I find Dr. Heaton in his
journal quoting in connection with his father's case
the declarations of Sterne and Archbishop Leighton,
in which they expressed their preference for a death
among strangers to one among sorrowing friends.

In the following November, the intervening period
having been fully occupied with the settlement of
important business matters in connection with his
father's estate, Dr. Heaton, accompanied by his wife,
went to London to witness a national ceremonial
which excited an immense amount of attention at the
time, and which has recently been the subject of an
animated controversy in the 'Times'—the funeral of
the Duke of Wellington.

'We reached London,' he says, 'soon after midnight on Monday the 14th of November, and the ·
following day we attempted to get access to the lying-
in-state at Chelsea Hospital. Aunt and Fanny, and
Mr. George Shaw and myself, commenced the attempt;
but the ladies soon found that it was impracticable
for them. A dense crowd, a mile or more in length,
extended to the entrance to the Hospital, and we had

to stand in a drizzling rain till the slow progress of the multitude brought us in turn to the building. It was five o'clock in the evening when I gained admission, and was passed rather hurriedly with the crowd through the hall, in which the coffin, covered with a magnificent pall and bearing the Duke's various insignia of office, lay under a splendid canopy. The hall was hung entirely with black, and lighted with massive candelabra. Mourners stood round the coffin, and soldiers were placed on guard round the walls. The funeral took place on Thursday the 18th. We had engaged seats on a platform erected in the church-yard of St. Mary-le-Strand. As there had been much rain during the night we felt some anxiety about Fanny, this being an open platform. We took plenty of wrappings and cushions with us, however, and at seven o'clock in the morning—in order that we might reach our places whilst the streets were still open —we drove off. We got very comfortably to our seats, which were on the west front of the platform, looking down the whole length of the Strand, and so commanding a very fine view of the procession during its approach. About half-past ten the head of the procession came in view, and it occupied an hour and a half in passing us. It consisted of the most distinguished civil and military officers of the nation in full costume, but all in mourning coaches ; representatives, I believe, of all the regiments of the

line; military bands; banners bearing the Duke's arms,
his charger and insignia of office, and the magnificent
bronze funeral car, drawn by twelve black dray-
horses, clothed in black velvet trappings, and with
lofty plumes on their heads. After eight in the
morning there was no rain; the day was hazy, with
occasional gleams of sunshine, which seemed appropriate to the occasion. The sun's rays produced
striking effects when glancing on the breastplates and
weapons of the soldiers as they passed. After the
procession was over we got home as best we could,
with no ill effects to any of us, and on the following
Monday we returned home to Leeds.'

It is not the purpose of this memoir to deal with
the domestic life of Dr. Heaton. I am, however,
tempted by many passages in his journal to throw
light upon this side of my subject. Whilst to the
outer world he seemed to be somewhat cold and
reserved in demeanour, very different was the impression which he made upon those who were
admitted to the familiar and unreserved intercourse of his own fireside. Here he was seen at his
best, unlike the many who, whilst making brilliant
figures in society, are dull and almost sullen under the
shelter of their own roofs. His marriage had turned
out most happily; he was devoted to his wife, and
full of affection for and interest in his children. Indeed, from the time of his union with Mrs. Heaton,

the journal from which I have made so many extracts
is almost exclusively occupied with the record of
domestic events, nothing that in any way concerned
his wife and children seeming to him to be too trivial
to be mentioned. It is only occasionally that one
catches glimpses in its pages of his public labours;
one must go elsewhere to find any full record of
them. But he is full of the details of family excursions to various places in the neighbourhood of Leeds,
or of trips with his wife to London and Paris; whilst
there is incidental mention of the books he was
reading, of the alterations and improvements he
was making in his house, of the transformation of his
father's old dwelling in Briggate—the birthplace of
Dr. Heaton and his sister—into a shop, and of other
events of purely personal or domestic interest. The
following, however, is a passage which, as bearing
upon Dr. Heaton's public work, ought to be given.

'I had for some time (1853) been the sole
physician to the Dispensary, my last two former
colleagues having resigned and left the town, so that
the work of these fell upon me alone. Neither Dr.
Wilson nor Dr. Chadwick would come forward to
help me, nor did the Committee trouble themselves at
all about the matter, so long as I was content to do
the work. As I had now been ten years physician to
the Dispensary, and sole physician for the last three
years, having likewise the physicianship of the House

of Recovery and the Infirmary, I thought it right
to give up this thankless and onerous charge. I
accordingly sent in my resignation to the Committee,
and received a very tardy and cool acknowledgment
of my communication, and vote of thanks for my
services. The Committee then advertised their three
vacancies, but received no response; they therefore
applied to Wilson, Chadwick, and myself, asking us all
to resume office. Dr. Chadwick was willing to accept
at all events a nominal appointment, and wished myself and Wilson, who were a good deal cooler about
it, to come into his views. Wilson consented, claim-
ing to be considered as senior, Chadwick claimed to
stand second, leaving me, after having been senior
for many years, and after having done all the work,
now to rank last. It was agreed that the question
should be referred to Mr. Garlick, who upon some
mistaken grounds adjudged that such should be our
relative standing as physicians to the Dispensary.
It was clear, however, that no one could object to
my signing my name as late senior physician to the
Dispensary. The result then was, that I returned to
office, now assisted by two colleagues; and that as a
reward for my ten years' service, in which I had been
successively third, second, senior, and ultimately sole
physician, I was put back to the position of third, or
junior physician, late senior physician, to the Dispensary.'

Leeds was now being agitated by the proposal that a new Town Hall should be erected, and that it should be upon a scale commensurate with the wealth and commercial importance of the town. It may seem a small matter to those who have not studied these questions of local politics, whether a Town Hall in a provincial city shall be of one style of architecture or another; whether it shall be large or small, handsome or the reverse. As a matter of fact, a great deal may depend upon the decision which is arrived at in such a matter by the authorities upon whose judgment the final issue depends. No one would wish to underestimate the importance of the metropolis; but, after all, it is not in London that we find the best specimens of our old English architecture. The grandest remains of that ' age of faith and stone,' when pious men were content to devote their lives to the task of rearing a single shrine which, by its beauty and magnificence, might be not unworthy in their eyes of the purpose to which it was to be devoted, are not to be found in London. It is in what were once provincial cities or hamlets that we discover the most venerable and the most striking memorials of the taste and self-consecration of our forefathers. And the time may come when the archæologist of a future age will look for the best specimens of the buildings of the present reign, not to the Law Courts or the Houses of Parliament. but to some provincial town, where possibly the hurry and rush of life have not been so great as in the capital, and where, in consequence, public buildings have lived a little longer than they are apt to do on the banks of the Thames.

But quite apart from this aspect of the question, there is another side to it of greater and more immediate importance. Those who know anything of the older cities of the Continent must be well aware of the extent to which the taste of the different communities dwelling in those cities has been educated and elevated by the character of the public buildings in their midst. We are naturally inclined to ' live up to ' the things of beauty by which we are surrounded. Let a town once possess a single building which is an architectural ornament to it, and all meaner edifices will at once be put to shame, and will begin to pall upon the taste of the people. This was the view held by Dr. Heaton, as well as by many other enlightened inhabitants of Leeds at the period to which we refer. The reader will have gathered from previous pages that the great Yorkshire town had little to boast of in the way of architectural decoration down to 1854. The building of the parish church, in the midst of the squalor and desolation of Kirkgate, had indeed done something to redeem the character of the town. But, apart from this one building, there was not a single edifice in the town of which the inhabitants had any reason to be proud. Nor was it certain at this time that the Town Council, with whom rested the decision as to the character of the Town Hall which was to be erected, would prove worthy of the great responsibility intrusted to them. They were more than suspected of a leaning towards a discreditable parsimony, and the more public-spirited and intelligent inhabitants of Leeds feared lest the borough should be permanently disfigured by a building which should be a perpetual monument of the lack of taste and liberality on the part of the local governing body. In these circumstances a vigorous agitation was carried on for the purpose of enlightening public opinion, and of thus bringing indirect pressure to bear upon the Town Council. Naturally enough, the members of the Town Council resented the notion that any pressure of this kind was needed in order to bring them into the right path. But in spite of their protests the people of taste in Leeds pursued their course, and, by means of the local press and of lectures before the chief local societies, did all that was possible to stimulate and inform the public mind. It was not in Dr. Heaton's power to look on with indifference whilst a work of this kind was in progress. Foreign travel had done much to improve his taste and enlarge his ideas; he saw now more clearly than he had ever done before the glaring deficiencies of Leeds as a city; and he now laboured as earnestly to increase its beauty as to improve its sanitary state. On the evening of Twelfth Night, 1854, he delivered a lecture on the subject of Town Halls before the members of the Philosophical and Literary Society, in which, treating the subject from a historical point of view, he gave his fellow-townsmen a large amount of useful information on a question which, it will be readily understood, was at that time of more than ordinary interest to those whom he addressed.

A matter of infinitely greater importance than this local agitation respecting the architecture of a Town Hall, was now, however, beginning to absorb the attention of the people of England. After a peace of forty years' duration, this country was once more about to enter upon a great European War. It is interesting, even for those of us who are old enough to remember with distinctness the events of that epoch, to see how people in England were struck at the time by the resort to the arbitrament of battle. Three years before this date, the Great Exhibition had been opened in Hyde Park, amid rejoicings which might fairly be described as cosmopolitan in their character. Throughout Europe men believed that this festival of industry and art was to set the seal upon the reign of peace, and to mark with emphasis the repudiation of war as a policy or a means of attaining national ends. It was a terrible fall from the height of the expectations which were thus indulged into the depth of the passions which prevailed throughout the country in 1851. But once again Englishmen proved on that occasion that, underlying all professions of peace and all inclination for peace, there is a deep-rooted belligerent sentiment by which in the last result their natures are entirely dominated. With hardly an exception the nation was ready for the call to arms when it came. It forgot all about the Great Exhibition and the sentiments of universal brotherhood which had been everywhere preached in 1851 ; and the shopkeeping class in particular, those against whom the greatest poet of the day had launched the bitter invective with which the pages of ' Maud ' are loaded, showed themselves eager to support Ministers in carrying on a war. Of the real causes of that war, of the objects at which it aimed, they might know little. It was enough for them that it was waged under the flag of England, and in this fact they found a sufficient reason for throwing aside the professions of forty years of peace.

Dr. Heaton as a politician was a singularly calm and impartial person. He showed throughout his life a strong distaste for mere party politics. Not at all the man to find favour with a Caucus or with the wire-pullers of any particular political organisation, he had a habit of looking at questions upon their merits which is not without its value in a country where party reigns supreme. His own intimate friends hardly knew whether to describe him as a Liberal or a Conservative, and probably on neither side was there any reliance placed upon his vote at an election. That which he believed to be for the good of his country, whether it was advocated by Liberal or Conservative, was what found favour in his eyes. His singular power of cutting himself absolutely loose from the great movements of public feeling on the questions of the day, the power of standing aside as it were, whilst the contending currents of popular opinion were being dashed against each other in angry vehemence, enabled him often to see more of the game than was visible to those who were actually engaged in it. There are naturally not a few references in his journal to the Crimean War, but I need only make one extract in order to show the cool and dispassionate way in which he could look even at so absorbing and exciting a matter as this was.

'We were now entering on the Crimean War with Russia, together with our allies the French, and subsequently the Sardinians. This being the first European war in which England had been involved since 1815, created much sensation and considerable anxiety, an anxiety which the result fully justified, as this war lasted just two years, with a tremendous loss of life and waste of money, and was concluded finally with no very appreciable good result, although

the allies were the successful party. In England we
are pretty fully convinced that had this country
alone undertaken the war, it would have been ended
much more successfully, more speedily, and with
more glory to our arms. Rivalries, hesitations, and
differences of opinion, which so naturally arose
between the commanders of the two nations, much
retarded and obstructed the operations of the war,
and in the end peace was concluded by the determination of the French Government, their own
resources being exhausted, at a time when the
English were both able and willing to prosecute the
war to a more successful issue.'

But even in times of war the ordinary usages of
society are maintained. It seemed strange to many of
us during the dark days when our troops were facing
death on the cruel plains of the Crimea that at home
the ordinary round of feast and festival should be
maintained after the accustomed fashion, and that not
even the darkening of a hundred homes by the
presence of death in its most terrible shape could be
allowed to interfere with the gaieties of the London
season. Among the Mansion House dinners which
took place this year was one which had a special
interest for many persons in Leeds. Mr. Sidney, the
great tea-merchant, was at that time Lord Mayor, and
Mr. Sidney's business was not confined to London.
He had a branch establishment in Leeds, where he

was well known. On the occasion of his mayoralty, he invited many Leeds gentlemen to partake of the hospitalities of the Mansion House, and Dr. Heaton was a guest at a dinner thus given on May 11. ‘We reached the Mansion House soon after six, and were ushered into the drawing-room, which was guarded at the door by the Macebearer and Sword-bearer in their state liveries. Here we were introduced to the Lady Mayoress, as well as to her daughter Mrs. Moon, who is married to the son of the eminent publisher of engravings. The Bishop of Ripon, the Bishop of Sodor and Man, Archdeacon Thorpe, our borough members, and other notables were also gathered here, besides a large number of our Leeds acquaintances. About seven we were ushered into the Egyptian Hall to dinner, the number of guests being two hundred and seventy in all. Of course there was a magnificent display of civic plate, a great abundance of food of every kind, and many varieties of wine. After dinner the Lord Mayor drank to the company assembled in the peculiar fashion adopted at these City banquets. The toast-master announced the Lord Mayor's intention as follows : “The Lord Mayor drinks to all a kindly cup, and wishes all a kindly greeting.” Then all the guests pledged each other, a large two-handled cup being passed along round the table, each person and his neighbour in succession standing up, and each

holding the cup by one handle whilst the first repeated
the pledge to the second, who then turned round
and went through the same ceremony with his
neighbour on the other side. The company broke
up about twelve o'clock. The Lord Mayor was very
polite, and invited us and the ladies to go with some
of the company in his barge to see the launch of the
Royal Albert, 131 guns, on Saturday. This was a very
interesting excursion. We assembled at the Mansion
House, where Mr. Sidney introduced the party to his
wife and daughter. We also met there Dr. Croly,
the rector of St. Stephen's, Walbrook, in which
parish the Mansion House stands. The whole
company were taken down in carriages to Fresh
Wharf, where we embarked. Two river steamers had
been provided for our accommodation, and we were
asked to go in that which the Lord Mayor and his
attendants—Swordbearer, Macebearer, and water-
men—also took passage. Both the boats were hung
round with flags, and the second boat had a band of
music on board. We thus went down the river quite
in gala fashion, and about one o'clock reached Woolwich, where we were moored next to the Admiralty
steamer, the *Black Eagle*. This in turn was moored
close to the quay on which was the platform provided
for the Royal party, so that our position was
unexceptionable. We were indeed directly opposite
the immense shed under which lay the vessel whose

entrance upon her nautical life we had come to witness. Soon after one, the Queen, Prince Albert, the Princess Royal, the Prince of Wales, Prince Alfred, Princess Alice, the Duchess of Kent, Lord Aberdeen, Sir James Graham, and a brilliant suite of naval and military officers, made their appearance. They walked round the ship and then returned to the platform. The Queen then christened the vessel in the usual manner, and the launch took place most successfully, amid immense cheering and the playing of the national anthem by the numberless bands on board the many steamboats which were gathered on the spot. When the ceremony was over we sat down to a magnificent collation, which had been laid out in the cabin of the steamboat whilst we were engaged in viewing the spectacle. Every variety of delicate viand and unlimited quantities of iced champagne were provided ; and after luncheon, when we came on deck, port and claret were supplied *ad libitum*, as well as ices, hothouse grapes, and straw-berries. Both of these fruits were selling at that time in Covent Garden at ten shillings a pound. Meanwhile the steamer went further down the river to Erith Reach, when it turned back. On reaching the *Royal Albert*, which was now moored in the middle of the river, we came alongside, and the whole party was invited on board to inspect the ship, the size and strength of which impressed us greatly.'

After this pleasant indulgence in inter-municipal
hospitalities, Dr. Heaton and his wife returned to
Leeds and to their ordinary life there. A busy life
as usual, but not without its compensations in the
shape of Conversation Club excursions, as well as
private visits to many of the scenes of beauty and
interest by which the West Riding is distinguished.
In the beginning of October, at the request of the
Council of the Philosophical Society, of which he was
one of the leading members, Dr. Heaton, accompanied
by Mr. Denny, the secretary to the society, went to
Drewton Manor near Hull, to discharge a commission
on behalf of the society. Drewton Manor was the
seat of the late Mr. Baron, who had bequeathed a
large collection of ancient coins, and all his books on
antiquarian and topographical subjects, to the Leeds
Philosophical Society. The object of Dr. Heaton's
visit was to protect the society's interests under this
bequest, as there was considerable danger that some
of the books which came within the terms of this
bequest might through accident or misunderstanding
be put up for sale along with the other portions of
the library. Dr. Heaton bought in many books
which seemed to him and Mr. Denny to be the
property of the Philosophical Society, and the justice
of their contention on this point being subsequently
admitted by Mr. Baron's executors, these books were
duly added to the library of the society in the build-

ing in Park Row. The following month, at the annual conversazione of the society, it fell to Dr. Heaton's lot to read a paper descriptive of the various books forming part of the Baron bequest which he had thus been in a measure instrumental in securing.

The year 1855 was made memorable in the domestic annals of the household by the birth of a son, John Arthur Dakeyne Heaton. This event happened in June, and some weeks later Dr. and Mrs. Heaton went to Paris, where the Exposition, an imitation of the Great Exhibition of 1851, was being held at the time, and where they had the opportunity of witnessing the public rejoicings for the victories in the Crimea.

It was shortly after their return from Paris, in the beginning of 1856, that Dr. and Mrs. Heaton took the first steps in a matter which led to a not inconsiderable change in the course of their daily life in Leeds. Up to this time they had continued to reside in the house in East Parade which had been provided for him by his father when he began practice in the town. Now, however, circumstances led them to contemplate the purchase of a larger detached house, situated on the north side of Woodhouse Square, which was at that time still almost in the suburbs of Leeds, and in the most fashionable quarter of the town. A man's house, it is justly said, is always an indication of his character, and the house which Dr. Heaton

was about to purchase, and which under the name
of Claremont subsequently became so well known to
the inhabitants of Leeds and to many persons of distinction in all parts of the country, affords no exception to this rule. But there is another side to the
aphorism, and it is not less true that men are to a
not inconsiderable extent influenced by the characteristics of the houses which are their homes. We are
all more or less the creatures of circumstances, and of
all the circumstances by which we are surrounded
few can be more powerful than the atmosphere of our
daily life in our own homes. Removal from East
Parade to Claremont was, in the case of Dr. Heaton,
evidence of the fact that he had become, so far as
wealth and social position were concerned, one of the
leading inhabitants of the town. It may seem absurd
to alter one's estimate of a man merely because he
has changed his place of residence : but it is the way
of the world. Dr. Heaton at Claremont was in no
respect different from Dr. Heaton at East Parade.
He was still the indefatigable and unselfish servant of
the public ; never neglecting his duties to his own
household, never failing to take tender charge of
those who were nearest and dearest to him ; but at
the same time successfully combining attention to
public matters and care for the welfare of the whole
community with this devotion to those interests
which were naturally of the first importance to a man

of his temperament. But although he had not
changed in any way in his devotion to his work,
men began to regard him in a different light after he
had established himself in his new home, and henceforth he played a more important part in the affairs
of Leeds than he had done before.

Nor was it quite without reason that this change
in his position took place. At Claremont, as the
occupier of a large and commodious house, occupying
a most convenient situation, he was able to be the
host of many of the persons of distinction or usefulness who visited Leeds on matters of public business.
Thus he was brought into contact with a wider circle
than that in which he had hitherto moved, and
became in due course the leader in the literary, scientific, and artistic society of the town. The visitors'
book at Claremont contains the names of many who
are known to the world at large, and who had an
opportunity of enjoying the pleasant hospitalities of
the master of the house. But those hospitalities were
never limited to people of note or fashion, and for
more than twenty years that house was the recognised
centre of much that was brightest and best in the
social life of Leeds.

After purchasing Claremont, and before entering
upon the occupancy of it, Dr. Heaton had to experience another of the risks incident to his profession.
He had been absent from Leeds for a few days visiting

friends in the south of England. Returning (in October 1856) he found Mr. Sleigh, a newly appointed medical man at the House of Recovery, ill of fever. He himself had through all these years maintained his connection with this most useful institution, although, as we have seen, he had suffered seriously in health in consequence of his attendance upon the patients who were in the hospital. He now at once devoted himself to the care of Mr. Sleigh. Unfortunately the case was a very bad one, and after a short but distressing illness Mr. Sleigh died within six weeks of his appointment as resident officer at the House of Recovery. His widowed mother, who had been summoned to his bedside, did not arrive until after his death. Immediately after Mr. Sleigh's death, Dr. Heaton himself fell ill of continued fever, and, although he was able to attend to the greater part of his duties, he was reduced to a condition of great feebleness and depression. This condition was the more trying to him, inasmuch as he was at the time engrossed in preparations for the removal to Claremont, where he had been carrying out extensive alterations of the house in order to make it more suitable and convenient as a residence. Under these circumstances he felt it to be his duty to resign his post of physician to the House of Recovery. The fact that he had been twice attacked by fever during his attendance there proved that he was more than ordinarily susceptible to infection, and made it clear that it was not prudent for him to continue his services to his fellow-townsmen in that capacity.

On November 27, 1856, he occupied Claremont for the first time, and as the early days of his residence in this house were marked by at least one incident of a somewhat extraordinary character, an extract from his journal bearing upon the subject may be inserted here with advantage.

'The only two rooms then habitable were the day-nursery for our sitting-room and the night-nursery for our bedroom. Workmen were in nearly all the rooms, but we gradually got some of them put into some degree of habitable condition. In December we got into our own bedroom, and used my dressing-room for a sitting-room. Before Christmas we had the drawing-room and library nearly completed, but the dining-room was still without a fireplace. We arranged, however, to have a large family gathering on Christmas day. On the night of Sunday, December 21, a large hungry rat got shut up in our bedroom when we went to bed. In its efforts to escape it gnawed and tore up the carpet near the door, as we found next day, but being unable to escape it got upon the bed and attacked me as I lay asleep. I was aroused by a sudden sharp pain on my nose, and the feeling of the animal's claws upon my face. Starting up I found my face covered with

blood from a severe bite across the bridge of the
nose. I got some hot water and bathed the wound
for some time, and while so engaged I actually saw
the rat crawling over the white counterpane towards
the face of my wife who still lay asleep. The animal
evidently intended to make a similar attack upon her.
Of course I gave chase, but it got away, and I saw
no more of it that night. The following morning my
nose was sore and much swollen. During the day I
found the rat in my dressing-room. It escaped into
the green-room, where it ran up the chimney. I put
some strychnia on bread and butter on the hearth.
and shut the door. Presently I found the rat lying
still on the hearth-stone beside the remains of the
meal I had provided for him, so greedily had he
eaten and so rapid had been the effect of the poison.
After a few days the swelling of my nose subsided.
and up to Christmas day I continued well in general
health. On rising on that day, however, I had some
curious giddy feelings, and while at church I was
chilly and uncomfortable. On returning home before
dinner, and while our guests were assembling, I was
seized with shivering, and felt so sick and ill, that
instead of sitting down to the Christmas dinner, I was
obliged to go to bed. This was the beginning of a
serious illness, and I fear the Christmas dinner went
off rather flatly under the circumstances. I had a
variety of curious symptoms in the course of the

illness; a patchy eruption somewhat like measles on my head and face, afterwards red patches, very painful and tender, which became large purplish blotches, from which the cuticle afterwards slowly exfoliated. I had also a peculiar inflammatory sore throat on which patches of lymph were effused, and a troublesome convulsive cough and distressing attacks of dyspnœa, as well as a considerable amount of general fever. Towards the middle of January 1857 I began to make some recovery, and to sit up part of the day in my bedroom; but I then had much rheumatic pain and swelling in my feet, knee, and arm. On January 18 I first came downstairs. On Saturday, the last day of January, I left the house for the first time. From this time I gradually made a complete recovery. This illness was so singular in its commencement and progress, that there were various conjectures as to its real nature. Chadwick and S. Hey both attended me. The former thought I must have been poisoned by eating oysters on Christmas eve, the evening before the attack began; the latter thought it was gout, and there was also the question whether it was not the result of the bite by the rat which I had received some days before.'

Fortunately, the recovery from this very unpleasant and curious illness, when it did take place, was complete; and within a few weeks large house-warming parties at Claremont celebrated not only

the entrance upon the new home, but the restoration
to health of the master of the house.

During the two years immediately succeeding, we
find Dr. Heaton engaged in his professional and public
work on the old lines. The new Town Hall which
had been erected in Leeds, and which will long remain
a monument of the public spirit of the generation
which raised it, was about to be opened by the
Queen ; and immediately afterwards the meeting of
the British Association was to be held in Leeds.
Both of these events necessarily occupied much of
Dr. Heaton's attention, for not a little work in connection with both events was thrown upon him.
They did not, however, so completely engross his
thoughts as to prevent his attending to matters which
came more directly within the scope of his labours as
a physician ; and in May 1858 we find in his journal
a record of the fact that he had commenced, at the
suggestion of his wife, an effort to form a library in
the Infirmary, for the benefit of the patients, who
were at that time thrown very much upon their own
resources during their hours of weariness and pain.
The effort was happily successful. A large number
of books were procured ; Mrs. Heaton and one or two
other ladies undertook the duty of inclosing them in
suitable covers, stamping and cataloguing them ; and
in a very short time they were placed in the Infirmary,
where they proved, it need hardly be said, a source

both of amusement and instruction to the patients. It may seem strange to many that so recently as 1858 a great public hospital should not have been provided with a library for the use of the inmates. The progress of public opinion in these matters has, however, been extraordinarily rapid during the last twenty years, and efforts the utility and even necessity of which are now universally recognised were comparatively novel in 1858.

CHAPTER VII.

PROGRESS OF LEEDS, AND PUBLIC WORK.

MENTION has already been made in the course of this narrative of the erection of the Leeds Town Hall, and of the controversy which accompanied the selection of a design for that building. It may seem to some persons that the building of the municipal offices of a provincial town is a matter of little importance either local or national. As a matter of fact, the erection of this Leeds Town Hall was important both locally and nationally. Those who are acquainted with the town are aware that from that event dates the great development which has taken place in local architecture. Down to 1858 there was hardly one really beautiful building in the town, with the exception of one or two of the churches, and utility in its baldest and most offensive shape seemed to be the object sought after by all the inhabitants. Row after row of houses was built in accordance with the needs of the population, but not the slightest attempt was made to introduce any change into the meagre and squalid architectural styles which had prevailed for

more than a generation. Briggate, the main thoroughfare of the town, and the street in which Dr. Heaton's
father so long carried on his business, was one of the
plainest and poorest streets in England. It might
almost have been thought that those who were re-
sponsible for it had deliberately conspired together to
produce the worst possible effect. Boar Lane, the
street which gave access to the railway stations, and
along which an enormous traffic was constantly being
carried, was as ugly as Briggate, and had the additional disadvantage of being so narrow that at certain
points two-wheeled vehicles of ordinary size could
not pass each other. The rest of Leeds consisted of
long terraces of tasteless suburban houses, or streets
occupied by mean and paltry dwellings allotted to
the poor.

All this was changed by the erection of the Town
Hall. But the change was not wrought without a
great struggle. The public-spirited men of the
borough saw that a splendid opportunity had presented itself for revolutionising the architecture of
Leeds. They believed, and as it proved with entire
justice, that, if a noble municipal palace that might
fairly vie with some of the best Town Halls of the
Continent were to be erected in the middle of their
hitherto squalid and unbeautiful town, it would
become a practical admonition to the populace of the
value of beauty and art, and in course of time men

would learn to live up to it. Furthermore, they saw that the time was approaching when provincial life would regain some of its lost importance, and when cities like Manchester, Birmingham, and Leeds, ceasing to be mere humble dependants upon the capital of the nation, would themselves become the capitals of the districts in which they were situated, just as the old county towns had been one or two hundred years before. They felt, therefore, that a rich town like Leeds, having to consider the necessity of erecting a Town Hall, was bound to approach that question in the most broad and liberal spirit, and to incur that which might even seem to some to be an extravagant expenditure, rather than fail in a duty which it owed to the rest of the community and to posterity.

But it need hardly be said that farseeing and public men are not the only active members of a community. Leeds, like other towns, had a considerable number of citizens whose one idea of the duty of the local government was that it should avoid all expenditure which could not be proved to be absolutely necessary. It is to be regretted that this false idea of economy should be so generally prevalent in provincial communities. We must remember, however, the character of the great majority of the population in these communities. It does not consist of men of wealth and culture. Very few persons belonging to the leisured classes are to be found in a manufacturing town; and, so far as nineteen men out of twenty are concerned, life is a hard struggle for money. When we remember the kind of education to which these people have been subjected, when we think of their painful and squalid surroundings, and of the efforts which each must make in order to gain not wealth but a bare subsistence, we cannot pretend to wonder at the fact that the false notion of economy which leads people to prefer that which is cheap to that which is good or beautiful, should so largely prevail.

The cultured classes in Leeds were, however, determined to win this battle if they could. Their only chance of doing so was of course by converting the mass of the people to their side—for the municipal franchise in a manufacturing town is very democratic, and town councillors are only too apt to render obedience to their masters whatever may be the nature of the orders which they receive from them. Among those who threw themselves into the fray with eagerness was Dr. Heaton. He had now made several rather extended tours on the Continent, and could speak from actual observation of the state of things in those famous old cities whose Town Halls are the permanent glory of the inhabitants and the standing wonder and delight of visitors from a distance. Accordingly, in order to aid in the enlightenment of his fellow-townsmen on this great subject, he had delivered on January 6, 1854, a lecture before the members of the Philosophical and Literary Society on the subject of Town Halls, which had attracted considerable attention. It ought to be explained that the Town Council had by this time gone so far as to select a very fine classic design for their municipal palace, the author of which was a young and unknown architect named Brodrick. Mr. Brodrick's design had many noble qualities, as all who have seen the Leeds Town Hall can testify. But persons were of opinion that its effect would have been greatly increased if the building he designed had been crowned by a tower of sufficiently stately proportions. To this the economical section of the inhabitants objected, on the ground that a tower would cost money and would be only good to look at, not to use. It was at this particular juncture in the great local controversy that Dr. Heaton delivered his lecture before the members of the Philosophical and Literary Society. After giving a sketch, at once clear and scholarly, and affording strong proof of his own delight in beauty of every kind, of the great Town Halls of the Continent, and of their intimate connection with the public spirit and municipal life of the places where they were to be found, Dr Heaton proceeded to deal with the case of Leeds.

'In 1207,' he said, 'a charter was given to the

burgesses of Leeds by Maurice Paganel, their feudal lord, confirming them in the possession of various privileges.   But the first Royal charter of incorporation was granted in 1626, in the second year of Charles the First.   Previously to the granting of this charter, however, the burgesses had already erected for themselves a Moot Hall.   We find a charge against John Metcalfe, under bailiff of the town, before a jury empanelled at Wakefield, April 28, 1620, in pursuance of a commission issued the previous year for inquiring into the due administration of public charities ; the charge being that he had appropriated to himself for two years the rental of part of that building, then recently erected, which should have been employed for the relief of the poor, the Moot Hall having been erected out of money and stocks belonging to the poor.   This was not the Moot Hall which stood in the middle of Briggate within the recollection of many of my hearers.   It was not till 1710 that this latter building was erected on the old site, in front of which stood the pillory and the stocks.

' This was the sole municipal building for just a century.   In 1809 an Act of Parliament was obtained for better lighting the town with gas, and supplying it with water, and also for the erection of a Court House and prison for the borough.   Under the provisions of this Act the present Court House was erected, the foundation stone being laid in 1811, and the whole completed in 1813. For some years longer the old Moot Hall continued to obstruct our principal thoroughfare. But in the year 1825 it was taken down, together with the Middle Row and Market Cross above it, by which the upper part of Briggate had till then been divided into two narrow alleys known as Cross Parish and the Shambles. This brings us to the present time. Till now the Court House has been the sole building for the transaction of all municipal business; but a necessity has long been felt for ampler accommodation and for architectural display more worthy of the wealth and importance of the town. All parties have gladly acquiesced in the resolution of the Town Council that this want shall be worthily supplied.

'The municipal buildings about to be erected by the burgesses of Leeds, besides the primary object of furnishing convenient accommodation to their officers in the transaction of public business, are intended to present an appearance worthy of the wealth and prosperity of the town; to show that in the ardour of mercantile pursuits the inhabitants of Leeds have not omitted to cultivate the perception of the beautiful and a taste for the fine arts, and to serve as a lasting monument of their public spirit and generous pride in the possession of their municipal privileges. They will form a monument which shall present an object of beauty not merely for their own contemplation and that of their children for successive generations, but which may be famous beyond their own limits, and, like the noble halls of France, of Belgium, and of Italy, may attract to our town the visits of strangers, dilettanti tourists, and the lovers of art from distant places.

'We have seen how the citizens of free towns in the middle ages erected for their public meetings, and as the seat and outward symbol of their public government, the most sumptuous buildings, decorated with all the grace which architecture and sculpture could confer upon the exterior, and whose interior halls added to these effects the rich variety of colour which the painter's art supplies. With the selection of the architectural designs for our Town Hall now in course of erection, I believe the inhabitants of Leeds have expressed a very general sentiment of approval and satisfaction. And perhaps it is not too much to anticipate that the completion of its construction will not be the end of the work, but that in it the memory of our Leeds worthies, and of the great men of our country, may be hereafter preserved by the statuary's art, and that native artists may depict upon its inner walls the more memorable events in the history of our town and country, the progress of manufactures and of our commercial prosperity. The work has been begun in no merely utilitarian or unduly economic spirit, and I trust that the same enlightened liberality and taste will watch over its progress, and still from year to year, and indeed from century to century, add to its embellishment and completeness.

'It is in such a spirit that I would have discussed the question of the propriety of adding a tower to this building. Were this a question to be decided on merely utilitarian grounds, I believe the tower must be condemned, for it is not my opinion that any of the possible uses suggested, to which such an erection might be applied, are of sufficient practical importance to warrant the expense of such a structure, were these the only or the chief consideration. But let us ask what is appropriate to a building for the purpose of the one in question, and what will be conducive to its dignity and beauty? And should we decide that a tower may be made and indeed is essential to fulfil these conditions, let us not, after having nobly determined on the expenditure of so large a sum upon the body of the work, grudge a few additional thousands to give this completion to the whole.'

I have given this extract from Dr. Heaton's lecture, not merely because of its direct bearing upon the subject of which I am writing, but in order that I may show the spirit in which he approached these questions of town improvement. Severely practical as he was in most matters, he was yet well able to appreciate the value of art and of the more genial and elevating influences which it brings to bear upon life ; and whenever it became a question between mere utility and utility *plus* beauty, his voice was unhesitatingly given in favour of the latter. The state of a community in which no men of this stamp were to be found would be poor indeed. In Leeds, happily, Dr. Heaton was but one of several public-spirited inhabitants whose public spirit was guided and informed by a cultured mind and a wide knowledge of men and things. In the present controversy the advocates of the tower got their way. It was a curious circumstance that the tower itself had not formed any part of Mr. Brodrick's original plan. He had been hampered by the restrictions laid down for the competition in designs, and had accordingly prepared a plan of a building which did not require this adjunct. Everybody knows how perilous in such circumstances is the experiment of making that which is almost a revolutionary change in the architect's conception. Yet by common consent the experiment was successfully performed upon this occasion. The Leeds Town Hall, with its noble tower crowning the finely proportioned building itself, is one of those edifices which command admiration and disarm criticism.

It was on September 6, 1858, that this noble building was opened by the Queen, who visited

Leeds for the purpose of assisting in celebrating the completion of a task which did so much honour to the taste and public spirit of the inhabitants. The diary of one who took so lively an interest in all that concerned the welfare of the town as did Dr. Heaton cannot be uninteres'ing when describing such an event as this, and therefore I do not hesitate to transcribe the following passages from his narrative.

'The Queen was to arrive on Monday the 6th of September, and as she would proceed direct to Woodsley House, which had been placed at the disposal of herself and suite by the Mayor, Mr. P. Fairbairn, the procession would go up Clarendon Road and pass our house and garden. We invited a large party of guests for the occasion, and put up two platforms behind the garden wall, so that our visitors might occupy these and look over the wall, and so command a perfect view of the Royal party and their escort as they passed. The platform was of course hung with drapery and gaily decorated with flags. We had about one hundred and twenty guests on the after-noon of that day. Our visitors began to assemble about four o'clock, and left us about eight o'clock. There were slight showers, but at the time that the Queen passed it was very fine. A few plain Royal carriages, drawn by four horses, and escorted by a troop of Yorkshire hussars, formed the principal part of the cavalcade. The Mayor, in his own carriage,

preceded the procession, and the road was kept by
the police. When our visitors for the day had left
us, the party staying in the house set out to walk
through the streets to see the illuminations and other
decorations, which were on a large scale and very
general. The crowds were enormous, but we got
back safely without any misadventure, though thoroughly tired. The following day was that fixed for
the opening of the Town Hall by the Queen. Early
in the morning Prince Albert accompanied some of
the Leeds merchants, members of the Chamber of
Commerce, to the Coloured Cloth Hall, where a very
good Exhibition of local industry had been got up,
exemplifying the great varieties of manufacture and
workmanship carried on in this district. At a later
hour the Royal procession started from Woodsley
House across the moor, where a large assemblage of
Sunday scholars, arranged on platforms, sang various
hymns and 'God Save the Queen,' as the Queen
passed ; then down Woodhouse Lane and by a long
circuit through the principal streets, finally arriving
at the Town Hall. Several triumphal arches were
erected, and the whole line of route was most
elaborately decorated with evergreens, festoons, flags,
drapery, mottoes, artificial flowers, and pictorial
representations, so that the town was so disguised by
its holiday dress as to present not the slightest
resemblance to its usual appearance. The whole

extensive front of Messrs. Gott's mill, for instance, in Wellington Street, was hung with crimson cloth, elegantly draped. The whole line of route was guarded with barricades, and no carriages were allowed to pass after a certain time. We did not attempt to see the procession, as we had tickets admitting us to the Town Hall to see the opening ceremony. A little after twelve o'clock the Queen entered the hall, accompanied by Prince Albert and the Princesses Alice and Helena. She was preceded by the Mayor in his robes, walking backwards with as much grace as he could command. They walked to the end of the hall, where gilt chairs of state were arranged upon a dais, but I think the Queen did not sit down. The Corporation in their robes, together with the magistrates and other officials, stood around. An address was read, the Queen replied, the hall was declared open, and the ceremony was at an end. Before leaving the hall her Majesty knighted the Mayor. On the four following days there was a great musical festival in the Town Hall, the chief apartment of which now took the name of the Victoria Hall. We went to Woodsley House, after the Queen's departure, to see the rooms as they had been fitted up for her Majesty. The whole had been done very elegantly, and no doubt at great cost. The Queen afterwards presented Lady Fairbairn with a diamond bracelet.

But the visit of the Queen and the opening of the

Town Hall were not the only events of importance in the history of Leeds at this time with which Dr. Heaton was closely identified. Perhaps a better idea of the extent of the work of a public or semi-public character in which he was constantly occupied will be gained by a further extract from his diary for the year 1858, than by any other means.

'Now commenced,' he says, 'the work of preparing for the meeting of the British Association in Leeds. I was one of the secretaries of the Section of Physiology, and had a good deal of correspondence to manage previous to the commencement of the meeting, which began on Wednesday, September 22. On the previous day Mr. Ward of Clapham Rise, known as a botanist and the inventor of the close glass cases for growing ferns, &c., came to be our guest, accompanied by two daughters. Mr. Ward was the examiner in botany for the Apothecaries' Company at the time when I gained the prize in 1840. On Wednesday Mr. Monckton Milnes (Lord Houghton) also arrived, having been allotted to me as a guest by the local committee. Our whole party went in the evening to hear the opening address by Professor Owen, who was the president of the year. On Thursday we had a dinner in honour of our guests, at which I had Dean Erskine, who came with Mr. J. H. Shaw, and Hare, who was in Leeds staying with some relatives, as well as a large number of others. . . . On Monday, October 4, I read the opening address at the School of Medicine, being president of the Council this year. On November 23 (my forty-first birthday) the annual conversazione was held at the Philosophical Hall. I read a short notice of some of the recent more important acquisitions to the museum, as one of the papers in the programme of the proceedings for the evening. My address at the opening of the session of the Medical School was revised and printed for publication about this time at the request of the Council. Early in December I commenced my part of the course of lectures on the Practice of Medicine at the Medical School.'

Thus the busy useful life ran its course, not quite uneventfully, and yet most unostentatiously. Engagement was heaped upon engagement, duty upon duty, but a time was found for the discharge of all the work thus undertaken for the benefit of others; and not only time for this, the serious business of life, but time also for its lighter duties and pleasures. Some of the sentences contained in the extracts just given will show that Dr. Heaton was at least 'given to hospitality.' His house was now in fact becoming one of the recognised headquarters of the hospitality of the town, and many strangers found there a warm and genial reception. It is worth noting, too, as illustrative of the development of provincial customs, that the old-fashioned 'tea and evening party' of which mention was made in a previous chapter, had by this time well-nigh disappeared, so far at least as Claremont was concerned, the conventional seven or eight o'clock dinner-party known to all of us taking its place. So another link with the simple customs of the past was snapped, and the life of the great Yorkshire town brought a little nearer in its social customs to that of the capital.

The year 1859 opened amid just as much activity, social and public, as that which had distinguished the preceding year. It began indeed for Dr. Heaton by his undertaking the secretaryship of the St. George's schools, an office which involved a good deal of labour, and which he held a few years, until he was persuaded to undertake the still more troublesome and more laborious office of treasurer. About this time also a scheme was set on foot, by Mr. Edward Baines chiefly, to raise a fund for the decoration of the Town Hall with paintings and other works of art by eminent artists. A committee was formed and a subscription list opened, but the effort, in which Dr. Heaton took his part, was not successful. The times were not then ripe for such a movement. The people of Leeds had been induced to see the necessity of making their Town Hall one creditable to themselves in size and general appearance, but they had not advanced far enough to feel emulous of the local patriotism which distinguished the good Flemish and German burghers of the middle ages.

It was in the spring of this year, 1859, that a new departure took place in the history of that little body called the Conversation Club, of which some account has already been given in these pages. Of this event, which was not without its influence upon the social history of Leeds, Dr. Heaton gives the following account. 'The club had been for some time discussing whether any means could be adopted for bringing together the society of Leeds so as to make acquainted with each other the different little coteries into which it is divided. It was at length decided that such members of the club as were willing should from time to time open their houses for a reception of the visiting acquaintances of all the members and other residents distinguished either officially, by position, or in the literary or scientific world. The invitations being given in the name of the club would obviate all appearance of intrusion or undue familiarity on the part of the member who received the club at his house. Mr. Sykes Ward offered his house for the first experiment, and from that time two receptions have been held by the club each season. The refreshments are limited to tea and coffee, with cakes, &c., and the entertainment consists of any objects of scientific or artistic interest which can be procured for the occasion. The number of 'visitors is generally between two and three hundred.'

Towards the close of 1860 a new question of great importance to the people of Leeds began to attract public attention. This was the proposal to erect a new Infirmary in place of the old building which had for many years done good service to the suffering poor of the town and district, but which was now practically obsolete. Much controversy arose both as to the site on which the new building should be erected, and as to the character of the building itself. In the discussion of this question, naturally, Dr. Heaton took an active part. He was not placed upon the Building Committee when at last the battle of the sites had been decided, inasmuch as the senior physician to the Infirmary, Dr. Chadwick, had precedence of him. But the interest of Dr. Heaton in the work was too great to be stifled merely because he had no official connection with it. He had given his time and energy for so many years to the service of the Infirmary that he could not fail to entertain the strongest desire that the new building should be one worthy alike of the great community which was to erect it, and of the purpose for which it was designed. Accordingly, such aid as it was in his power to render to those who had undertaken the task of superintending the erection of the Infirmary was most cheerfully and systematically given.

The new building, a large and handsome edifice, designed upon what is now known as the pavilion plan, by Sir Gilbert Scott, was one of the first of the great new hospitals erected in England under the reformed system, and as such some account of it may not inappropriately be given here. It took the place of a large and commodious edifice of the old style which had been erected about the year 1770, in what was then a pleasant suburban district of Leeds, at the west end of the Coloured Cloth Hall Yard. This building itself had taken the place of a small edifice temporarily used for the purpose of the hospital in Kirkgate. The Leeds Infirmary had been for many years the most important of all the medical institutions of the West Riding. It was in connection with it that the admirable Medical School of the town had been formed, and its reputation had extended far and wide throughout the country. Mr. Carr's building was, as has been said, in the old style. Carr was an architect of eminence who had designed many handsome buildings, among them Harewood House, near Leeds. The Infirmary was not unworthy of his reputation. It was a massive and stately building of fine proportions. But it had been built at a time when our knowledge of hygienic laws was in its infancy. Like all the old hospitals, it was erected with an idea that it was impossible to bring the different wards too close to each other, or to make them too large. As a consequence the medical staff of the infirmary had, long before 1861, come to the conclusion that it was altogether defective so far as the purpose for which it had been erected was concerned. When first the idea of replacing it by a new building was mooted, there was strong opposition in certain quarters to the scheme, and it was proposed as an alternative merely to enlarge the existing building. Fortunately, this proposal, as we have seen, was overruled, and after much delay and discussion it was finally determined, towards the close of 1861, to buy the site east of St. George's Church, on which the present building stands. For the following account of this remarkable edifice—the first large infirmary, as has been stated, which was built in England on the pavilion principle—I am indebted to Dr. Chadwick, who was for so many years Dr. Heaton's colleague on the staff of the Leeds Infirmary. At the meeting of the British Medical Association at Leeds in 1869, Dr. Chadwick, who was president of the meeting, gave a description of the building. The Leeds new Infirmary and the Herbert Hospital at Woolwich, he stated, are the first complete hospitals built in England on the pavilion principle. The Leeds Hospital is arranged on the normal plan of a cloistered quadrangle in the centre, from which the pavilions branch out north and south. The width of the ground only permits three pavilions on either side of the central court, and administrative requirements other than the special objects of the infirmary necessitated the use of one of the southern spaces, so that the hospital really consists of five pavilions. Owing to the fall in the ground on which the hospital is built, one-half of the building has an extra ground story of full height. This is appropriated mainly to the several purposes of administration. The result is, that on reaching the hospital level the entire space is devoted to the actual uses of the patients, and the culinary or other administrative work is transacted on this floor. The exact measurement of the wards is as follows :—Upper ward, 32 beds, 19 feet high, 122 feet long, 27·6 feet wide. Lower North, 32 beds, 16 6 feet high, 122 feet long, 27·6 feet wide. Upper South, 28 beds, 19 feet high, 112 feet long, 27·6 feet wide. Lower South, 28 beds, 16·6 feet high, 122 feet long, 27·6 feet wide. The large amount of window space in the Leeds Infirmary, and in all modern structures for the same purpose, affords a striking and advantageous contrast to those of earlier construction. There are eight large windows on each side of the southern, and seven large windows on each side of the northern, wards, besides one at the end of each ward. These are all divided by mullions, and so contrived as to admit of opening and shutting, as the need for ventilation demands. Standing in the central line of the wards are two detached and open stoves, by which alone the warming of the wards is effected. They have descending flues which pass into the chimney shafts within the walls. They have been carefully constructed in every particular, and, having a large radiating surface, are well calculated to effect their purpose. The water-closets, sinks, lavatories, and baths are situated at the terminal extremities of the wards. The pavilions are approached from the central court by means of lofty, well-proportioned halls, having the staircase on one side, the ward nurses' room and scullery on the other. The external features of this noble hospital are furnished by a fine adaptation of mediæval architecture; and Sir Gilbert Scott has shown all his usual skill in making the very best of a site that presented no ordinary difficulties.

It was determined, when the building was approaching completion, to celebrate its opening by holding an Exhibition of Art Treasures in the wards, which were well adapted for the display of pictures; and it was hoped that a sufficient amount of public support would be obtained for the Exhibition to enable the trustees of the infirmary to reduce by a considerable amount the heavy debt which remained upon the building after the receipt of the various subscriptions which had been promised. This scheme made necessary a considerable delay in the opening of the new infirmary for the reception of patients, a delay to which the medical staff somewhat grudgingly assented, in view of the beneficial results they hoped to secure from the Exhibition. Dr. Heaton, along with many other residents in Leeds, was now much occupied in making preparations for this Exhibition. The collection of pictures formed at the infirmary was such as had never been gathered together before in any provincial town. On Tuesday, May 18, the Exhibition was opened by the Prince of Wales. 'The Prince,' says Dr. Heaton, 'was expected soon after twelve, but it was after one o'clock before he made his appearance. After a tedious delay, his arrival was announced by a salute of twenty-one guns, fired from a battery of the Royal Artillery stationed in the vacant ground at the foot of my garden. The Prince, after inspecting the collection of pictures, returned to the hall where the guests invited for the occasion were assembled, and declared the Exhibition open.' The day was not altogether a successful one in Leeds. as the rain fell in torrents during the afternoon, drenching the thousands of pleasure-seekers who had been brought together to greet the Prince and to celebrate the opening of the Exhibition. In the evening a ball was given by the Mayor. Mr. (now Sir Andrew) Fairbairn, in the Town Hall, at which the Prince of Wales. the Duke of Devonshire. and other distinguished guests were present.

Unfortunately, the Exhibition. though from an artistic point of view so brilliant a success. proved a failure in another, and perhaps a more important, respect. Instead of adding some twelve thousand pounds to the infirmary building fund, it resulted in a small deficiency. That there must have been some want of good management in the business arrangements was certain. The committee apparently allowed themselves to be led into a needlessly lavish expenditure, and, as a consequence, the infirmary suffered in a double sense. Its appropriation to the special purpose for which it was intended was delayed for twelve months, and no pecuniary advantage was gained. To anticipate the course of this narrative, it may be stated here that, in March 1869, the medical faculty of the infirmary generously commenced a movement for wiping off the debt left upon the building, Dr. Heaton and five other members of the staff each contributing a hundred pounds for this purpose. Under the stimulus of their example, the public bestirred themselves vigorously in the matter, and 20,000*l.* was quickly raised. It was at the time when this effort was being made that the small but beautiful chapel connected with the infirmary was opened for service. One of the distinguishing features of this chapel is the number of fine stained glass windows which it contains. A contemporary record says: 'The three two-light windows which form as many sides of the east apsidal end are exceedingly beautiful, the colours employed in the designs being brilliant and rich in hue, and most harmonious in tone. The right and left windows are the munificent gift of Dr. Heaton, of Leeds. Each window contains four figure compositions and two emblematic designs. The designs in the upper part of the left window represent the "Faithful Servant" and the "Widow's Mite"; beneath designs emblematical of the texts, "Your heavenly Father feedeth them" (the birds of the air), and "Consider the lilies of the field"; the lower figure compositions representing the Good Samaritan and the Good Shepherd. The inscription at the foot of this window is as follows :—"To the memory of John Heaton, 24 years a member of the Weekly Board of this Infirmary, died July 22, 1852, aged 83 ; and his wife, daughter of William Deakin, of Attercliffe, died May 2, 1841, aged 66 years." The right window is similarly designed, the subjects being illustrative of the texts, "To the poor the gospel is preached ; " "Come ye blessed of my Father;" "Suffer little children to come unto me ; " "I was sick and ye visited me." Two other texts are also illustrated—"The desert shall blossom as the rose," and "I am the true vine." The centre window is the generous gift of Sir Andrew Fairbairn. At the foot there is the following inscription :—"Dedicated to the glory of God by A. F. and C. F. F." The figure compositions portray Christ healing the sick and restoring sight to the blind, the forgiveness of sins and the restoration of the dead to

life, the texts being, " Thy sins are forgiven thee ; "
" Young man, I say unto thee arise ; " " Their eyes
received sight ; " and " Thy faith hath made thee
whole." Separating these compositions are two works
suggested by the words, " Instead of the briar shall
come up the myrtle tree." There is a very pretty
rose window in the west gable, which has been filled
with stained glass by subscription among the gentlemen
immediately connected with the management of the
infirmary.' It may no doubt seem a small matter
that this little chapel in this ' House of Pain ' should
have been beautified in this way, but those who
know anything of the bare and unredeemed ugliness
of the hospital chapels of the past will admit that
there is something significant of the age in which we
live, and of the greater gentleness and sympathy with
the poor and suffering by which it is characterised,
in this adornment of the Leeds Infirmary Chapel.

But we must return to the year 1868, and to the
Art Exhibition. Mention has already been made
more than once in these pages of another most important public institution of Leeds with which Dr.
Heaton was closely identified. This was the Philosophical and Literary Society. We have seen how,
as a very young man, he had become connected with
that society, and how constantly he had aided in the
good work which it accomplished by the delivery of
lectures on various subjects to its members. For the

long period of thirty-five years his interest in it was maintained, not merely unabated, but with ever-increasing warmth and zeal. In 1857 he was appointed to the post of honorary curator of the library, and that position he held for the remainder of his life. It was by no means a sinecure. The library of the society, consisting of rare and valuable books on scientific and philosophic questions, called for constant attention, and a considerable portion of Dr. Heaton's time was devoted to the discharge of the duties he had undertaken in connection with it. In 1866 he became one of the vice-presidents of the society, and, after holding that office for two years, he was appointed president—an office which he held until 1872.

The president of such a society as the Leeds Philosophical and Literary Society has to fill a position of no ordinary importance. He is, or he ought to be, the head of the literary and scientific society of the town in which he lives. It is his chief duty to hold aloft the torch of culture for the benefit of a community which has little time to spare for thought about anything save the hard practical business of life. Some idea of the difficulty of securing suitable persons for such a post in a great manufacturing and commercial town may be found from the fact that it has become already a tradition in Leeds that the president of the Philosophical Society must be either

a doctor or a clergyman. For many years it seemed
to be supposed that no one who did not belong to
one or other of these orders could have sufficient
sympathy with art or with science or literature to be
qualified to fill this office. Your business man might
perhaps condescend occasionally to read a scientific
book, or to attend a lecture upon some subject which
happened at the moment to be exciting public attention ; but nobody expected him to devote any portion of his leisure to the careful and intelligent study
of any of those great subjects of human interest
which lie outside the dull arena of commerce, unless
they happened to be subjects closely connected with
party politics. Engrossed from early morning till
late in the afternoon in the severe task of money-
making, the man of business, when he reached home
in the evening, was expected to devote himself to the
pleasures of the table as his chief occupation for the
remainder of the day. Not many years ago, a very
wealthy and prosperous merchant of Leeds, renowned
as much for his hospitality as for his riches, found to
his annoyance one evening that he had made a slight
mistake in the character of the guests whom he was
entertaining. Two of them, instead of joining in the
usual animated talk over the characteristics of particular vintages of port, the price of iron, or the
gossip of the Exchange, positively insisted upon discussing a subject so dull and void of all human

interest as books. They were in the midst of a brisk conversation about the treasures of their respective libraries, when their host, whose patience was exhausted by their unseemly conduct, interrupted them. ' Gentlemen,' he said, ' did you ever see my library ? ' They both confessed ignorance of the fact that he possessed such a thing. ' Come along with me then, gentlemen, and I'll let you see *my* books.' The wonder with which they received this invitation was not lessened by the devious and mysterious way that led to the apartment they were thus invited to inspect. Their host, candlestick in hand, seemed to be taking them down to the very foundation of his handsome mansion. Suddenly he flung open a door, and ushered them into—a spacious wine cellar ! ' There, gentlemen !' said he, with a flush of pride upon his face, as he pointed to the well-filled bins in which many rare vintages were nestling snugly side by side, ' *that's* my library ; and I'd like to know if that ain't a long sight better than a lot of your fusty books ? '

It would be a libel upon the people of Leeds to say that this story affords a fair representation of the state of culture in that town at the present moment. From the days of Priestley down to those in which we now live, there has always been in Leeds society a not inconsiderable representation of culture both literary and scientific, though it must be said that few towns approaching Leeds in size have given so few men of eminence, either in science, art, or literature, to the world. But despite the 'little leaven' of this cultivated clique, it cannot be doubted that the great mass of the society of Leeds, until a comparatively recent period, took but a feeble interest in the progress of culture. The Philosophical and Literary Society was the second of the important institutions established in the town for the purpose of ministering to the higher intellectual needs of the inhabitants. The first had been the Leeds Library, still a flourishing and most valuable institution, for the foundation of which Leeds was indebted to Dr. Priestley. Something has been said in a preceding chapter of the foundation of the Philosophical and Literary Society, and of the manner in which it grew out of a chance seed cast into the ground by one who still survives—the venerable Sir Edward Baines. It started under excellent auspices, that 'cultured clique' of which mention has been made taking the warmest interest in its progress, and freely advancing money for the erection of a building on the site now occupied for the same purpose. In 1861 it was found that this building was too small, and money was obtained for the enlargement, or rather the rebuilding, of the original edifice. In this work Dr. Heaton took a very active part, and at the close of 1862 he had the satisfaction of seeing the new and very commodious premises in Park Row thrown open for the accommodation of the society. Between five and six years later, he was elected president.

It so happened that he entered upon the presidential office at the time when Leeds was engaged in preparing for the Art Treasures Exhibition in the new infirmary. The council of the Philosophical Society had wisely determined to celebrate the occasion by a series of special lectures in the theatre of their institution, illustrative of the Exhibition. It became Dr. Heaton's first duty, after his election, to visit London for the purpose of securing suitable lecturers for this special course. How successful he was will be gathered from the fact that among those who undertook to deliver lectures in Leeds during the summer, to illustrate the collection of art treasures at the infirmary, were Mr. Tom Taylor, Mr. Digby Wyatt, Mr. Redford, Mr. R. N. James, Mr. Hailstone, Mr. J. C. Robinson, Mr. B. B. Woodward, and Mr. H. O'Neil. For the next four years much of Dr. Heaton's time and attention was necessarily devoted to the work of the office he held in connection with the Philosophical and Literary Society. Upon the president rests necessarily the heaviest part of the duties in connection with the annual session of the society. He is expected to arrange for the course of lectures held during each successive winter, to preside at these lectures, to entertain, on all suitable occasions, either those who are engaged in lecturing or those who are specially interested in science and literature, and generally to represent the town of Leeds in movements connected with the advance of culture in Yorkshire.

No one who knew Dr. Heaton can doubt that he discharged the duties thus laid upon him with zeal and efficiency. Not a fluent speaker himself, nor one who delighted in obtruding himself upon the notice of the public, he nevertheless did not shrink from any part of the responsibilities he had assumed when he accepted the office of president of the Philosophical and Literary Society. His interest in the welfare of that society had been proved by years of unremitting labour in its behalf; and even now, when he had attained the post of highest honour which its members could confer upon him, he refused to allow the duties of the presidency to interfere with the more obscure but probably not less trouble-some duties of the librarianship. For the whole four years of his presidency he continued to act as curator to the library. As an occupant of the presidential chair he was distinguished by the clearness with which he grasped the point of each successive lecture and the common-sense of the views which he enunciated in the customary discussion on the subject of the papers read before the society. Not having the faintest ambition to shine in oratorical display, he was devoid of all temptation to occupy the time of those whom he addressed by means of long set orations. But he had full possession of the secret of the art of public speaking. He never spoke unless he had something that he really wished to say, he always knew exactly what that something was before he rose to his feet, and he invariably expressed himself clearly and concisely. Thus, though the term of his presidency was not marked by any brilliant displays of oratory, or even of exceptional learning, it was one that was singularly successful so far as the comfort of the members and the prosperity of the society were concerned. The president was not seeking to ' show off ' on his own account. He was well content, indeed, to sink his own individuality in that of the body of which he was the head ; and though in consequence men probably formed a much lower estimate than they ought to have done of Dr. Heaton's personal abilities, he had his reward in the great success of the society during his administration of its affairs.

His connection with it unquestionably marked something like a new era in his own social life. As president he was placed by virtue of his office in the front rank in the society of Leeds. The personal reserve, almost amounting to shyness, which characterised him, had prevented his hitherto making any attempt to cultivate the society of those whom—with perhaps a mistaken idea of their relative importance —he had regarded as his social superiors. Whilst delighting in the company of men of culture and genius, he had shrunk from any attempt to cultivate their acquaintance, from a fear that they might regard him as an intruder. But as president of the Philosophical and Literary Society it became his duty, as we have seen, to show hospitality to the many men distinguished in science and literature who visited Leeds. How admirably he discharged that task is known to all who lived in Leeds during that period. Claremont had already become one of the centres of social intercourse so far as Leeds itself was concerned. It now became something more, however; and the leading residents of the town frequented it not merely to meet each other, and the host and his amiable wife, but to make the acquaintance of not a few of the most eminent men of the day who had visited Leeds upon some literary or scientific mission. The visitors' book at Claremont bears the signatures of not a few men of rank and fame, who had from time to time enjoyed the hospitality of Dr. Heaton. His house became now the recognised meeting point of all sections of society in the town, and both the host and those whom he entertained so pleasantly and genially benefited by the step in advance which he had thus made.

An extract from his journal at this particular period gives an interesting account of his visit to the meeting of the British Medical Association at Oxford.

'The annual meeting of the British Medical Association having been fixed by anticipation to be held in Leeds next year (1869), it seemed desirable to attend the meeting at Oxford this year, so as to acquire some knowledge and experience of the mode of procedure and the nature of the business. I accordingly wrote to say that I intended to be present at Oxford, and got in reply an intimation that I should be accommodated at the house of Sir Benjamin Brodie, son of the eminent surgeon of the same name, and Professor of Chemistry in the University. I left Leeds for Oxford on the evening of Monday, August 3, and on reaching Oxford on Tuesday morning I learnt at the reception room that I was to consider myself as the guest of Dr. Acland, president of the association, though I should be accommodated at the house of Sir Benjamin Brodie, who at that time was staying with his family at his country seat. I therefore left my card at Dr. Acland's, and then drove to Cowley House, which is just beyond Magdalen Bridge. I was there received by the housekeeper, who, with her husband, seemed to be left in sole charge of the house. Other visitors had been expected, but none had yet arrived. Sir W. Wilde, of Dublin, came in the course of the day, but the rest never made their appearance, so that we two had the house to ourselves. In the course of the day I called on the W.'s, and in the evening attended the general meeting to hear the president's address in the hall of Christ Church. The next day, Wednesday, there was the conferring of honorary degrees in the Sheldonian Theatre and the Rev. Dr. Haughton's address on " Food in relation to Vital Force." This lecture, although on a dry scientific subject, sparkled with wit, and the audience was kept in a state of continued merriment and delight. In the evening I dined with Professor Phillips. Dr. Shann, of York, and Dr. Aquila Smith, of Dublin, who were staying at his house, being the other guests. I left them after dinner to go to Mr. Waring's, and after that to the president's soirée in the Museum. This was a very successful entertainment on a large scale, the chief objects, in addition to the permanent museum, being Dr. Lionel Beale's large series of microscopic preparations of tissues, shown in from fifty to one hundred microscopes, M. Marey's exhibition of sphygmographs and cardiographs, and the " annual museum," which is a collection of new inventions, apparatus, illustrated books, &c. All these were admirably arranged and classified. Unfortunately, the arrangements for distributing tea and coffee, iced drinks, &c., were most imperfect. For these there was a great fight, and the classification of hats was so deficient that the men in charge soon lost their heads and could find nothing. Then the company broke down the barriers and tried to help themselves, soon reducing the whole to complete confusion.

' Thursday morning I spent in an excursion to Blenheim in company with Mr. Hey and others. We went in an open wagonette through the village of Woodstock, and before alighting at the house had a long drive through the park, through herds of deer, amongst ancient oaks or on the open plain. . . . After seeing the house we had some lunch at the Bear, and then drove back to Oxford. In the evening I went to the large public dinner of the association in the hall of Christ Church. Chadwick was elected as president for next year, and made a speech in reply.'

Going on from Oxford to London, Dr. Heaton tells us how he was admitted to the Fellowship of the Royal College of Physicians, to which he had just been nominated.

' At five o'clock Hare went with me to the College of Physicians, where a Comitia was to be held to admit the new batch of Fellows. All the nine new Fellows were present. Each had to pay a fee of 56*l*. 10*s*. After some delay in the reading-room, we were ushered into the library where the Comitia sit. Dr. Alderson, the president, sits in the middle of the room in his black silk gown trimmed with gold lace, with the large silver-gilt mace placed on the table before him. The president read a declaration to the new Fellows, to which all assented, and then each signed his name and place of birth in a book, and

x

went round the table shaking hands with the Fellows present. All were then allowed to sit at the table and take part in any proceedings.'

The meeting of the British Medical Association for 1869 had, it will be seen from the foregoing extracts from Dr. Heaton's journal, been appointed to be held in Leeds. Naturally enough, Dr. Heaton was one of those most actively engaged in preparing for the meeting, and early in the year he became treasurer of the local committee. He had not, however, anticipated that through a melancholy event in the family of Dr. Chadwick, the president-elect, a still more prominent position would be assigned to him at the meeting.

'On Monday, July 26,' to quote once more from the diary, 'Dr. Farr, of the Registrar General's Office, arrived here, the first of the guests coming to stay at Claremont during the week of the British Medical Association meeting. Chadwick was the president of the association. Unhappily, his second daughter was dangerously ill at Manchester—a double trial to him at a time when so much devolved on him. A gloom was necessarily cast over the meeting in consequence. It was arranged that the directors of the Grand Hotel, Scarborough, of whom I am one, should give a dinner to a select number of the leading medical men attending the meeting. I had the work of filling up and sending out the invitation cards, of which nearly three hundred were issued. Also, as president of the Philosophical Society, I was to give a soirée at the Philosophical Hall during one evening of the meeting, and of this all the responsibility, trouble, and expense fell upon me. My other guests arrived on Tuesday, namely, Dr. Banks, of Dublin, Dr. Stewart, of Dublin, and my old friend Augustin Prichard, of Bristol. During the day there was a council meeting in the Town Hall, and the first general meeting to hear the president's address and transact general business was held in the evening. Dr. Chadwick's address was chiefly a description of the new infirmary. Just as he finished it he received a telegram summoning him to his daughter at Manchester, supposed to be dying. He left immediately, and Dr. Sibson took the chair in his absence, the meeting not breaking up till midnight. At the meeting on Wednesday morning Sir William Jenner read the address in Medicine, and I proposed the vote of thanks to him at the conclusion. We had lunch on the table for all comers. The business of the sections commenced in the afternoon. Of the section on Medicine Dr. Gairdner, of Glasgow, was president, and Dr. Banks and myself were vice-presidents. We all went to the opening meeting, when Dr. Gairdner read an address. At six o'clock I had a dinner party to which I had invited several of the medical men visiting Leeds. We broke up at nine, to go to the

president's soirée in the Town Hall.   Most unhappily,
Dr. Chadwick's daughter had died in the course of
the afternoon.   He of course was absent, and the
incident threw a gloom over the meeting.   Mr. Hey
received the guests for the president.   During the
evening a meeting of the local committee was hastily
summoned, at which it was decided that in Chadwick's
absence I must take the chair at the public dinner
the next evening, and a great part of the evening was
spent in arranging toasts and making other preparations.   On Thursday I was up early, thinking over
my speeches for the dinner in the evening, the responsibility of which had come upon me so suddenly and
unexpectedly.   I got this pretty well arranged before
breakfast, and wrote out a list of toasts and speakers
which I sent to the secretary.   During the morning
I took a party consisting of my guests and other
gentlemen round the infirmary, showing them every
part.   I had a very large gathering after at my public
lunch.   In the afternoon I attended the Medical
section, and at half-past five I went to the Town Hall
to prepare for the dinner.   I was a good deal alarmed
to find preparations apparently very backward.   However, Wheelhouse soon arrived with the toasts written
out, and things began to look more hopeful.   I received the guests in the Mayor's room, where I had
to stand at the door for more than twenty minutes
shaking hands with each new-comer.   About half-

past six we sat down to dinner in the Victoria Hall. I had the Mayor of Leeds on my right hand and the Vicar on my left, and distinguished medical men from various parts of the kingdom on each side beyond. I got through my own duties and speeches as well as I had expected, and I think satisfactorily. The chief speech I had to make was in giving the toast of 'Success to the association and its president.' When I had made a start, I found that I got on without hesitation, and I thought I made myself pretty well heard, so far as it is possible in the Victoria Hall. When this was over I felt at my ease, and capable of enjoying myself during the remainder of the evening. On the evening of Friday my own conversazione, as president of the Philosophical Society, came off at the Philosophical Hall. During the morning I was very busily engaged in taking objects of art of my own in baskets, boxes, &c., in the carriage, and arranging them at the hall. I had a fine series of paintings of early Italian masters, lent to me from London for the occasion by Mr. Redford, who had been assistant commissioner at the Art Exhibition of last year. I had also the copy by Wheelwright of Titian's "Sacred and Profane Love," which Mr. Redford had sent, and which I ultimately purchased of him for 200*l*. The original is in the Borghese Palace at Rome. Mr. Redford had this copy with him during the Exhibition of last year, and he then asked 500*l*. for it. I much

admired it then. I had expected to be very busy all
this day in preparing the hall for the conversazione,
till I should have to go home to prepare for a dinner
party at my own house to several leading men of the
association and Mr. George the Mayor. My efforts
were, however, arrested by a summons to Halifax to
see a patient for Dr. Chadwick. When I reached
Halifax I had a drive of some two or three miles to
the house of the patient. . . . I drove back to the
station, hoping to catch a train to Leeds, and luckily
for me the train was late, so that I just caught it.
Reaching Leeds I drove to the North Eastern Railway
Station to complete arrangements for the special train
on the following day to the dinner at the Grand
Hotel, then to the Philosophical Hall to see if arrangements there were satisfactory, and then home to dress
as quickly as possible and join my guests, who were
in the middle of dinner when I arrived. After about
an hour at the dinner table we drove to the Philosophical Hall. I had to stand at the entrance to
receive my guests for some time, after which I mixed
with the company. I suppose between two and three
hundred visitors were present. There were many
beautiful objects of various kinds and works of art.
Tuffin West gave an address describing various
parasitic fungi, illustrated by very fine drawings, and
there were some experiments on the inhalation of
gases. I left Leeds on Saturday morning at eight

o'clock for Thorp Arch to see a patient, and got back just in time for the starting of the train for Scarborough, where I had to join the company who had gone by a previous train to dine at the Grand Hotel, by invitation of the directors. When I got there I found all the arrangements for the toast-list, &c., still required to be made, and this took up all my time until we sat down to dinner. I again took the chair as being chairman of the board of directors. The speeches were of the ordinary kind; the dinner, however, gave great satisfaction. We left at half-past nine to return to Leeds.'

This long extract from Dr. Heaton's journal is well worth giving, not only because it throws light upon the important social and public position which he had now reached in his native town, but because it sets very clearly before us the enormous pressure that falls upon one occupying that position at certain times, and shows us with what indefatigable energy and industry Dr. Heaton was able to meet the calls thus made upon him.

CHAPTER VIII.

THOUGH the study and practice of medicine was the chief business of Dr. Heaton's life, that life, as will have been gathered from previous pages of this book, embraced other interests of a still wider character. As he advanced in life it came to pass that in his native town he became familiar to the majority of the inhabitants less as a medical man than as one of the most active and energetic of the servants of the community in which his lot was cast. It was as the president of the Philosophical and Literary Society, as the chairman of the Council of the Yorkshire College, as the active supporter of all the chief movements for promoting the social and educational progress of the people of Leeds, rather than as a physician in actual practice, that he became best known to his fellow-townsmen. And yet all the time no man had a keener interest than Dr. Heaton in the practice of his noble profession, nor could any one have been more anxious to extend the sphere of usefulness which is open to the medical man. His work as a doctor resembled to some extent his public work generally. It was not of a kind to attract the notice of the general public; it was quiet and unobtrusive in its character. But among his medical colleagues his rank in the profession, and the great services which he constantly rendered to it, were fully recognised.

Before entering into any remarks upon Dr. Heaton's personal work as a physician, it seems desirable to say something about one of the great institutions of Leeds with which he was, almost throughout his whole life, closely connected, and of which, during no inconsiderable number of years, he was one of the chief supporters. This is the School of Medicine.

The School of Medicine was founded in Leeds in 1831. From a very interesting address delivered to the students at the opening of the session of 1881, by Mr. W. Nicholson Price, we take the following account of its origin and progress. ‘And so it came to pass, fifty years ago, that this School was established quietly and unostentatiously—without any flourish of trumpets—for its promoters evidently intended, silently but surely, to lay the foundation upon the solid rock of public usefulness. There was no general meeting of the nobility and gentry of Leeds and its vicinity called to consider the desirability of taking such measures as should be deemed necessary to promote

medical education in this district, and to secure to
its inhabitants the advantages which would naturally
flow from the establishment of a Medical School in
its midst. No; it might have been better if something of the sort had been done—there have been
those who thought so—but this was not the opinion
of the founders. They possessed a certain spirit of
independence and self-reliance (not bad qualities by
the way), and so set to work to do the labour and
undertake the responsibility of it themselves. For
they were men of Old Leeds, and imbued with the
Old Leeds spirit, the nature of which may be expressed in two words—" hard work." This is what
succeeded here, and to-day we celebrate the jubilee
of their effort.

'Of course they began in a very humble way.
A few back rooms in the old Dispensary in North
Street, which would hardly have compared favourably with the traditional two-pair back of a London
lodging, and a dissecting room, the ascent to which
was difficult and the descent dangerous, typical no
doubt of the steepness of the path of knowledge, and
of the peril which may result from slipping thereon,
completed the local habitation of our good beginning.
I remember well the little back-yard in which the
carriages of the professors waited the conclusion of
the lectures. Professors, did I say? That must have
been a *lapsus linguæ*, or perhaps a portion of that

prophetic spirit which is apt to fall on certain people at certain periods, but they were only lecturers then: for carriages I ought to have said gigs, for they were less pretentious times than the present. Those were the days when the name of Stanhope was a power among the coachbuilders, while that of Brougham, however well known in legal and literary circles, had not yet begun to influence the mode of locomotion, medical or general.

'I do not know that I can give you a better idea of the mode in which the medical education of that day, so far as a Medical School was concerned, was conducted, or of what was required of the student at that time, than by reading to you the advertisement of the second session :—

LEEDS SCHOOL OF MEDICINE.

Dispensary, North Street.

The NEXT SESSION will commence on Monday, October 1, 1832, in which the following COURSES of LECTURES will be delivered :—

ANATOMY, PHYSIOLOGY, and PATHOLOGY, by Mr. T. P. Teale and Mr. Garlick.

The LECTURES on the THORACIC VISCERA, by Mr. Thackrah.

DEMONSTRATIONS and DISSECTIONS, by Mr. Price.

PRINCIPLES and PRACTICE of SURGERY, by Mr. William Hey.

The Lectures on HERNIA, and on the DISEASES of the PELVIC VISCERA, by Mr. Thackrah.

OPERATIVE SURGERY, by Mr. S. Smith and Mr. Hey.

MATERIA MEDICA and THERAPEUTICS, by Dr. Hunter.
CHEMISTRY, by Mr. West.
PRINCIPLES and PRACTICE of PHYSIC, by Dr. Williamson.
BOTANY, by Mr. John Hey and Mr. Denny.
FORENSIC MEDICINE, by Dr. Disney Thorpe.
MIDWIFERY and DISEASES of WOMEN and CHILDREN, by
Mr. S. Smith.

'These lectures are recognised by the *Royal
College of Surgeons*, and the *Worshipful Society of
Apothecaries*, and certificates of attendance upon
them confer the same qualification for examination
as the certificate from the Medical Schools of
London.

'I should explain that Mr. West and Mr. Denny
were not on the council, or even members of the
medical profession. The former was an eminent
chemist and toxicologist in this town, and subsequently became a Fellow of the Royal Society. The
latter was sub-curator of the Philosophical and
Literary Society, and, along with Mr. West, took an
active part in its scientific and literary labours.

'Suffer me to trouble you with a few remarks
respecting some of the men referred to above. And
first let me say that, for obvious reasons, I shall omit
the mention of those whose names live after them by
a process of direct descent, and whose works, nay
whose very thoughts, are still active forces among
us, daily working out the beneficent designs of their

authors. That their influence was great, not only in the establishment of this School, but also in the building up of the medical reputation of this town, is known to all in any way acquainted with its history. But there are others who in course of time might be forgotten, and to their memory the passing tribute of my remark is due.

'The first president of this Council was Dr. Williamson, a man who held the leading position, not only in the profession in this town, but also in its civil life ; for, if my memory serves me rightly, he was Mayor of Leeds in 1836–37, and presided over the festivities which celebrated the attainment of her majority by Her Majesty the Queen, then Princess Victoria. He was for several years physician to the Infirmary. He evidently took an active part in the establishment of this School, and afterwards facilitated its removal to its more commodious home in East Parade, at that time quite adequate to all that was required of it. He was actively engaged in the formation of the Leeds Philosophical and Literary Society, was one of its first honorary secretaries, served in other offices, and was its president during two sessions.

'In point of time, in energetic professional work both in practice and teaching, if not in actual position in the Council, this School was very greatly indebted to Charles Turner Thackrah, who before its establishment had already given lectures to his private pupils and other professional pupils who were invited to attend—a great boon in a provincial town at a time when, even in the metropolitan centres, professional teaching was a very irregular and haphazard proceeding when compared with the great facilities of acquiring knowledge and the hard-and-fast regulations of the present day. He was one of the earliest members of the Philosophical and Literary Society, and was selected to deliver the Introductory Discourse, April 1821. He delivered a course of popular lectures on Physiology before that society, some of which were afterwards published. He also published an 'Inquiry into the Nature and Properties of the Blood in Health and Disease'—a work fully abreast of the most advanced scientific researches of the day, and subsequently published his work on the 'Effects of Arts, Trades, and Professions on Health and Longevity,' perhaps one of the most comprehensive, as it was one of the earliest works, upon a subject even yet but little studied. He died at the early age of thirty-eight, and to this end his incessant toil in no small degree contributed. . . .

'Dr. Hunter was a physician to the Infirmary and lectured at the School on Materia Medica and Therapeutics. He was member of the council of the Philosophical and Literary Society, and served the office of president. It was at the meetings of that society I

chiefly remember him by the tenacity with which he
maintained his own opinion.

' Of Joseph Prince Garlick I speak to an audience
many of whom knew him well, and they will bear me
out when I say that a more kindly or genial soul there
was not among us. He was a man who worked hard
to promote the prosperity of this School, was its first
treasurer, and carefully tended it during its earlier
years. He was full of good work in every relation of
life. He enjoyed the professional confidence of a large
circle of friends, for if I say that he was indeed a
friend to his patients, there are still many in this town
who can prove my saying true. He lectured first on
anatomy and subsequently on surgery : the plain
practical character of his teaching will long be remembered by his old pupils. He was for many years
surgeon to the Dispensary.

' One there was who, though not an original member of the Council, joined it as early as 1835, in
company with the late Thomas Nunneley. I refer to
George Morley. He did excellent work here, and
rendered most important service to this School.
Originally designed for business, for which I should
think that he was utterly unfitted, he turned his attention to medicine as a profession, and eventually
attained to the highest rank as a scientific man in
this town. His absorbing interest in his studies and
devotion to his patients caused him to exert himself

to the serious injury of his health, and he was compelled to relinquish practice: he died a short time
after leaving Leeds. He lectured on Chemistry in
this School, and had also a considerable reputation as
a toxicologist. He was consulted by the law officers
of the Crown in the trial of Palmer for the murder of
Cook at Rugeley by the administration of strychnine
or antimony; and when I say that he was associated
with Sir B. Brodie, Drs. Todd, Alfred Taylor, Owen
Rees, Sir Robert Christison, and others, it will be seen
in what light his contemporaries regarded him. A
case of criminal poisoning by strychnine occurred in
his own practice. The late Mr. Nunneley was associated with him in its medical investigation. In the
evening, after the post-mortem examination, I was
permitted to assist in the chemical analysis, and well
remember the intense interest with which, after a long
night's work, the concluding processes were conducted,
which ended in the detection of the poison, and
helped to build up the evidence which hanged the
murderer in this case, as it had previously assisted in
moulding that which led to the execution of the
poisoner of Cook.

'Of Samuel Smith I would desire to speak in terms
of affectionate respect. He was for many years (fifty-
five, I think) surgeon to the Infirmary. For a period
of eighteen months I acted as his dresser, and had then,
as for many years afterwards, and particularly while

associated with him in the Midwifery course—a chair
which he filled from the origin of this School—an
opportunity of studying his character and appreci-
ating his worth. I always considered him decidedly
underrated both as a surgeon and a citizen. He was
a man of great industry, ingenuity, and resource; a
skilful and successful operator, a practitioner of sound
judgment and great experience. He was most assidu-
ous in his attention to his hospital duties, and kind to
his patients, with whom he was very popular. He
was to the last a valuable member of this council, for
he literally died in harness. His lectures on Midwifery were highly appreciated by the students for the
practical and graphic manner in which he placed the
subject before them, and his class was one of the best
attended and most popular in the School. There was
an air of freshness about his lectures which you will
easily realise, when I tell you that they were delivered at seven o'clock in the morning, and began
punctually as the clock ceased striking.

' The only living member of the band of founders
is Dr. Disney Launder Thorp, now of Cheltenham.
For some years he filled the chair of Forensic Medicine, a subject to which he was so enthusiastically
devoted that he has most generously endowed a valuable prize in this School for the purpose of encouraging the study of this subject. . . . I believe that Dr.
Thorp did not practise many years in Leeds, though

he was an early instance in this town of those who, to
quote the words of Sir James Paget when speaking of
the Heys and the Teales, " prove in so emphatic a manner the error of the belief that high capacity for science
and for art cannot be inherited ; " for his father, also
Dr. Thorp, held a leading position here many years
before the period at which our retrospective sketch
begins, as he must have been nearly contemporary
with my great-uncle, who was physician to the Infirmary a century ago, and whom, at no great interval of
time, he succeeded in that office.'

This interesting sketch, by one who knew them,
of the founders of the Leeds School of Medicine, is
confessedly incomplete. Mr. Price was careful, for
obvious reasons, to say nothing of those whose direct
descendants still survived and practised in the town
of Leeds ; yet any attempt to give an account of
those to whom Leeds was indebted for the establishment of the School would fail to convey any just idea
to the mind of the reader unless some mention were
made of the names of William Hey, Thomas Pridgin
Teale, and Mr. Price ; nor would it be fair to over-
look the fact that among the first to join the council
after the College had been established was the late
Mr. Thomas Kennedy. Dr. Heaton, whose medical
training, as we have seen, began in this College in the
winter of 1835, may be said to have been connected
with it continuously from that time down to his death.

In 1844 he became a member of the council, an office which he retained until 1878, when, having for some time been the senior member of the council, he thought it right to retire and thus make room for some younger man. But even then his connection with it did not cease. He had been elected treasurer in 1865, and this office, at the urgent solicitation of his colleagues, he continued to hold after his retirement from the council. He held it in fact down to the day of his death. By him and by others, whose names it would be invidious to mention as they are happily still living, the reputation secured for the Leeds School of Medicine among the great centres of medical education in England was happily maintained, and no small part of his busy life was devoted with characteristic energy and industry to the task of promoting by every possible means the welfare of an institution to which he was at all times so warmly attached.

How the School advanced may be gathered from another extract from the admirable address by Mr. Price from which I have already quoted so largely. 'In 1834 the school was removed to No. 1, East Parade, then a strictly residential street. In order that the privacy of the neighbourhood might not be disturbed, for the property was held under very stringent conditions, no outward indications of the purposes to which the house was devoted were permitted.

The students were obliged to enter and leave by a
side door in St. Paul's Street, so as to prevent crowd-
ing about the front and other interference with the
comfort of foot-passengers on the Parade. For
many years this house afforded the space that was
necessary. But the School continued to grow in
size and importance, the museums being constantly
enlarged, as they were added to by many kind
friends and former students as well as by the industry and liberality of the staff. On one occasion
the late Mr. T. P. Teale sent a very large contribution
from his private museum, and the names of Hey,
Smith, and Chorley also claim notice as contributors
of very valuable and unique preparations.

'It therefore became necessary to provide more
space, and that more adapted to the changing modes
of medical instruction. So the council erected the
present building, which was formally opened by Sir
James Paget, who delivered the inaugural address on
October 3, 1865.' The new building thus dedicated
to the purposes of the School presents, it need hardly
be said, a great contrast to the rude and limited
establishment in which the work was begun more
than fifty years ago. It was in the year 1865, in
which the change from East Parade to the building
now occupied by the school in Park Street was
effected, that Dr. Heaton became treasurer of the
council. From that time forward much of the

School's prosperity depended upon him. His surviving colleagues cheerfully recognise the work which he did for them during the fifteen years of his treasurership. The post was not so much one of dignity as of downright hard work. But it was one admirably suited to Dr. Heaton's character, and he devoted himself to it with intense zeal. Such leisure as he had from his other professional work was always at the service of the School, and until he had fulfilled his duties there he never allowed social engagements, or possibly more pleasant and exciting public labours, to seduce him from his task. Thus it came to pass in the end that his influence in the School was well-nigh paramount. It was not that he was famous as a brilliant lecturer. Care and scrupulous conscientiousness in the statement of facts were his chief characteristics in that capacity. Nor did he claim the attention of his colleagues as a man who had surpassed all his rivals in the practice of his profession. As a matter of fact his professional practice, apart from his gratuitous work in such institutions as the Infirmary and Dispensary, was never very large— never, indeed, so large as he had been warranted in expecting that it would be when he settled in Leeds at the close of his brilliant college career. To a certain extent he found himself thrown into the shade both by those who preceded and by those who followed him—men who were endowed with different gifts from those which characterised him, and who had a far greater power of taking the public by storm, as it were, than he possessed. His comparative failure to attain considerable practice in Leeds was often deplored by himself as a misfortune, and possibly he might be justified in thus regarding it. But it was a misfortune for himself alone. For the community in whose welfare he took so deep an interest it was an unmixed blessing. It set him free to do work in which men of more brilliant parts could not approach him. And this work, it is to be observed, was not one whit less important than that which would have employed his time and energies if he had ever become the leading consulting physician in a great town like Leeds.

It was not, therefore, either brilliant powers as a lecturer or a popular reputation as a successful physician that gave Dr. Heaton the influence he so long enjoyed in the council of the Leeds School of Medicine, and caused him to be during so many years one of the leading spirits, if not the leading spirit, in that institution. His influence depended in the first place upon the well-earned reputation he had secured at College, next, upon his known conscientiousness and diligence as a physician, but most of all, upon the unremitting energy and industry with which he devoted himself to any task which he undertook, and above all to the task which devolved upon him as treasurer to the School. There was no work—even

though others might have regarded it as mere
drudgery—that he disdained so long as it came to
him in the way of duty. A rich man, as the world
goes, he might well have withdrawn years before
he did from the hard work he had undertaken
in connection with the School of Medicine. But
he continued to lecture there with the greatest
regularity down to the close of 1877, long after men.
who were younger than himself had thought themselves entitled to leave the task in other hands; and
even when, by his retirement from the council, he
had ceased to have any personal interest in the
success of the School, he continued, for the benefit
of his old colleagues, to give his time to the discharge of the wearisome and often trivial duties of
the treasurership.

In the preparation of his lectures to the successive
generations of students whom he helped to prepare
for their profession, he spared no expenditure of
either time or trouble. In an earlier chapter something has been said of the number of these lectures.
His first class, as is there stated, was in Botany. To
illustrate his lectures he executed with his own hand
a very large number of coloured diagrams, enlarge-
ments chiefly of the engravings and woodcuts in
standard scientific works, which of themselves
furnished a wonderful testimony both to his graphic
skill and to his patient and conscientious devotion to

the work of teaching. It was noticeable, too, that he took the same pains year by year to keep his lectures abreast of the progress of science. With laborious exactness he constantly strove to give his pupils the very best that he could bestow upon them.

His delivery of his lectures, unfortunately, was not attractive in manner. It was altogether plain and unvarnished—a simple statement of the truths he wished to bring home to his class, devoid of all rhetorical ornament. The result was that his lectures did not produce the impression which they might otherwise have done upon careless or indifferent students. But by those who were anxious to learn they were appreciated at their true value, and there were few lecturers who succeeded in imparting a larger amount of knowledge to the diligent student than he did.

As a practising physician he won in a very marked degree the confidence of his patients, whilst in consultations with his professional brethren he enjoyed their high esteem and respect. As has been explained elsewhere, he never attained a large practice, except that which fell to him in connection with the work he performed for the various charitable institutions of the town. But those who came in contact with him as a consulting physician had much reason to admire the thoroughness with which he investi-

gated the cases with which he had to deal. In
diagnosing a disease he made use not merely of his
own personal experience, but of the knowledge
gained by the leaders in his profession ; for throughout his life he was most careful to keep himself
abreast of the advancing tide of medical discovery,
and at any moment he could elucidate the case of a
patient who was the subject of a consultation by
reference to the most recent investigations of scientific
men which happened to bear upon it. The declaration of his fellow-doctors in Leeds was that in consultations on difficult cases ' Dr. Heaton talked like a
book.' The fact was that he talked out of the fulness
of his knowledge of what other persons thought upon
the particular disease with which he was dealing, and
also out of his own readiness to suppress himself.
He was one of those men, rarely to be met with, who
are willing to accept the undoubted experiences of
others as being equal in importance and significance
to their own. He offered himself, as it were, as a
witness in the case with which he was dealing, but in
pronouncing judgment he relied upon the general
weight of testimony and experience rather than upon
his own evidence alone. ' I never,' says one of his
colleagues, ' knew a man who in his dealings with his
patients was more completely self-effacing—I mean
who thought less of himself and of the impression he
might make either on the patient, his friends, or the

practitioner in attendance. This indifference to outward effect doubtless had something to do with the
comparative smallness of his practice. He would
have disdained a reputation which depended in any
degree on graces of manner or the arts of insinuation.
Esse quam videri was the motto of his life, and in
nothing was his adherence to this principle more
clearly displayed than in his professional labours as a
physician.' It should be added to this that among
the poorer class of patients he enjoyed a very marked
degree of popularity. They liked him for his quiet
and unpretending manner and genuine kindliness,
and their regard for him was touchingly shown at
the time of his death, when one very poor woman
sent what she described as a ' reefe' of flowers to be
placed upon his coffin, and others testified in similar
ways their gratitude for his kindness to them.

CHAPTER IX.

EDUCATIONAL WORK—THE YORKSHIRE COLLEGE.

THE steady growth, not merely in usefulness, but in sympathy with all works which he regarded as likely to benefit his fellow-creatures, and above all those with whom by the accident of position he was brought into most immediate contact, which had marked the whole public career of Dr. Heaton, was never more conspicuous than during the last decade of his life. We find that during these closing years he was often complaining of decaying physical powers, and had evident forebodings of a comparatively early close to his life. His spirits had never been high, and as he advanced in life they did not improve. Like other men he had his disappointments, though it was fortunate for him that they were in no case of a serious character. Yet, if they were not serious in themselves, they weighed upon his spirits, from which the elasticity of youth was gone, and often compelled him to take a somewhat gloomy view of the future. This fact must be borne in mind by those who wish to appreciate the singular devotion which he showed

during these closing years of his life to the public
work in which he had taken so active and useful a
part. No feeling of physical weariness or mental dis-
couragement, not even the heavy pressure of sore
bereavement, was allowed to interfere with the discharge of the public duties he had undertaken. On
the contrary, with advancing years those duties increased in number and variety, and if, towards the
close, he felt himself compelled to abandon some tasks
in which he had long taken delight, it was only in
order that he might devote himself to others of larger
scope and more pressing importance.

In 1870, as all the world knows, a great York-
shireman succeeded in carrying through Parliament
that which is probably the most beneficent and useful
Act to which the legislature ever gave its sanction.
Mr. Forster's scheme for the education of the children
of England was hotly debated in Parliament, but far
more hotly and stubbornly out of doors. Little good
can be done by entering here into the details of a
happily forgotten controversy. The measure was
avowedly a compromise, and a compromise dictated
by a very stern necessity. If the Act had not been
passed in 1870, it is probable that it would not have
been passed till a dozen years afterwards. Certain
parties, however, on both sides refused to recognise
this fact, and opposed the measure with intense bitterness, on the ground that it did not do all that they

desired. Of these the most bitter and resolute were the advanced Liberals and Nonconformists. They discovered in the measure what they regarded as very dangerous concessions to the Church of England, and they opened a campaign against the Act and its author, which spread throughout the length and breadth of England.

Never probably was there a more profitless, never, certainly, was there a more painful or wearisome, political dispute than that which was waged over the ever-memorable 'Twenty-fifth Clause.' It terminated in the victory of Mr. Forster; for though certain changes were made in the wording of that clause, no substantial alteration was made in the provisions of the Act as a whole. Probably at this moment there is not a Nonconformist or Radical in England who will not admit that, in the fierce controversies of 1870 and 1871, Mr. Forster was mainly in the right, and his opponents mainly in the wrong.

One feature of the Act was the provision of School Boards for the purpose of administering it in those towns in which it was applied; and one of the first towns to take steps for the election of such a Board was Leeds. The character of the controversy which was at that time (1870) being conducted with regard to the Act itself, naturally resulted in the fact that the election of the School Boards throughout the country was contested upon religious rather than

political grounds. On the one hand were the representatives of the Church of England, devoted to the
cause of education, but determined that, so far as in
them lay, nothing should be done under the new Act
which would in any degree interfere with the successful working of the Church Schools upon which hitherto
the education of the children of the poor had so
largely depended. On the other hand were the members of the different Nonconformist communities, and
the advanced Liberals. A large number of these
were in favour of having simply secular teaching in
the schools, leaving religious training to be given at
home, or in the places of worship and Sunday Schools
attended by the children ; but the majority favoured
the reading of the Bible and non-sectarian teaching of
a religious character in the schools themselves.

The launching of a new system of administration
is always a matter of great difficulty as well as of
great interest, and the launching of the School Board
system formed no exception to the rule. A special
element of interest and uncertainty had been imported
into the work by the fact that the voting for the
members of the various Boards was to be conducted
upon the cumulative system. It is probably nothing
more than the truth to say that nobody, when that
system was in the first place adopted by Parliament,
knew how it would work. The desire of Mr. Forster
was that all sections of the community might have a

chance of being fairly represented on the Boards, and that really valuable men of the upper classes should not be excluded merely because they did not happen to be popularly known among the masses. But where fifteen members of a Board are to be chosen, and each elector has fifteen votes of which he may dispose as he pleases, either giving the whole fifteen to a single candidate, or splitting them according as his fancy dictates among any number of candidates, a tremendous weapon is placed in the hands of narrow sects and self-absorbed cliques.

Such was found to be the case when the Leeds School Board of 1870 was elected. When the time for the election of the Board drew near a strenuous effort was made by the friends of education in the borough to secure the appointment of a thoroughly satisfactory Board without a contest. A provisional committee on which, as far as possible, all parties in the borough were represented, was appointed for the purpose of drawing up a list of gentlemen whose election on the Board would secure the full representation of different shades of opinion on educational questions. Of this committee Dr. Heaton and Mr. Baines, then the senior representative of the borough in Parliament, were members, and Dr. Heaton was unanimously chosen as chairman. He and Mr. Baines strove earnestly to bring about a reconciliation among all parties. based upon their

common adhesion to the principles embodied in the
Education Act ; but their efforts failed, and at Leeds,
as elsewhere, the first School Board election involved
a somewhat bitter and exciting politico-ecclesiastical
controversy. Candidates were nominated on behalf
of the Church party, of the Radicals in the borough,
and of different Nonconformist bodies. The five
candidates put forward on behalf of the Church of
England were Sir Andrew Fairbairn, Dr. Heaton, and
Messrs. Armitage, Ellershaw, and Middleton. Thus,
for the first time in his life, the subject of this memoir
found himself in 1870 appearing before the public in
the prominent and not altogether agreeable position
of a candidate in a contested election. It was a great
sacrifice which he made in consenting to come forward on this occasion—a sacrifice to which nothing
but the strongest sense of duty could have led him.
Hitherto, busy and indefatigable as he had been in
public work, he had always shrunk from any appearance as an active politician. It was in the quieter
paths of life that he loved to walk, and he had at all
times been ready to bear the brunt of the effort
whilst leaving the honours of success, such as they
were, to others. To the tumult, bitterness, and agitation of a contested election he had the very strongest
aversion. But he felt too strongly on this question
of the Education Act to stand aside when he saw
that he might render some service to that which he

believed to be the cause of truth and justice. Although born of Nonconformist parents he had been, almost from boyhood, a sincere and devoted member of the Church of England; and he was prepared to make any sacrifice of his own comfort in a cause in which he believed that not only the interests of that Church but of the people of England were involved. His political opinions, though never very pronounced, had been growing somewhat more Conservative with advancing years; and, though the Church candidates at this Leeds election were not selected on political grounds, one of them indeed being a decided Liberal, there can be no doubt that Dr. Heaton's candidature on this occasion brought him into direct contact with the Conservative party in the borough, and probably tended to accelerate his progress in the direction of Conservatism. As for the education question itself, it was no new one to him. He had shown his practical interest in it during the many years in which he had officiated as one of the managers of the St. George's Schools, and by the good work he had accomplished in connection with the Yorkshire Board of Education. He had therefore strong reasons for throwing himself with heart and soul into the cause which he now espoused; and he accordingly did so with a vigour and thoroughness which surprised all who knew him.

One extract only need be made from one of the

many speeches which he delivered during the course
of the contest. It is inserted here merely for the
purpose of showing the views he held in this memorable struggle—for it must be remembered that the
contest which was being waged in Leeds in November
1870 was practically being waged simultaneously in
nearly all the other large towns of England. The
report itself is bald enough, and utterly devoid, as
will be seen, of any rhetorical ornament: still it will
not be the less valuable on that account as an expression of the views of the speaker.

'He said, though fully determined to give effect
to the Act in allowing religious instruction to be given,
yet he did not mean to carry out those provisions in
any unfair or partial spirit. He would have the
same pleasure, if returned, in working with his
Dissenting colleagues who entertained like views, as
with his Church colleagues. The Act laid down the
principle of religious instruction, and he thought that
it was those who were opposed to such teaching that
were endeavouring to evade the Act rather than those
who wished to introduce religious teaching. He
would never be a party to establishing new schools
that would tend to impair the efficiency of existing
schools, because he thought it was due to those who
had worked so long in the cause that they should be
allowed to continue their labours unimpeded. With
reference to the desirability of having free schools,

his feeling was against them, although he would educate free of charge those whose parents were unable to pay for them. With regard to compulsory attendance he would apply it, but only after all other means had failed to induce parents to send their children. He thought the election of a School Board was a matter of the utmost importance, and that the future welfare and prosperity of the country depended much upon the character of the men they should return. He would only say that, if returned, it would be his endeavour to promote conscientiously the objects they had in view.'

When the election took place it was found, as has already been remarked, that in Leeds as elsewhere the power conferred by the cumulative mode of voting told heavily in favour of comparatively small but thoroughly united and well-organised bodies of men. The candidates who had been brought out on behalf of the Liberal party pure and simple were defeated, with two exceptions. Mr. Jowitt, who had been nominated by the Congregationalists, was at the head of the poll with nearly fifty thousand votes; the five Church candidates came next—a Wesleyan candidate being returned in the middle of the little group of five—and the Roman Catholic candidates, independent Church candidates, and other Nonconformist candidates made up the list. The result was a surprise to everybody, and it is probable that what happened in this School Board election of November 1870 in Leeds, happened in almost all the other towns in which similar elections took place at that time. The purely political differences between the two great parties were for the moment obliterated, their place being supplied by the religious and ecclesiastical distinctions which prevailed in connection with the education question. So far as Leeds was concerned, however, the Board thus elected proved a great success. It laid wide and deep the foundations of a system of education for the town which has been carried out with the happiest results, and it was peculiarly fortunate in avoiding any difficulty of a religious character. This was in a great measure due to the fact that the Church and denominational candidates had, for the most part, been selected with great judgment by their respective constituents. They were one and all animated, as Dr. Heaton showed himself to be in the speech quoted on a previous page, by a most sincere desire to carry out not the mere letter, but the spirit of the Act of 1870. They were, in short, thoroughly loyal to that Act, and far more anxious to bring all classes of the population within reach of the blessings of education than to advance their own personal or sectional opinions.

The result was that, during the three years of its existence, this first School Board for Leeds not only performed wonders in the way of providing school accommodation for the children of the town, but got through its laborious and difficult work with an almost unbroken harmony. Mr. Forster had occasion repeatedly to refer to it in the course of his speeches, and he never did so without expressing his admiration of a body which was in so many respects a model for imitation elsewhere. So generally was approval of its proceedings felt in the town of Leeds, that when, in 1873, the time came for the election of a new Board, an almost universal desire was expressed for the re-election of the old Board *en bloc.* This wish unfortunately could not be realised, through the determination of one or two gentlemen to aspire to the honour of a part in the good work which had been so successfully carried on by the members elected in 1870, and a contest became inevitable.

Dr. Heaton resolved to retire from his place on the Board at the expiry of his first term of office, and he did not appear for re-election in 1873. Great as was his interest in education, and faithfully as he had discharged the duties laid upon him as a member of the Board, there were some respects in which those duties were not altogether congenial to him. They imposed upon him the necessity of taking a more active part in public meetings than he cared for or was fitted for. His delight had always been to work modestly and unostentatiously behind the scenes ; and though he had never shrunk from taking his full share in the more prominent departments of public work—as when he acted as president of the Philosophical and Literary Society—he had a strong feeling of aversion to anything like needless platform display. Satisfied therefore with having done his utmost to assist in the laying of the foundations of a system of education for his native town, he retired from the Board in 1873, and left others to carry on the great work in the inauguration of which he had been privileged to take part.

There was, however, another reason for this step on Dr. Heaton's part. He had now in view an undertaking more serious and important, as well as more laborious and difficult of execution, than probably any other with which during his long public career he had been connected. This was the establishment of a College of Science for Yorkshire in the town of Leeds—a movement which has led in the end to the creation of the Yorkshire College, and indirectly to the formation of the Victoria University.

Dr. Heaton's first mention of the subject is to be found in his journal, under date March 1873.

'At this time, and at intervals throughout this year, I gave much time in endeavouring to promote the establishment of a College of Science for Yorkshire, and to obtain contributions for its foundation from the rich men of Leeds and other parts of the West Riding. It had been suggested some years ago as a work for the Yorkshire Board of Education, and was at first taken up by some influential county men who attended some meetings and talked, but did little else. These have gradually ceased to act, and the affair has been left very much in my hands as Chairman of the Committee of the Yorkshire Board. Sir Andrew Fairbairn and I have been elected vice-chairmen of the Committee for the College of Science, and Lord Frederick Cavendish chairman. Lord Frederick continues to take much interest, and will help from time to time and attend a public meeting, but we do not get other influential men to act continuously, so that at this time the work of keeping the thing going at all, and avoiding its collapse and the loss of all that has already been done and secured, seems very much to rest on myself. It is a heavy task and responsibility.'

From this time forward, frequent entries are to be met with in the journal relating to this subject. They chiefly speak of visits paid to various towns in Yorkshire, or to influential residents in the county, for the purpose of inviting subscriptions to the College. It was essential, as a preliminary even to drawing up the scheme of the new institution, that a very considerable amount of pecuniary support should be obtained for it. Eloquent speeches at public meetings, and newspaper demonstrations of the need of such a College and the benefits which might be expected to result from its establishment, were all well enough in their way. To those outsiders who have never had to do actual work in connection with an undertaking of this description, it may seem that such speeches, newspaper articles, and pamphlets form the chief part of the labour connected with their beginning. But practical men are well aware that this is not the fact. Besides all the speaking and writing by means of which the new movement was brought before the public, it was necessary that there should be, in this as in all such cases, an enormous amount of dogged hard work accomplished by some one. It was not pleasant work, this personal canvass of hundreds of more or less unwilling givers. No one who has ever undertaken a begging expedition of this kind can labour under any delusion as to the character of the occupation. But in the case of the Yorkshire College of Science, as it was then called, this was work which it was absolutely necessary that some one should undertake, and Dr. Heaton accordingly devoted himself to it with the zeal and patience which had distinguished him in so many other works of public usefulness.

The tedium of a begging expedition on behalf of some great public object is occasionally relieved in the manufacturing districts of the West Riding by the native humour of the people appealed to. A ' self-made ' man in one of the great manufacturing towns of Yorkshire, if he should happen to be asked to contribute to some object which does not happen to meet with his personal approval, will never hesitate to say 'No' with a plainness and emphasis which must be somewhat startling to the visitor from the more polished south. He sees no advantage, however, either in making believe to 'think over the matter,' and thus giving his visitor the trouble of a second unprofitable call, or in wrapping up his refusal in any euphemisms. He says what he means, and he says it with a clearness and firmness that admits of no dispute. Nor will he be much affected by the social position of the applicant who has waited upon him, and sought to obtain admittance to his purse. A duke would probably be refused with the same bluff but not ill-natured decision as that which meets the appeal of a local clergyman or town-councillor. A story is told of the manner in which a wealthy Leeds merchant dealt with an appeal made to his benevolence by two very influential gentlemen residing in that town. It was at the time when the whole county was stirred by the terrible condition of affairs in Lancashire, owing to the failure of the cotton supply during the American civil war; and the gentlemen in question had undertaken to canvass some of the richer inhabitants of Leeds for subscriptions for the dismissed operatives. Arriving at the warehouse of Mr. X., they were duly shown into his counting-

house and bidden to wait for his arrival. Presently
a rattling noise was heard, apparently in the room ;
a hidden door was thrown open, and Mr. X. was
revealed standing in the hoist by means of which
heavy goods were transported from floor to floor of
the lofty building. He eyed his visitors with evident
suspicion. Their wealth and social position were
well known to him, but they were not in the cloth
trade, and they were both men of benevolence.
X. suspected at once that they had not come with
the view of entering into any business transac-
tions, and he received them with cautious reticence,
retaining his position meanwhile in the hoist. 'What
can I do for you, gentlemen ? ' he demanded. ' Well,
Mr. X., you are no doubt aware of the terrible
distress there is in Lancashire among the cotton
operatives just now, and of the fund which is being
raised in Leeds for their relief. We have called upon
you to solicit a subscription——' But the sentence
was never completed. No sooner had the word
' solicit ' escaped the speaker's lips than Mr. X.,
his doubts now converted into a dismal certainty,
pulled the cord that set the hoist in motion, and,
shooting instantaneously upwards, left his two inter-
viewers staring at an empty hole in the wall : nor
did he descend to his counting-house again until he
was well assured that the intruders had departed. It
was at times among men of this description that Dr.

Heaton laboured in his indefatigable endeavours to obtain the funds needed for starting the College of Science. Often rebuffed, he still persevered, and with such considerable success that in April 1864, the sum of 25,000*l.* having been got together, it became possible to take the first public steps for launching the College.

On April 30 in that year a meeting was held at Leeds of the subscribers and donors to the proposed College, for the purpose of considering and agreeing upon its constitution and electing a board of governors. This meeting was presided over by Lord Frederick Cavendish, the warm and consistent friend of the undertaking, and Dr. Heaton read the report detailing the steps which had been already taken in connection with the work. As this report gives an accurate and succinct account of the rise of one of the most important of the educational institutions of the provinces, it will not be inappropriate to quote it here.

The report said—'The first action in promotion of a Yorkshire College of Science was taken at a meeting of the Executive Committee of the Yorkshire Board of Education on September 20, 1869, when a report was read by Mr. Sales, the honorary secretary, strongly recommending the formation of a College of Science for Yorkshire. A special meeting of the Yorkshire Board of Education was held in the Leeds Town Hall

on November 5 in the same year. A considerable
number of influential gentlemen were present from
Leeds and other parts of Yorkshire. Lord Frederick
Cavendish was in the chair; Colonel Akroyd, M.P.,
Colonel Morrison, M.P., the late Mr. James Garth
Marshall, Mr. James Kitson, junr., Mr. Huth, Mr. R. W.
Ripley, Mr Lomas, Mr. Isaac Holden, Mr. Baines, M.P.,
Mr. Fitch, and Canon Woodford spoke. Resolutions
were passed enforcing the desirability of a College for
Yorkshire, and appointing a committee to consider
and propose the best means for its establishment.
That committee met many times in Leeds, Bradford,
and at the house of its chairman, Lord F. Cavendish,
in London, and drew up a preliminary report in the
course of the year 1870. During that year also the
committee visited Colleges of Science or similar institutions in different parts of England, including King's
College and the School of Music in London, and Owens
College, Manchester. Other schools were corresponded
with, and ultimately a more detailed report and
scheme was prepared and published in 1872, which
was signed by twenty-one members of the committee.
It now became necessary to take measures for providing the means of founding the College, and for this
purpose a subscription list was opened, headed by
the munificent donation of 1,000*l.* by Sir Andrew
Fairbairn. Many other liberal donations soon followed. The work of canvassing and making known

the objects intended has gone on since. We have now overpassed the sum of 20,000*l.* which the committee proposed as the minimum sum with which they would be justified in commencing. Besides this, there are offers of valuable help both in money and in science exhibitions from the Endowed Schools Commissioners; and the Clothworkers' Company of London offer 500*l.* a year to found a chair of textile fabrics. The committee for a considerable time carried on its work independently of the Yorkshire Board, as a provisional committee of the College of Science. Having now carried the work with which it was entrusted to the present stage, in which it is proposed formally to constitute the College, with its own governing body, this committee will naturally cease to exist. Many of its members have worked zealously and sincerely to accomplish the work entrusted to them. They have met with much encouragement and with many disappointments. The work is far from being completed : it may be said to be only commencing. The governing body have an arduous task before them, both in organising the College and in still prosecuting the canvass for subscriptions. 20,000*l.* does neither represent the amount to be expected from the large and wealthy West Riding of Yorkshire, nor does it approach to the amount necessary to give permanency and full efficiency to the institution which we desire to establish. Although it is proposed to

commence operations in a rented building, both
because our present means would not permit of the
purchase of a site and erection of buildings thereon,
and because of the long delay which would be occasioned by waiting for the completion of a building yet
to be erected, yet it is most desirable, indeed essential,
that the College should ultimately possess its own
buildings, appropriately constructed and arranged for
carrying on its work with the greatest efficiency and
convenience.   We have often been asked if Government should not assist the work we have in hand.
Continental Governments do provide for scientific
teaching as applied to industry, and it might be well
if our own Government did more to promote this
great national work.   In this country we have always
been left to do more for ourselves by individual action
and by voluntary benevolence : and our national self-
reliance and powers of organisation and practical benevolence are no doubt strengthened and developed
by our people being left to their own resources.   But
inasmuch as all are interested directly or indirectly in
the commercial prosperity of the nation, this does
seem to be an object towards which (when it is once
commenced by private exertions) some assistance and
encouragement by the Government would be peculiarly appropriate.   Elementary learning is now enforced and aided by Government ; science and art are
also assisted by the South Kensington Department in

various ways, and much scientific teaching is provided in London. The fourth report of the Royal Commission on Scientific Instruction, recently issued, recommends, among other things, that lectures on science accessible to all on the payment of small fees should be promoted by the Government in the great centres of the population, and that the system of instruction of this kind established by Government in the metropolis should be developed.'

This report, it will be observed, is marked very strongly by one characteristic not often to be found in documents of this kind. That is, its unswerving fidelity to truth, even where the truth is not altogether agreeable. No attempt is made to hide or colour painful facts. It is admitted that whilst much encouragement has been given to the promoters of the scheme, they have met with many disappointments; and the friends of the movement are even told, with as much plainness of speech as is consistent with the laws of politeness, that only a portion of the members appointed on the provisional committee have attended to the duties imposed upon them. No one who knew Dr. Heaton can doubt whose was the hand that impressed this character upon the report. It was, as some persons thought, the defect, as others believed, the virtue of his character, that he invariably showed in connection both with public and private affairs an unswerving sense of rectitude, an unbroken fidelity to the truth even in the smallest matters, on those points on which our social usages permit to us a certain degree of latitude. If it happened that the truth was a painful one, so much the worse ; but still it *was* the truth, and must be stated as such. No wish to gain applause, to conciliate, to please, would lead Dr. Heaton on any occasion to blink the facts of any case with which he had to deal. There were some who were repelled by this characteristic of his, but those who knew him best were rather attracted by it than repelled. They knew that they could at least rely upon him on all occasions to deal faithfully as well as fairly with any question submitted to him ; they knew that when Dr. Heaton had once said his say upon any subject it was quite certain that the whole truth, so far as it was known to him, had been given to the world ; that there were no exaggerations and no concealments or evasions in the statement he had made. A public man in whom such confidence as this could at all times be reposed, was, it need hardly be said, of enormous value to his fellow-townsmen, and to those who were his colleagues in public labours of any kind.

This digression has been suggested by the report read at the meeting of the promoters of the Yorkshire College of Science which we have quoted in the foregoing pages ; for that report, as the reader cannot fail to perceive, is very strongly marked with this characteristic of Dr. Heaton's mind. It need hardly be said that the views expressed in the closing passage of the report, with regard to the claims of the College upon the aid of Government, have not yet been accepted by the Treasury, and that the College, such as it is to-day, is purely the result of the voluntary labours of a small band of devoted men, among whom Dr. Heaton long held a foremost place. The constitution of the College having been agreed upon by the meeting to which this report was submitted, and a council formed, of which Dr. Heaton was appointed the first chairman, the work was not allowed to languish. Renewed and strenuous efforts were made to increase the amount of capital at the command of the founders of the College, and a temporary building in Cookridge Street, Leeds, was obtained for the commencement of the work of the College. In July 1874 matters had got so far advanced that, as an entry in Dr. Heaton's diary informs us, two professors were elected at a council meeting held in that month, the election of a professor of Chemistry being postponed. In October work in the temporary building occupied by the College in Cookridge Street was fairly commenced, four professors having been engaged by the council. There was no formal inauguration of the session. An introductory lecture was delivered by Professor Green, who had been appointed to the chair of

Geology, in the presence of a few friends of the College, Dr. Heaton acting as president, and thus modestly and informally a new educational agency of no small importance was set in action. Subsequently Professor Rücker, Professor Thorpe, and Mr. Walker, the instructor in the textile departments, delivered the introductory lectures of their respective courses, in the presence of a number of the friends of the College, and on each occasion under the presidency of Dr. Heaton.

At the end of this chapter will be found statistics showing the work of the College at the time when it was thus begun, as well as its gradual progress from year to year since then. Those statistics show that though progress may not have been rapid, it has been steady, and has been accompanied by a regular development not merely in the numerical strength of the classes, but in the character of the work accomplished. The formal inauguration of the College did not take place until a year after the commencement of work just recorded.

' I was then,' says Dr. Heaton, writing on Monday, October 5, 1875, ' much occupied with the preparations for the inauguration of the College of Science on the approaching Wednesday. On Tuesday some guests arrived whom we had invited to stay here to take part in the proceedings of the following day. These included Dr. Lyon Playfair, and Mr. Macrae, of

Halifax. *Wednesday, October 6.*—This was a busy and important day, being that of the inauguration of the College, in preparation for which our thoughts and our exertions had been employed for some time. I took my guests to the College about noon, after which I went to the station to meet the Duke of Devonshire, coming with Sir Andrew Fairbairn from Goldsbrough, where he had passed the previous night. On going to the College, we found a considerable number of visitors assembled there, and many introductions took place; after which the Duke of Devonshire and other visitors, accompanied by Lord Frederick Cavendish, Mr. Baines, and myself, were conducted over the different parts of the building. On our return to the large lecture room, after making the round of the College, we found it filled with visitors. Lord Frederick gave an address, at the end of which he called upon me, and I spoke, describing the work that had already been done. The Duke then declared the College open, and the proceedings in the building were at an end. We then went to the Great Northern Railway Hotel, where about 150 sat down to lunch, filling the room but not overcrowding it. There were numerous speeches by the Duke, the Marquis of Ripon, Dean Lake, Canon Robinson, Mr. Baines, Lord Hampton, Sir John Lubbock, Mr. Forster, Lord Frederick Cavendish, Mr. Powell, Mr. Fielden, myself, and Sir Andrew Fairbairn. All the

speeches are reported at length in an account of
the inauguration subsequently published, of which a
copy printed on large paper, and elegantly bound in
morocco, was presented to me. A subscription list
went round during the proceedings, headed by a
second 1,000*l.* from the Duke of Devonshire, and
several thousands in all were added to our previous
list. We did not break up till after five. The
visitors then went to Claremont. At a quarter
before eight I took the Duke to the Town Hall, to
the Mayor's rooms, where the speakers and other
leading gentlemen assembled previously to appearing
in the Victoria Hall. At eight o'clock we entered
the hall, and found it quite crammed with an audience
which proved itself very enthusiastic and appreciative.
Many good speeches were made. The Duke gave an
opening address which was very good, and was said
to be the longest speech he had ever made. . I considered Mr. Forster's the most hearty and effective
speech of the evening. Dr. Lyon Playfair's was also
very good. All the speeches are given in the report
of the inauguration. As I had no speech to make I
was at ease and free from much responsibility, but I
had to take care that Lord Frederick got off for
London at ten o'clock, and then to send the Duke,
Lord Ripon, and Sir Andrew Fairbairn in my carriage
to catch the train to Harrogate at a quarter to eleven ;
all which was accomplished successfully. Only Dr.

Playfair returned to Claremont, all the rest having dispersed. Between four and five thousand pounds were added to our funds this day.'

The simple details of the ceremony which have been transcribed from Dr. Heaton's diary will at least bear witness to the heartiness and good will with which all parties joined in launching the Yorkshire College upon its career. Whilst the Duke of Devonshire and other men of high rank in the State came forward with the utmost readiness to give their assistance to the movement, it enjoyed at the same time the support not only of the intelligent middle class, to whose self-devoted exertions its very existence was so largely due, but of the great masses of the working population in Leeds, who flocked in thousands to the Victoria Hall to show their appreciation of a work with the object of which they could so heartily sympathise.

At the close of the year's operations, the council had an encouraging report to present to the supporters of the College. They were able to show that 80 day students, 145 evening, and 101 afternoon students had entered the College during the year, and that the progress made in all departments of work had been highly satisfactory. At this time the curriculum of the College was somewhat limited, the only professorships established being in Mathematics and Experimental Physics, in Chemistry, in Geology

and Mining, and in Biology, in addition to the class
formed under the care of a practical instructor for
study of the Textile Industries. The instructor or
professor in this class, as has already been mentioned,
enjoyed the benefit of an endowment from the Clothworkers' Company of the City of London. The same
Company had also founded four scholarships of the
annual value of 25*l.*, available for students in Yorkshire, and four other scholarships of the value of 30*l.*,
available for students from the West of England. A
year later, in 1877, Dr. Heaton and his colleagues
were able to give a very different report of the progress which they had made in connection with the
College. They could now show that the number of
day students had increased to 113, and of evening
students to ; the 161 afternoon students being 69 in
number. This, however, was by no means the most
important sign of progress which they had to report
during the year.

'On October 27, 1876,' says the report, ' the
professors brought the question of including
Literature and Classics in the curriculum before the
Education Committee as one of urgency, having had
repeated applications from students for advice as to
the best mode of obtaining instruction in subjects
which are requisite for University degrees, but which
the College does not teach. The professors expressed
a decided opinion that the number of students in the

science classes would be considerably augmented if the curriculum were enlarged so as to embrace the subjects in Literature and Classics necessary for the science degrees of the University of London; and the Education Committee at the above meeting passed a resolution recording their sense of the desirableness of such a step. The matter duly came before the council on November 3, and the importance of the recommendation was unanimously recognised, but as the existing funds of the College did not allow of any immediate action being taken to carry it into effect, the council simply recorded their approval of the scheme, and added an expression of regret that they were unable to do anything further then. On January 26, 1877, a deputation from the University Extension Committee (consisting of the Rev. Dr. Gott, Mr. Baines, and Mr. Legard) attended a meeting of the Education Committee of the College. They stated that the term of three years for which they had undertaken to supply literary teaching in Leeds was on the point of expiring, and inquired if any arrangement could be made by which the College should undertake, in a more systematic way, the work hitherto carried on by the University Extension Committee. The discussion was adjourned, the professors being requested to consider the whole question in the meantime, and to report to the next meeting. Their report was accordingly presented and adopted, and was brought

up to the council on February 2, when a resolution
was passed to the effect that after careful consideration of the question, especially as influenced by the
communications with the University Extension Committee, the council considered that the matter was
now ripe for action on the part of the College, and
a committee was appointed to confer with the University Extension Committee, and to prepare a
scheme for carrying their suggestions into effect;
such scheme to be laid before the Board of Governors.

'Several meetings of the committee were held in
accordance with this resolution, and ultimately the
scheme resolved itself into one of creating two additional Chairs, viz. one of Classics, and another of
Literature and History, the stipend of each professor
to be fixed at 300*l.* a year. It was thought desirable
to raise the necessary funds by means of annual subscriptions, the proportion to be collected by the University Extension Committee to be 350*l.* per annum,
and the time for which such annual sum should be
contributed to be three years certain.'

This scheme was discussed by the council on
March 28, when it was resolved :—

'That the council recommend the Board of
Governors to sanction the experiment of an extension
of the curriculum, by providing the means of giving
efficient instruction in Modern Literature and Classics
to students in the College, upon the condition that the

expense to be incurred by this extension shall be provided without trenching on the existing funds of the College.'

Speaking on the question at a meeting in Leeds, Mr. Forster, who had from the first been one of the warmest friends of the College, took occasion to make the following remarks :—

'I would put it whether the time has not come for that, and so far from it being in the slightest degree likely to derogate from the scientific success of the College, I cannot help thinking that if you were to add literature you would in all probability find it add to the scientific success ; and for this reason I think that the young men who come to this College ought to be able to get the fullest advantage for obtaining a degree by attending it. So long as the teaching is confined to science I do not imagine there is any University at which they would be allowed to matriculate, if their knowledge were confined to science.' Mr. Forster added that if, with the aid of annual subscriptions, a Literary Institution were added to the College of Science, it was perfectly certain that subscriptions would not fail, and they would soon be added to by permanent endowments.

Thus Dr. Heaton and his colleagues on the council of the College found themselves embarking upon a still more extensive undertaking than that which they had originally contemplated. The College of

Science, which had grown from the first idea of a
mere technical school, was now in turn becoming
merged in the much larger idea of a College, with all
the necessary means of providing a liberal education,
not in science only but in literature and the classics:
and this idea again, it is hardly necessary to point out,
inevitably opened up one still larger—that which has
since been realised under the name of the Victoria
University.

In this same report for 1876–77, from which the
foregoing extracts have been made, another matter of
much importance to the College was mentioned.
'One of the most important acts of the year,' says the
report, ' has been the purchase from John Lawson,
Esq., for 13,000*l.*, of the Beech Grove Hall estate, containing about three and a half acres of building land.
This is situated within a mile from the railway station,
and in proximity to the Grammar School and Woodhouse Moor.' It is more than probable that the
council would not have ventured to undertake the
responsibility involved in this purchase, but for the
fact that they were enabled to report, among the events
of the year, a fresh display of liberality on the part of
the Clothworkers' Company. ' The council have just
received from the Worshipful Clothworkers' Company
the munificent offer of 10,000*l.* for the purpose of
securing permanent and efficient accommodation for
the department of Textile Industries. The conditions

upon which this offer is made will be laid before the Board of Governors. The council believe them to be such as will be gratefully accepted by the Board.' Furthermore, in this report, we find the first mention of a movement which was subsequently destined to have important results. It was announced that the council had been observant of the movement set on foot by the authorities of Owens College, Manchester, to obtain for their institution the charter of a University, with power to confer degrees. The proposal having been adopted by the Board of Governors of Owens College, at a meeting presided over by the Duke of Devonshire, its probable influence upon higher education in Yorkshire needed to be carefully considered. The council of the Yorkshire College announced that, pending the receipt of further information on the subject, they must reserve any opinion upon 'the scheme for providing another University for the North of England.'

In October 1877 the story of the College advanced a step further. On the 23rd of that month the foundation stone of the College buildings, on the Beech Grove Hall estate, was laid by the Archbishop of York. Among others present, in addition to the council and officials of the College, were Lord Edward Cavendish, M.P., and the Master of the Clothworkers' Company. The building of which the foundation stone was then laid was intended to be little more

than an annexe to the College buildings proper, for
which a design was now being prepared by Mr. Alfred
Waterhouse, the eminent architect. This building,
begun in 1877, consisted in fact of the lecture rooms,
museum, and weaving shed used in connection with
the ‘textile industries’ class.

How far the general work of the College had
advanced during the year was shown by the fact
that the list of professors, lecturers, and instructors
published in the annual report for 1877–78, included the names of a professor in Mathematics and
Experimental Science, and his assistant; a professor of
Chemistry, and two assistants; a professor of Geology
and Mining; an instructor in Coal Mining; a professor
of Biology, and a demonstrator in the same class; a
professor of Civil and Mechanical Engineering; a professor of Classical Literature and History; a professor
of Modern Literature and History; lecturers in French,
German, and Oriental languages; a teacher of Latin,
and an instructor in the ‘textile industries’ class. This
year, too, the report gave further evidence of the
development of the scheme for the completion of the
work of the College, in the fact that the name originally adopted, that of the Yorkshire College of Science,
was no longer used, that of the Yorkshire College
being adopted instead.

Reverting to the proposed foundation of a new
University for the North of England, the report of

1877–78 said : 'It is now well known that the Owens College, Manchester, applied in 1877 to Her Majesty's Privy Council for the grant of a charter of incorporation as the University of Manchester, with power to grant degrees in Arts, Sciences, Medicine, and Law. A step the influence of which upon the higher education in the North of England might be so important, necessarily attracted the attention of the council of the Yorkshire College, which after due consideration came to the conclusion that the proposed scheme was open to several grave objections.   In this opinion they were confirmed by that of the representatives of Liverpool and of other towns whom they consulted. The Owens College scheme provided for the admission of other Colleges to the University, but the provisions that the charter should be granted to the Owens College, and that the University should be named after the city of Manchester, were very generally considered incompatible with the future incorporation of institutions situated in other towns.   Hence, in May, a deputation waited upon his Grace the Duke of Richmond and Gordon, K.G., now President of the Council, and Sir Stafford Northcote, M.P., Chancellor of the Exchequer, to lay these views before them. In the unavoidable absence of his Grace the Archbishop of York, the Marquis of Ripon introduced the deputation, forcibly stated the grounds on which their objections to the scheme were based, and presented a memorial to the Privy Council, in which they were briefly expressed. The influential character of the deputation, including representatives of sixteen municipal and other corporations, and of an equal number of scientific societies, and the fact that the prayer of the memorial was supported by many gentlemen of the highest authority in educational matters, give reason for the belief that a more satisfactory scheme will ultimately be adopted. The Yorkshire College has held friendly communications with the authorities of Owens College on the subject, but is at present unable to make them the subject of a public report.'

The anxiety which Dr. Heaton felt with regard to this question of the new Northern University, and of the position which the Yorkshire College was to hold in connection with it, was very great; whilst the labour which the negotiations and deputations in regard to the matter entailed upon him was enormous. The appeal to the Lord President of the Council, which is mentioned in the foregoing extract from the report, could not be made without much previous preparation, and in Dr. Heaton's diaries there is abundant evidence of the time and toil which he had to expend upon it. As in all other public matters, however, which engaged his sympathies, there was no disposition to spare himself, and he cheerfully devoted several hours of every day to the necessary though unostentatious work involved in the development of the College.

A year later (1879) the annual report of the College mentioned the successful conclusion of the negotiations with the Owens College, Manchester, which followed the sending of the deputation to the Duke of Richmond. The result of those negotiations was that a second deputation waited upon his Grace, as Lord President of the Council. On this occasion, however, the deputation included the representatives of Owens College as well as of the Yorkshire College. The spirit in which the reconciliation of the apparently conflicting interests of the two bodies had been brought about may be gathered from the following passage of the memorial which was presented on behalf of the Yorkshire College by Lord Frederick Cavendish, M.P.

The memorial prayed that Her Majesty might be advised—

1. To create a new University, in which the Owens College, Manchester, and such other institutions as may now or hereafter be able to fulfil the conditions of incorporation laid down in the charter, may be incorporated Colleges.

2. To grant to each of such incorporated Colleges a share in the government of the University, depending only upon its magnitude and efficiency, in accordance with the suggested constitution.

3. To be graciously pleased to allow the said University to be called the Victoria University.

Dr. Heaton did not take part in the second deputation to the Lord President of the Council, the result of which is given above. When that deputation waited upon the Duke of Richmond on May 15, 1879, Dr. Heaton had just returned to England from a somewhat lengthened Continental tour, and he found that many matters at home required his attention. But he had never been in the habit of subordinating the public duties he had undertaken to his personal convenience, and he would without doubt have sacrificed any private plans he might have formed which stood in the way of his being present at the interview of the Duke of Richmond with the deputation, but for one fact. This was, that he did not agree with his colleagues on the council of the Yorkshire College with regard to this question of a Northern University.

Whether he was right or wrong in his view of the question need not be argued here. It would, however, be unfair to allow this disagreement between himself and the colleagues with whom he had so long been associated to be passed over in silence. Dr. Heaton's view was that the formation of a new Northern University was not really required, inasmuch as the existing Universities of Oxford, Cambridge, and London served all practical purposes. He was jealous of any step which might seem in any degree to reduce the value of degrees gained at the older Universities, and he did not look with favour upon the attempt to establish rival Universities in which the standard of scholarship might possibly be reduced under the pressure of a brisk competition for students. But over and above these reasons he felt a natural jealousy on behalf of the interests of the two great educational institutions with which he was himself so closely identified, the Leeds School of Medicine and the Yorkshire College. He recognised the fact that several years must elapse before, under the conditions prescribed, the Yorkshire College could claim admission to the University of which Owens College became at once, and as a matter of right, a member. His fear was that both the School of Medicine, whose high traditions no man cherished more jealously than he did, and the College, might begin to droop and suffer in prosperity and reputation so soon as the Owens College was able to afford the privileges of a University training to its students.

But whilst these were the views which he had formed, and to which he clung to the last, he did not allow his zeal on behalf of the Yorkshire College to abate one jot because on this question his colleagues on the council differed from him. All through the negotiations concerning the establishment of this

Northern University, and despite the fact that he
found himself in a minority on the council, he clung
to the work in which he had from the outset taken
so active a part. Other people might get their way
in questions of high policy, and for good or for evil
his views might be overruled, but at least he could
persevere in the task about which there was no
difference of opinion, that of laying the foundations
broad and deep of the structure. What precise form
the structure was to take when it was completed was
a matter upon which everybody could not agree,
and, as we have seen, it was one upon which Dr.
Heaton did not agree with his colleagues. But in
the meantime there was a duty which excited no
controversy, and as to the immediate importance of
which all were agreed. So with the sturdy, quiet
spirit of resolution and self-effacement which distinguished him, he went on with the laborious and not
always pleasant task of collecting funds for the
College, and securing for it influential support in all
possible quarters. Visits to London were frequent
for the purpose of enlisting the co-operation of the
City Companies and other influential bodies on behalf
of a movement which was really designed in part to
accomplish in the nineteenth century the work which
these Companies were originally intended to accomplish in the middle ages. As we have already seen,
the Clothworkers' Company rendered munificent aid

in the task, and, as will be related in fuller detail in the next chapter, that Company recognised Dr. Heaton's disinterested labours in the work by conferring upon him its freedom. But he was not always fortunate in his efforts to secure aid in such quarters, and at times he had to submit with patience to somewhat rude rebuffs. Upon the whole, however, he had great success in this most important though unostentatious department of work, and the Yorkshire College, such as it is to-day, may fairly be described not merely as a monument of the enterprise and public spirit of the Yorkshiremen of this generation, but as a memorial of the unremitting diligence, perseverance, and self-denial of John Deakin Heaton.

The following are the statistics showing the progress of the Yorkshire College from its establishment in 1874 down to the autumn session of 1882 :—

Sessions	Number of students				Professors and instructors	Assistants	Total fees received		
	Registered	Medical	Occasional	Evening			£	s	d.
1874–75	24	—	—	—	4	1	148	15	6
1875–76	39	26	121	145	5	2	653	2	8
1876–77	55	38	178	166	6	3	937	6	3
1877–78	90	38	37[1]	192	11	7	1233	18	5
1878–79	113	28	140	143	11	8	1455	6	0
1879–80	142	52	148	121	12	9	1769	18	11
1880–81	153	65	115	131	12	10	2446	2	3
1881–82	146	56	215	162	12	10	2330	15	5

[1] No afternoon class held this year.

Courses of lectures have also been delivered by the professors in Wakefield, Bradford, Halifax, Harrogate, Darlington, Hull, Keighley, Rotherham, Sheffield, Barnsley, and Mirfield.

CHAPTER X.

CLOSING DAYS.

WE have seen what were the chief incidents of the last ten years of Dr. Heaton's life as a public man. He had during that period been busier than ever in his labours for others. He had at the same time been concerned in public works of much greater importance than those to which he had devoted his energies in early life and middle age, and he had also taken a much more prominent place in the eyes of his fellow-townsmen than he had ever aspired to before. During all this time, indeed, he had been advancing both in power and in usefulness, and his progress had been steady and uninterrupted. It was an almost noiseless, an altogether unostentatious progress. Those about him, who had known him from his modest beginnings, never realised, until after he was gone, how large a place he had gradually come to fill in the provincial society to which he belonged, how numerous were the interests and the varieties of public work which converged upon him. A busy, unpretending, careful man : apt to speak home truths with blunt precision, resolute to do that which he believed to be the right, with little fear of the consequences either for himself or others; reserved in his intercourse with the outer world on all points save the special point on which it happened for the moment to be his duty to enlarge; always ready to take his share in work that needed to be done for the public good, and never anxious to secure for himself what the world would have thought the best part of that work—the shining, showy part—such was Dr. Heaton as he appeared in the eyes of his fellow-citizens between 1870 and 1880. He had filled such posts of dignity as the presidency of the Leeds Philosophical and Literary Society, he had been a member of the first School Board, which laid deep and wide the foundations of the educational system of the town, he had been the most active and untiring of those who were building up, brick by brick, the great edifice of the Yorkshire College. All these and other offices and duties had been imposed upon him, and in none of them had he been found wanting. Rather, it had been discovered by those about him, that their old friend was still developing in power and character, and that he could be trusted to be equal to any task which he undertook, nay, to some which he would rather not have undertaken, but which were forced upon him by the persistency of others; for all through his life he had entertained but a humble idea of his own powers, and had been anxious to begin no work which he did not feel himself able to finish *well.*

Those about him saw that as he grew older, though his labours became more abundant than ever, there was a certain loss of elasticity in his gait which marked the advance of age, and that with it came an inclination to take a somewhat sombre view of life, and to feel with exaggerated sensitiveness some of those disappointments which are inevitable in the lot of any man. This fact must be noted to Dr. Heaton's credit, because, whilst he thus suffered in health and spirits, he never allowed any public work which he had undertaken to suffer with him. The last chapter furnishes some idea of the extent of his public labours during the closing decade of his life. It is a remarkable story, for it shows that this quiet and unpretending professional man was spending his days in the most laborious and thankless tasks; but the story of these never-ending labours, these incessant journeyings to and fro, this interminable writing of letters, these numberless meetings and interviews and begging expeditions, were carried on amid the pressure of social and professional engagements by one whose health was failing, and who too often had occasion to remark upon his loss of strength and vigour.

In his journal at the close of the year 1875

appears the following passage regarding his daily life at that time, which throws some light both upon his habits and his thoughts :—

'My daily life at this time, and now for several years, has been to rise early, frequently before six in the summer, and between six and seven in the winter, and to come down to my library in my dressing-gown, where I write or read till it is time to return to my dressing-room to complete my toilet before family prayers and breakfast. At this hour I have no fire in the coldest weather, being commonly down-stairs before any of the servants. This, of course, is a very cold and comfortless time during the winter, but it is pleasant enough in the summer, and it is the time when I can now best apply myself to work. Clinical and other lectures are chiefly prepared at this time. We have prayers at 8.15, and then breakfast. Then I look over my correspondence, arrange the work for the day, and see patients and other callers on business until after 10. Then I go out in the carriage or on foot, returning at 2, when I am at home to callers till 3 or 3.30. After 3 I go out again, returning by 6, either to tea or dinner ; after which I stay at home when I have no evening engagement.

'My reason for rising early is that I am a poor sleeper, unable to sleep much after five o'clock ; and at this hour my mental reflections, retrospects, and anticipations are always uncomfortable and unhappy when I am unoccupied, partaking, in fact, of the nature of " blue devils." I find that I best escape this discomfort (which, when anything goes wrong, is really extreme) by rising early and occupying myself. Moreover, the time is very valuable to me. But the shortness of my sleep during the night often causes me to be uncomfortably drowsy during the day, and must tend to wear out both mind and body, of which result I am increasingly conscious.'

Again, at the close of 1877 there is the following passage in the journal, marking still more strongly the increasing weakness and depression of the writer :—

'In looking back upon this year, when past, it does not give me the impression of having been a very successful or encouraging period. My sixtieth birthday having passed, I had entered upon another decade of my life ; what remained to me of existence could not be very long, and the rapid decline of vigour which I had experienced during the last few years suggested the great uncertainty of my surviving for another decade. . . . Naturally the present experience of declining powers, and the prospect of continually increasing failure, and the rapid abbreviation of life, must tend to cast a shade of melancholy over one's existence continually.'

Such are but a few of the reflections which are to

be found scattered over the pages of Dr. Heaton's journal during these years between 1870 and 1880, and they prove the accuracy of what has been said as to the growing tendency on his part to look rather upon the dark than the bright side of things. But in contrast with this hidden melancholy must be set his noble devotedness to the duties assigned to him, his constant regard for the interests of those around him. Characteristically enough, on the next page of the journal to that on which may be found the passage above quoted, Dr. Heaton has transcribed, as his motto for the opening year, Mrs. Browning's sonnet on Work.

> What are we set on earth for? Say to toil;
> Nor seek to leave thy tending of the vines
> For all the heat o' the day, till it declines,
> And Death's wild curfew shall from work assoil.
> God did anoint thee with His odorous oil,
> To wrestle, not to reign ; and He assigns
> All thy tears over, like pure crystallines,
> For younger fellow-workers of the soil
> To wear for amulets. So others shall
> Take patience, labour, to their heart and hand,
> From thy heart and thy brave cheer,
> And God's grace fructify through thee to all.
> The least flower, with a brimming cup may stand,
> And share its dew-drops with another near.

So no consciousness of failing physical powers, or growing disappointments and clouded hopes, led Dr. Heaton to abandon the wise course he had marked out for himself, when he deliberately chose a life of useful and unselfish public work, in preference to one of ease and pleasure.

It might be well, before proceeding with the story of his personal life during this closing decade, to say something of the change which had taken place in the social institutions of the town in which he played so active a part. But no formal statement on this subject can be needed. Like Dr. Heaton himself, Leeds had made great progress during the term over which his life extended. It was now altogether different from the slow and somewhat narrow and old-fashioned provincial town which he had known in his boyhood, and of which something has been said in previous pages. Railways, telegraphs, daily newspapers, Free Trade, the progress of invention, the growth of rapid communication by sea with all parts of the world, had done their work, and Leeds had emerged from the dulness and obscurity which had so long weighed upon it, and stood forth as the competitor in public spirit and commercial and manufacturing enterprise, not only of the largest of provincial cities but of the capital itself.

We have seen something in these pages of the growth of some of the agencies by which these changes were effected, and we have also seen the share which Dr. Heaton had in supporting many of these agencies. In the mere outward appearance of the town a wonderful transformation had been wrought since he entered upon public life. To say nothing of the railways and railway stations, which were of course entirely new, Leeds had become possessed of a noble Town Hall, and was already rejoicing in the erection of Public Buildings for the administration of the town, equal in architectural distinction to the Town Hall. The old Infirmary had been replaced by the great edifice in which Dr. Heaton spent so many anxious and useful hours; the Philosophical Society, the Mechanics' Institute, and the Grammar School had all been adequately housed; many fine churches, schools, banks, and other public buildings had been added to the adornments of the place; the first portion of the buildings designed by Mr. Waterhouse for the use of the Yorkshire College was in course of erection, new streets had been opened up, old streets had been widened and straightened; a noble park, unequalled as a public recreation ground in England, if not in Europe, had been acquired by the town; the country surrounding Leeds had been dotted with handsome villas, the residences of the rich merchants who thirty years earlier had been content to crowd together in what were then the suburban districts, where Clarendon Road and Wellington Street now show their long rows of houses. Everywhere there had been change and growth and progress. One thing indeed remained unchanged in Leeds, and we

might almost say one thing only. The long absent
townsman, who after an interval of fifty years came
back again to see the place in which he had been
born, would find himself, soon after leaving the railway station, in front of a well-remembered building,
unaltered in any particular, even by half a century
of rough usage; grim, ugly, uncompromising, obtruding itself upon the attention of astounded strangers as
a monument of the bad taste and ignorance of our
forefathers; and he would welcome with joy the one
familiar object in the midst of the busy scene. But
if he turned his back upon that old though by no
means venerable Cloth Hall, it mattered not in what
direction his footsteps carried him, he would find
himself amid scenes wholly strange to him. Where
he had left narrow and crooked alleys, great streets
now stretch themselves before his eyes: where he
remembered green fields and quiet suburban houses,
huge manufactories and warehouses, the homes of an
immense commerce, are now everywhere to be met
with. Such a man would be filled with a profound
amazement at the change which within a comparatively limited period—a period that is at times
covered twice over in the life of a human being—
had wrought itself in the town he had once known.
And yet this extraordinary transformation, so familiar
to all the older inhabitants of Leeds, is but an example of what has happened in most of the great pro-

vincial towns of England within the last half-century.
That change would not, however, have been possible
if the people had been a weak and nerveless race,
unable or unwilling to assist themselves. Great deeds
can only be wrought by men who have the elements
of greatness in them ; and therefore it is that the life
even of one whose reputation is wholly local and
provincial, but who, within the limits of his own
province, exerted himself so wisely and so well, is not
unworthy of being recorded, and ought not to be
devoid of some useful lessons. Even though the tale
may seem to some to be more than a trifle monotonous, and though the scene upon which it is set may
not be one that has attractions for all, a faithful
record of duty done and progress made in one of
these great provincial towns of England, during the
last half-century, cannot be altogether without profit
to those who read it.

The change, however, of which we speak has not
been one merely of a material kind. Whilst wealth has
increased, and great buildings have been multiplied,
and vast districts, which fifty years ago were in the
open country, have been included in the embrace of
the town, there has been a corresponding change in
the mental and moral condition of the people. In
this change, so far as Leeds was concerned, a worker
like Dr. Heaton had a larger share than in the extension of what are commonly known as 'local improve-

ments,' though we have seen that with regard to these he held sound and public-spirited views, and lost no opportunity of impressing them upon the minds of his fellow-townsmen. When he began his life of labour in Leeds the schools for the poor were few in number and by no means excellent in quality, whilst we have seen something in his own story of the state of matters at the Grammar School where the middle-class youth of the town were trained. Conscious of the deficiencies of his own education, Dr. Heaton was throughout his whole career a most zealous educationist. The Grammar School, of which he was during the later years of his life one of the trustees, enlarged its boundaries and brought its curriculum into greater conformity to the spirit and the requirements of the age, a work in which all his sympathies were on the side of progress. Strongly attached to the Church of England, he was naturally more favourable to the increase and development of the parochial schools than to the establishment of Board Schools. For thirty years he had been the treasurer of the schools connected with the church at which he was a regular attendant—St. George's— and had given all the needed time and labour to the support of a work in which, both as an educationist and a churchman, he was so deeply interested. But he was not blind to the necessity laid upon all the friends of education by the progress of the nation.

and, whilst a member of the School Board, he did all that he could to give the young of Leeds for generations to come a complete and efficient system of education. The cause of higher education had undergone a marvellous development within his time. The Medical School and the Yorkshire College were doing their work, and raising the standard of culture in the community generally. Of the part which he played in connection with both of these institutions nothing need be said here in addition to what has been stated in preceding chapters.

It was of course impossible that all these agencies should have been in operation during a long term of years without a marked effect being produced upon the population as a whole. But these were by no means the only causes which had contributed to bring about the change which caused the Leeds of 1880 to present so marked a contrast to the Leeds of 1830. The quickening of intellectual life which has been so marked in London during the last thirty years has penetrated to the provinces. Books are bought far more freely in provincial towns than was formerly the case. It would be too much to say that they are read more carefully, but even a slight knowledge of books, widespread over the population, affords a grateful contrast to the condition of the masses—including the mass of the well-to-do—in the early decades of the present century. The spirit of scientific

research has, again, permeated the more intelligent
classes in the provinces. It is no exaggeration to say
that in this respect the country has attained a certain
degree of supremacy over London. At all events
some knowledge of science, some interest in scientific
pursuits, and some study in a special line of investigation, are far more commonly found among the
middle classes in the provinces than in London.
Lastly, the increased facilities for travelling which
have been afforded in recent years have made an
enormous change in the tone of provincial society.
When Dr. Heaton paid his first visit, as a young man,
to the Continent, he was regarded by his friends in
Leeds as the hero of a truly remarkable adventure.
He continued to be fond of travelling all his life, and
always he used his great powers of observation with
care and industry, so that the diaries of his successive
journeys abroad are both interesting and valuable as
records of the peculiar features of the places which
he visited. But long before he died. he found himself surrounded at every dinner-table in Leeds by
people who had also travelled, and to whom the
Madonna of Dresden, the silver shrine of St. John
Nepomuc at Prague, and the Temple of Isis at Pompeii
were as familiar as they were to himself. All this
afforded a wonderful contrast to the quiet. sleepy.
limited life of Leeds when Dr. Heaton began his
career as a professional man there. A great revolu-

tion had been wrought, and, for good or for evil, our provincial towns had emerged from the chrysalis stage of existence into one that bears at any rate some slight resemblance to that of the butterfly.

In tracing, in this closing chapter, the last years of Dr. Heaton's life, we find that whilst his domestic life ran its course chequered only by those incidents which are inevitable in the history of all families, his activity in public work continued to increase until the last year of his life was reached. Then, as though some premonition of the end had come to him, we find him gradually withdrawing from many of those engagements in which he had spent so large a portion of his time. His membership of the council of the Leeds Medical School was given up, as was also his treasurership of the St. George's Schools. Work of other kinds was brought to a close; whilst labours which he had no wish to abandon so long as any strength was left to him were kept up as it were from day to day, so that, at the moment when the call to rest came, there seemed to all around him to be a singular completeness about his life's work. It appeared to have been rounded off as it were in anticipation of an event which, though it happened at last unexpectedly, had not for several years been out of Dr. Heaton's mind.

Taking up the thread of the personal narrative of his life at the point where it was dropped in a previous chapter, we see him continuing to play a leading part in the social life of Leeds, and his house still recognised as a centre of local society. As his public engagements in connection with the Yorkshire College and similar institutions increased, so the stream of visitors of distinction who enjoyed the hospitalities of Claremont increased also, and a larger number of men of mark found their way thither than were received in any other house in Leeds.

In July 1876 his domestic life underwent a change through the marriage of his second daughter to Mr. Arthur Rücker, professor of mathematics at the Yorkshire College. A few days later (July 26), Dr. Heaton received some recognition of the great efforts he had made on behalf of the Yorkshire College by being admitted an honorary member of the Clothworkers' Company, a body which had given generous aid to the College. As the mysteries of the City Companies are still hidden to a great extent from the outer world, it may not be uninteresting to quote Dr. Heaton's own account of this event.

'We arrived at the Clothworkers' Hall, Mincing Lane, at 5.30, and were ushered with much ceremony into the binding room, so called as serving formerly for the binding of apprentices. The Master. Mr. Wyld, soon came to us and received us very politely We were invited to take " bitters," which I declined, and after a little delay we were introduced to the

court room, a large handsome apartment, with some
stained glass in the windows, several large portraits
on the walls, and shields bearing the arms of past
Masters. A large table of the form of a horse-shoe,
and covered with green cloth, occupies the middle of
the floor, the Master's chair being placed at the con-
vexity or head of the table. Soon the Master, robed in
a gown of purple cloth trimmed with sable, with the
jewel or badge hung round his neck, took his chair,
the four Wardens in similar gowns, and having badges
like large gold medals, sat two on each side, and other
Clothworkers in their gowns sat along the table. Three
chairs in the interior of the horse-shoe were placed for
Lord Frederick Cavendish, who had not yet arrived,
myself, and Mr. Nussey. After waiting some time Lord
Frederick arrived, and then the proceedings commenced. Mr. Owen Roberts, the clerk, produced a
large folio minute book, from which he read the minute
of the resolution that we three should be admitted
honorary members of the Company, and minutes of
the resolutions of donations to the College of Science.
Then from another book the clerk read a form of declaration to be signed by each of us on admission, that
we would loyally keep all the secrets of the Company,
and attend meetings and dinners when summoned,
unless unavoidably prevented, &c. After we had
each signed a copy of the declaration, a purple gown
was put on each of us, and then we three, standing

opposite the Master, were addressed by him with congratulations and assurances of the pleasure the Company had in admitting us to association with them. Then he shook hands with each of us, we each spoke shortly in reply acknowledging the honour, and the ceremony was at an end.

'After we had been divested of our robes, Lord Frederick went away at once, not being able to stay for the banquet owing to a public engagement in the House of Commons. There was some delay and chat, during which the band of the Coldstream Guards played in the entrance hall, and we were then invited to ascend to the drawing-room. The grand staircase is most gorgeous, with elaborate gilt metal-work balustrade, and marble hand-rail, the steps being covered with a thick crimson pile carpet. The Master had already placed himself in front of his chair of state in the middle of the room, Wardens and Clothworkers standing on each side. Servants at the entrance inquired the name of each visitor as he arrived, and if he were a Clothworker, the Master shaking hands with each as his name was announced. " Dr. Heaton, Clothworker," was my description as I approached the Master. I saw many among the company whom I knew, but after a few salutations I had time to look round the room. The drawing-room is large and handsome, but not strikingly magnificent. It has a sumptuous pile carpet, and

there were tables in the room on which books and
periodicals were laid. Soon a servant in the livery
of the Company announced that dinner was served.
The Master took me on his right hand and Mr. Nussey
on his left, and led the way through another large
room, which serves as a tea-room, to the banqueting
hall, the beauty and gorgeous effect of which at once
struck me. The four Wardens followed us, the rest
of the very numerous company coming after. The
Master led us to our places at the cross table at the
head of the room, with the sideboard of plate illuminated by numerous wax candles behind us. In the
absence of Lord Frederick Cavendish I sat on the
Master's right hand, and Mr. Nussey on his left,
other invited guests and the Wardens sitting on each
side. After all were seated, and when, the chaplain
having said grace, the dishes were being handed
round, I had a little leisure to survey the novel scene,
in which I found myself to be holding for a time so
conspicuous a position. I think that the sumptuous
display of wealth, magnificence, and luxurious good
cheer surpassed anything that I had previously seen.
The dining-room is an oblong well-proportioned hall,
of Palladian architecture. The side walls are divided
into numerous bays by Corinthian columns of polished
granite, with gilded capitals. The spaces between
the columns on the side opposite to the entrance have
large circular-headed windows, filled with stained

glass, having the armorial bearings of distinguished Clothworkers and past Masters. Corresponding spaces on the other side are filled with mirrors. The mouldings around the windows and panelling are of polished marble. The pillars support an entablature from which springs a coved ceiling. There are large spandrils above the entablature, in which are bold reliefs of female figures, personifying the principal towns of England concerned in the woollen trade or in the manufacture of other textile fabrics. Among these is a figure representing Leeds, with a view of the Town Hall in the background. The coved ceiling is in panels, and is relieved with gilding and colours. Numerous rich silk banners, bearing the arms of distinguished Clothworkers, hang from the upper part of the walls on each side of the hall. At the further end of the hall, opposite the daïs, is a gallery for musicians; in the middle, underneath the gallery, is a door, on either side of which is a gigantic banner furled round its pole. These banners, I was told, are only unfurled on some great occasion, such as a visit by royalty. They are then borne before the guests in the procession to the banqueting hall.

'The cross table and three long tables along the length of the room were laden with plate, fruits, wines, dishes, and large pyramids of clear ice at intervals, to keep the air cool. The effect of the whole, brilliantly illuminated as the hall was, was very grand. In niches, one on each side of the sideboard, behind the Master's chair, are two gilded statues, rather less than life size, of two of our Kings—I think James the First and Charles the First. The Master was exceedingly kind and attentive, and gave me much information about the company and the hall during dinner. After dinner the loving-cup was passed round. A lofty cup by Benvenuto Cellini, a gift of Pepys, the author of the Diary, who was a Cloth-worker, was passed round on the right of the Master, and a companion, a modern facsimile of the original, passed in the other direction. After this began a long series of toasts, many of them being merely formal toasts given by the Master and repeated in a loud voice by the toastmaster. Each was followed by a song by a party of male and female vocalists.

'When several toasts had been disposed of a curious ceremony took place. I must explain that this was the election dinner, as I learnt during the evening, when the officers elected for a year resign to their successors the offices which they have held, and the ceremony which now took place had relation to this change of officers. The beadle in his gown came to the Master and summoned him into the adjoining room. He left the chair and went out, followed by the four Wardens. Some other gentlemen at the same time left their seats and joined them, and several officials in gowns retired at the same time.

In the meantime another Clothworker temporarily occupied the chair. In less than ten minutes the party returned, forming a procession. First came some beadles, bearing long black staves tipped with silver, others bore staves surmounted with large silver badges. Then came the Master, bearing a silver two-handled loving-cup; the Master elect; two of the Wardens bearing silver cups; other gentlemen, a trumpeter and beadles. The whole procession walked slowly down one side of the room and up the middle to the cross table, when the head of the procession wheeled round, walking down whilst the rest still went forward. When the whole line was thus divided into two halves—one ascending, the other descending—they halted and each made a half-turn, so that the two lines faced each other. Then the trumpeter sounded a flourish, and the Master declared that Mr. Farnan was elected his successor, and made a short speech upon his merits. Mr. Farnan replied, and then they drank to each other in the loving-cup borne by the Master. Then again there was a flourish on the trumpet, and the retiring senior Warden announced his successor with similar ceremonies. The second Warden and his successor went through the same process, and then all retired in the order in which they had entered. Soon the Master reappeared and resumed his chair. the other actors in the ceremony also returned to their places. and the

business of the toasts proceeded. In due course the
Master proposed the healths of the newly elected
liverymen, Lord Frederick Cavendish, myself, and
Mr. Nussey, with high eulogiums upon each. Of
myself he spoke in terms far too exalted.'

Though this description of a great civic banquet
and ceremony will probably convey nothing that is
new to some readers of these pages, there must be
many who will wish to have some record of the
impression produced upon a stranger by the sumptuous hospitality of the great City Companies; and it
is possible that a time may come when this story of
the way in which the Clothworkers' Company entertained their friends in the middle of the reign of
Queen Victoria will have a distinct historical and
archæological interest. No apology need be offered,
therefore, for the length at which the account has
been transcribed from the pages of Dr. Heaton's
diary.

The remainder of the year was uneventful, either
as regards public or private affairs in Leeds. The
country was at the time engrossed with the agitation
on the subject of the atrocities in Bulgaria, which was
commenced and carried on with so much vigour by
Mr. Gladstone. Enough has already been said of
Dr. Heaton's political opinions and of his general
temperament to show that he was not a man likely
to have much sympathy with any emotional excess

such as that in which the nation at that time indulged.
Far as he was from sharing the extreme views on the
other side, he was quite capable of standing aloof
from all participation in a movement which for the
time being carried nine-tenths of the English people
along with it. The year 1877 was devoted to sedu-
lous labour on behalf of the Yorkshire College, Lord
Frederick Cavendish, as usual, being the zealous
co-operator with Dr. Heaton in the work. During
the summer Dr. and Mrs. Heaton made a prolonged
tour in Brittany, on which he brought back copious
notes. In May of the following year he again went
abroad for the purpose of visiting Germany, a journey
which occupied some six weeks ; and in July of that
year he records the fact that he was nominated for
election as a Fellow of the Royal Society. The
nomination paper described him as having been ' for
four years President of the Philosophical and Literary
Society of Leeds, an influential promoter of the Yorkshire College of Science, and Chairman of the Council
of the College from its foundation ; Senior Physician
to the Leeds General Infirmary, Senior Lecturer on
the Practice of Medicine in the Leeds Medical School,
and formerly lecturer on Botany and Materia Medica
in that School ; author of papers on Mineral Vegeta-
tion read before the British Association at Dundee and
at Exeter ; generally attached to science. and an earnest
promoter of science in his native town of Leeds.'

Dr. Heaton did not live to secure the honour of election ; but it is worth while putting on record this description of his qualifications, which was subscribed with the names of Sir John Hawkshaw, Dr. Sharpey, Professor Huggins, Dr. Lyon Playfair, Mr. James Glaisher, Professor Erischen, Dr. Quain, the Right Hon. W. E. Forster, Sir John Lubbock, the Duke of Devonshire, Dr. Ferrier, Dr. Haughton, Lord Houghton, the Archbishop of York, Lord Ripon, and others who had enjoyed many opportunities of witnessing the useful and unostentatious labours of his life.

On Friday, July 12, the annual meeting of the council of the Leeds Medical School was held, and Dr. Heaton, as treasurer, presented his balance sheet of the accounts of the School, which at this time were in a highly satisfactory condition. Referring to the meeting he says: 'On this occasion I tendered my resignation of membership, and of course of my office of treasurer, having been connected with the School for thirty-five years and being the last survivor of my generation remaining in the council, and having reached my sixtieth year. I felt the separation very much as the first mark of declining years, and of withdrawal from public life, from pleasant association with my colleagues, and from work which has been agreeable and beneficial, though now becoming burdensome. I withdraw at a time when the undertaking is becoming increasingly remunerative, after having been carried on for a great part of my time for very small pecuniary profit.' But though his colleagues on the council could not deny that Dr. Heaton was entitled to the repose which he thus sought to obtain, they had far too high a sense of the value of his services to allow him to quit the work in which he had been so long engaged without making an effort to retain him in it. 'The result was,' he writes, ' that at a subsequent meeting of the council I was elected an extraordinary member, and requested to continue to act as treasurer, though no longer sharing in the profits.' In the following November there was a pleasant sequel to this arrangement, which came at a time when it was greatly needed, to cheer Dr. Heaton, then suffering under the influence of great depression.

A deputation from the council of the Medical School called upon him at Claremont, and presented him with a handsome silver gilt salver in token of the gratitude of his old colleagues for the services which he had rendered them. In acknowledging the gift, which was formally presented to him in a graceful speech by his friend Dr. Eddison, Dr. Heaton said :—

' I feel it difficult to explain to you the gratification which this handsome present affords me, accompanied as it is by your kind expressions of esteem and approval. Throughout a life now of considerable duration, I have, since reaching the age of independence and responsibility, made it my endeavour to be usefully occupied, not merely for my own personal interests and those of my family, but also for friends, for associations with which I have been connected, and for the community among which I have lived. Success does not always reward our efforts, even when they are made earnestly and with the best intentions, but I have not been always without that best reward which consists in the evidence that some good has been effected and that worthy objects have been secured.

'It is indeed a great additional personal gratification, and a great encouragement to continued exertion, when those with whom I have worked in the furtherance of a common cause are prompted to evince their kind appreciation of the efficiency of my endeavours by such a testimonial as this. For more than half of my life I have been associated with the Leeds Medical School; and at a still earlier period I was a student upon its benches, when as yet it had existed only for a very few years. I have witnessed, therefore, its early rise and its gradual development to its present influential position and great efficiency. For thirty-five years I have been engaged in lecturing to its classes, which have doubled and trebled their numbers during that time. During this long period I have enjoyed much pleasant intercourse with my colleagues, scarcely shadowed by any cloud of difference, and when, having reached my sixtieth year, and having been for several years the only one of my generation actively engaged in the work of the School, I felt that the time had arrived when it was my duty to resign the task to younger and more energetic workers, you will believe me that the pain of separation was very deeply felt.

'But you, gentlemen of the council, have alleviated this pain, and have indeed afforded me a very great counterbalancing gratification, by still retaining me upon your councils, and still confiding to me for a time the care of your finances, and by presenting to me this very gratifying evidence of your esteem.'

It has been said that this recognition of his work came to Dr. Heaton from his old professional brethren in Leeds at a time when he was not a little cast down. In the previous month of August a great blow had fallen upon him—one from which he never recovered. Mention has been made of the happy marriage of his second daughter, May, with Mr. Arthur Rücker, one of the professors of the Yorkshire College. On August 2, Mrs. Rücker, to the great joy of her parents and other relatives, gave birth to a daughter. She did not, however, recover satisfactorily; untoward symptoms made their appearance, and on August 12 she died.

This work is so much more a sketch of Dr.

Heaton's public work than of his private life, that
little can be said in these pages of any domestic
incident in his history. But it is impossible to pass
over his daughter's death without saying something
of the effect which it had upon him. Reserved in his
general demeanour, even towards those with whom
he had long been on terms of intimacy, he was apt to
give those who knew him but slightly the idea that
his temperament was naturally cold. No one who
had any opportunity of seeing how the death of his
daughter affected him, how it remained with him
an abiding sorrow to the end of his days, casting
a gloom over his life, and filling him with unavailing
pain, can entertain this idea of his character. 'Even
now,' he says, writing more than a year afterwards,
'to recount this most unhappy period of my life
seems to fill my mind with horror and bewilderment.'
Yet so strong was the sense of duty within him, so
little accustomed was he to consider his own feelings
when any public work had to be discharged, that we
find him recording in his diary, on the very day on
which he had seen the child, whom he loved so
tenderly, snatched from him and from her husband,
his attendance at a meeting of directors. To do his
duty, without thought of his own convenience, had
been his custom throughout life, and even this great
blow could not drive him from his usual line of
action. Yet a few days after we find him saying,

with reference to his state, ' Except absolutely
necessary duties I was quite unable to do anything.
I could in no degree reconcile my mind to this
removal of the bright and happy May, on whom the
promise of a life of happiness and usefulness had
opened so auspiciously ; whilst we old people, who
had already accomplished the brightest, most useful,
and perhaps the most important portion of our
possible existence, were left to mourn her loss with
this additional shadow cast over our declining years.
And then, when I thought of her widowed husband,
and the perfect happy love which existed between the
young couple thus prematurely sundered, and the
blank desolation in which he is now overwhelmed,
my heart ached with actual physical as well as mental
pain, and I felt too truly that happiness could no
more be mine, but that I should go sorrowing all my
days.'

It is right that these words should be quoted.
They might be largely supplemented ; but enough has
been transcribed to show how strong and tender were
the ties which bound him to his children. and how
terrible was the blow which overwhelmed him in this
death of his second daughter. In literal truth he
' went sorrowing all his days ' after that event : and
those who watched him daily saw how his step was
losing its elasticity, how his form was becoming
bowed and his hair growing white under the burden

T

of his grief. But such strength as was left to him
was given to the work he felt he had to do, and it
may be confidently affirmed that neither the Yorkshire College nor any other public body with which
he was officially connected was permitted to suffer
in the slightest degree in consequence of his own
bereavement and bitter sorrow.

The work of the Yorkshire College, and of other
public bodies, continued to engage his attention,
though he was compelled to admit in his diary that
his physical powers were declining, and that he could
not hope to enlarge his sphere of labour. 'All that
I can do is to hold on to what I am already doing.'
So 1878 closed amid gloom, and 1879 opened in-
auspiciously. A visit to Italy in April did something to restore his spirits and his health, though
even on his return he complained that he was ' still
feeling feeble, inelastic, depressed, and experiencing a
rapid advance of all the deteriorating effects of old
age.' He devoted himself with vigour to his various
public and private engagements, however, attending,
according to his custom, the annual meeting of the
British Association, which was held this year at
Sheffield, and showing his usual active interest in all
that concerned the welfare of his native town. The
local newspapers continued to receive frequent communications from his pen on such matters; sanitary
affairs, in particular, still engaging much of his

attention. It is no exaggeration to say that since his
death Leeds has lacked a public censor who seldom
failed when the occasion arose to make his voice
heard, in connection with any matter on which the
dispassionate and common-sense views of a man who
was singularly free from partisan bias, and who had
never entangled himself with either of the two great
political organisations, could be of service to the
public.

And here it may be well to add a few words to
what has already been said regarding the local public
life of a town like Leeds. In Leeds, as in most other
great towns in this country, local affairs have become
inextricably mixed up with national politics. When
a gentleman comes forward as a candidate for a
vacancy in the Town Council or the Board of
Guardians, the question asked by the overwhelming
majority of the electors is not, ' Is he qualified to
make a good town-councillor or a good guardian ? ' as
the case may be ; but, ' Is he a Liberal or a Conservative ? ' It seems absurd to make the election of
a man whose duty it is to look after questions of gas
or paving-stones, of police or sanitation, dependent
upon the political creed he holds, and no doubt the
services of many an excellent man have been lost in
consequence of the adoption of this system. On the
other hand, those who are practically concerned in
the working of local politics have found themselves

forced to the conclusion that it is only by associating
these questions, from the choice of a parish beadle
upwards, with the great questions of Imperial policy,
that a party organisation can be maintained in full
efficiency. The consequence is that active and zealous
politicians of both political parties, even though
they may deplore the necessity imposed upon them,
believe that it is a necessity that they should bring
municipal and national life into this close connection.

But, on the other hand, those who care little about
politics or political parties see only the evils of the
system under which the local affairs of large towns
are managed, and are strenuous in insisting that the
interests of the ratepayers, the fitness of candidates for
the offices to which they aspire, and the merits of the
special questions at the moment under consideration,
should be considered, rather than the struggle for
supremacy between two rival political parties. Dr.
Heaton, it need scarcely be said, belonged to this class,
and he often gave vent to his bitter indignation at
what he conceived to be the sacrifice of the welfare
of the town to that of the contending political armies.
It is a nice point that is involved in this question
and it is one upon which different men may fairly
hold different opinions. Dr. Heaton had, however,
no hesitation as to his opinions, and up to the close
of his life he continued to protest against the introduction of politics into municipal elections. The

'Leeds Mercury,' which, after battling for many years on the same side as Dr. Heaton, had at last been compelled to acknowledge the force of accomplished facts, was severely condemned by him on account of the inconsistency of which he deemed that it had thus been guilty.

In summing up in his diary the events of 1879, we find him saying: 'I am now nearing a time of life when I find myself looking back on my past career as on a course which is already run, and the results of which I may now estimate. My professional work has certainly been a failure; I have never commanded a valuable practice. This I recognise as due to faults of disposition and defects of ability which I have been unable to overcome. I have never been able to make myself popular and practise the arts of self-exaltation, nor to assume the manners of superior authority, even within the limits of what is fair and honest, much less to the full extent which may command the multitude. I have worked hard, and I have striven, after my own unsuccessful methods, to succeed. If I have failed to command success, I have commanded a degree of esteem and respect. That I should have been elected a Fellow of University College in my early days, and afterwards a Fellow of the College of Physicians, is some evidence of this. . . . Some years ago I could look back upon my past life with some satis-

faction and encouragement, when I reflected on
various successes, and the distinction, and position,
and material prosperity which I had attained. . . .
No doubt my state of mind is somewhat morbid and
exaggerated. I derive from my mother an anxious
disposition. Success over exhilarates me; perhaps
makes me too confident. But failure, and especially
many successive failures, leaves a most injurious influence upon me. With the encouragement of success I can work earnestly; failures seem to destroy
self-reliance and to quench all energy. This, of
course, is very bad, but it is too much my case.

' Each year latterly, its termination has marked
some decided failure of strength and physical ability.
I think during the past year I have made more
decline than during any former year ; and now, what
is more distressing, I fear that I find my mind giving
way in some respects. I have less power of application, less inclination to read, less ability to acquire
knowledge, and, especially and most markedly, my
memory fails me ; partly so as to passing events, but
especially so as to new facts or freshly acquired
knowledge. If I read a book, in a few months it
seems to have quite passed away from my recollection. Proper names, both of persons and places,
even such as are familiar to me, I continually find
myself unable to recall when I want them. This.
is most inconvenient and depressing.

'Though there is a natural desire to prolong one's life, I begin to be sensible of the disadvantages of an old age in which both the ability and the inclination for an active, useful life have failed. If one is taken away from a life still given to good works, one's loss may for a time be felt and one's memory respected. But to live past this period, and to pass a life of years in incapacity and retirement, is to be forgotten ere one ceases to exist, and results in one's final removal being regarded only as a relief. Such a result is surely to be deprecated by any one who desires that his life and example should be, to some extent, and however imperfectly a legacy of example and credit to his children.'

These are sad words, though they must have a distinct psychological interest. It is only right to say, however, that to outsiders Dr. Heaton's case seemed to be by no means so bad as he believed it to be. That he was suffering from depression of spirits and from increasing weakness was evident to most persons; but no one else perceived those signs of mental failure of which he spoke. On the contrary, during his visit to Italy during the spring of this year 1879, he had shown the same lively interest as of old in all that he saw, and his diary, kept with the usual fulness and regularity, testifies to his appreciation of scenery and historical associations. Still a man's own account of himself and of his feelings may be trusted before that which is given by anybody else, and the foregoing extract, which has so deep an interest in connection with the event by which it was so shortly to be followed, can hardly be omitted from this work.

On February 13 we find in the diary the following entry: ‘At the Weekly Board of the Infirmary this afternoon, I told Mr. Brown, the chairman, that I intended to resign my physicianship in April.’ On February 26 occurs another entry as follows: ‘Clinical lecture at the Infirmary this morning; perhaps the last I shall ever give.’

It must not be supposed, however, that there were any signs at this time of the end that was now so near. We find him actively engaged with the other trustees of Emmanuel Church in looking for a suitable person for the incumbency, and undertaking a journey to Nottingham for that purpose; then, a few days later, he is at Halifax attending a meeting of the Ladies’ Council of Education, and on Sunday, March 7, he records his attendance at the farewell sermon of Mr. Adams, the old incumbent of St. George’s Church, with which he had been connected during so many years. There are many committee meetings, too, which are mentioned in his record of the dull March days of that hard winter. One of the last of these was at Scarborough, on March 19. It was a meeting of the directors of the Grand

Hotel, with which he had from the first been connected, and of which he had for many years been chairman. In mentioning the meeting in his diary, he says: 'We passed a resolution of condolence on the death of George Buckton. This is the fourth director removed by death since the formation of the Board. Botterill, Anderton, Nunneley, Buckton. Who next?'

It is impossible at times to avoid a conviction that premonitions such as occurred to Dr. Heaton during these last months and weeks of his life are not accidental. Probably, in the case of a medical man especially, they are founded upon what may be called an unconscious self-diagnosis. At all events, though Dr. Heaton complained of no particular illness, and seemed to his family and friends to be as cheerful and active as usual, he was undoubtedly impressed during this last winter of his life with the idea that he had not long to live, and he made many arrangements that seemed afterwards to his mourning friends to have been made in view of his approaching death.

On March 24, on which day he made his last entry in that journal from which so many extracts have been made, and which had been kept during so many years with so scrupulous a care, he passed a particularly busy day. Friends who had been visiting at Claremont left in the morning, and he accompanied them to the railway station ; then there was shopping to be done—a wedding and a birthday present to be bought—and this duty also was accomplished; though neither the wedding-day nor the birthday for which preparation was thus made arrived during his lifetime. Then in the afternoon the usual round of public duties commenced, truly, in his case, 'the daily round, the common task.' There was a meeting of the council at the Yorkshire College, and afterwards meetings of the trustees of St. George's and Emmanuel Churches. All these he duly attended. The day was cold and raw, and on leaving the meeting at the Yorkshire College, where he had been seated in a comfortably warmed room, he felt greatly chilled. He reached home about six o'clock in the evening, evidently ill, though no one imagined that he was suffering from anything more than an ordinary cold.

On the following day, Thursday, March 25, he was no better ; but he came down for a short time, in order to keep an appointment on business, and took a cup of tea in the drawing-room. This was the last occasion on which he was downstairs. His illness rapidly developed into acute pneumonia, and very soon its exceedingly grave and even desperate character was recognised by all. Dr. Eddison and Dr. Barrs gave him the most zealous attention, and he was nursed with unremitting solicitude by his wife and children

But there was no abatement in the rate at which the disease advanced, and his suffering became most acute. Never once, however, did he lose the characteristic presence of mind and coolness of judgment which had distinguished him in other days. Evidently conscious that his end was approaching, he yet spoke no word that would distress his wife and children, and, whilst submitting cheerfully to all the directions of the medical men, he showed a curious professional interest on his own account in each successive stage of his illness. So calm and collected was he that on Saturday, the 27th, he was able to give many directions on matters of business that it seemed necessary to attend to, and even, in his magisterial capacity, to witness the signature of a neighbour to his proxy vote as a member of the London University. He was very anxious to record his own vote at this election, and had resolved to vote for the Conservative candidate. His wife, seeing what his wish was, endeavoured to secure the attendance of a Conservative magistrate in order to witness his signature, but failed to do so. She then proposed to send for one of his old friends who was a Liberal. But his strong, it might almost be said his intense, sense of fairness once more came into play. 'No,' he said, ' I could not find it in my heart to send for a man in order that he might witness a vote for the party to which he was opposed.'

On Easter Sunday, March 28, a consultation was
held at which Dr. Clifford Allbutt, who had returned to Leeds from Grange for the purpose, and
Mr. Teale took part with Dr. Eddison and Dr. Barrs.
The result was to establish the fact that the end
was fast approaching, and two of the children of Dr.
Heaton who were absent were at once sent for. One
of these, his eldest daughter, by great exertions
succeeded in reaching Claremont about half past
three on the morning of Monday. At that time Dr
Heaton was conscious, and was able to welcome his
daughter. His sufferings, which had been intense for
many hours, were over, and he was perfectly calm.
He told his wife and children, as they were gathered
round his bed, that he ' had always prayed for a prepared life and a sudden death,' and he seemed not
ungrateful that the prayer had been in a measure
answered. At twenty minutes before five o'clock,
just as the dawn was peeping into the room where
the sorrow-stricken watchers were waiting for the
end, that end came, and their loved one, after his long
years of ceaseless labour and untiring effort, entered
into his eternal rest.

Born on November 23, 1817, Dr. Heaton had
reached his sixty-third year at the time of his death.
He was buried on Friday, April 2, in the vault at
the side of St. George's Church, which he had prepared many years before, and in which the bodies of

his father and mother already lay. The funeral took place at the very height of the excitement connected with one of the most exciting political contests ever waged in this country. But the members of both political and of all religious bodies in the town of Leeds made a solemn truce for that day, and joined together to pay the last tribute of respect to one whose citizenship had been so full of useful and honourable work, so free from taint of selfishness or of self-seeking. The church in which Dr. Heaton had laboured so long was crowded to the doors, among those present being the representatives of all the great public bodies in the town, and of many humbler charitable institutions that had now to mourn the loss of a faithful and unwearied friend. It was a touching tribute that was paid by the presence of this great host of men and women, representing so many different ranks in life and shades of opinion, to the career of him who was gone. No one who was present at that sad ceremony—so simple in itself, so free from all the mechanical appliances of fictitious woe, and yet so profoundly and genuinely pathetic—could fail to acknowledge that the dead man had gained a greater hold upon the respect and esteem of the community with which he had been so long associated than he himself had been aware of during his lifetime.

CHAPTER XI.

PERSONAL CHARACTERISTICS.

THIS little record has been occupied, as the reader will perceive, chiefly with the public side of Dr. Heaton's life ; and, so far as his personal character has been touched upon, the sketch has been copied from the portrait drawn by himself in the diary he kept so faithfully during many years. Perhaps if it had been possible to print that diary in full, a correct idea of its writer's character would have been gained by the reader ; for Dr. Heaton was as severely faithful and almost as minute in his record of his own sayings and doings and of his household life during the long term over which the diary extends, as was Pepys himself. Indeed it is difficult to resist the conclusion that he had taken the great diarist of the Restoration as his literary model. A hundred years hence, the laborious and comprehensive story told by Dr. Heaton in the seven or eight closely written quarto volumes, each of many hundred pages, which formed the work of so many years, will be exceedingly valuable as a picture of domestic life in an English provincial town in the reign of Queen Victoria.

But for the present it is of course impossible to give such a story to the public, and there is not a little risk that the partial and limited extracts made from the diary may have a misleading effect upon the mind of the reader. In one respect, indeed, Dr. Heaton's picture of himself, if left uncorrected, would be certain to produce a wrong impression. It has been shown in the preceding chapter with what gloomy reflections his mind was at times filled during his closing years, and it has also been seen that throughout his life he was subject to fits of despondency. I have already stated that he never allowed these feelings, fanciful though they were, to interfere with his public duty. But in justice to the subject of this sketch it must be said that he was equally scrupulous in hiding from the members of his own family all traces of the gloom to which he appears to have given way in private. In the family circle he was regarded not merely as the faithful and tender husband and father, but as the life and soul of the family life. From the oldest to the youngest, all knew that he would sympathise with them in their pleasures and their sorrows, whilst his manner towards his children was, down to his latest days, marked by a brightness and gaiety that are quite inconsistent with the ideas of gloom and despondency conjured up by some of his own declarations.

One who knew him intimately throughout his life

has furnished me with the following sketch of his
personal characteristics, which to a large extent
confirms what I have just said : ' It has been noticed
that there was at times a sadness or despondency
about Dr. Heaton which the circumstances of his life
did not justify. Probably a vein of mournfulness
was natural to him, which, if he had been brought
up in a large and cheerful family, he might have out-
grown. Having been in childhood and early youth
one of a very small circle, however, and not having
undergone the developing influences of a large and
joyous houschold, his natural temperament was
fostered. Sources of sad thought were dwelt upon,
and discouragements that might easily have been
thrown off were allowed to weigh upon the mind of
the lonely boy. Yet though his was not a hopeful
nature, it was one in whose deep affections lay large
possibilities of happiness, and these in a married
union of many years were fully realised. His conversation was marked by a tone of playfulness which,
little seen in his more public life, sparkled in the
circle of his home. After his death one of his sorrowing children said, " There will be no one to answer
my little jokes any more." When he did not laugh
himself he was often the cause of laughter in others.
He had to a remarkable extent the capacity of
gathering up in a word the essence of the question
under discussion, and there was a fine irony in his

humour that was at times irresistible. Looking at
his character as a whole, credit ought to be given to
one who, under whatever private discouragements,
was always able to work for others. Schemes for
effecting individual and public good were his daily
business, the occupation of half his life. The strong
sense of duty, the habit of conscientious work, led
him on through those portions of his life where hope-
fulness failed. From boyhood it had been natural to
him to be helpful to those around him and forgetful of
himself; and in his medical work the strongest tribute
to his skill and kindness was the constant desire of
the poor among whom he laboured to be his patients.
His countenance expressed in a wonderfully vivid
manner the nobler characteristics of his mind ; and it
was often observed by those about him that the
estimate of character formed on a first acquaintance by
others was in exact proportion to their knowledge of
physiognomy. If the whole town did not love him, at
least it may be said that all Leeds mourned for him.'

As a further illustration of that brighter and gentler
side of his character which is not depicted in his own
diary, the following extracts from a few of his letters
to his children will be of service. Some of them, it
will be seen, were addressed to them when they were
still very young ; but in all cases they afford proof of
his humorous insight into the weaknesses and his
sympathy with the aspirations of childhood.

To Arthur D. Heaton.

Claremont, Leeds : November 19, 1866.

My dear Arthur,—It is rather long since I have written to you, and mamma says I must now write to tell you about the falling stars.

I am very sorry that you did not see them, as it was a grand sight, and would have been something for you to remember and talk of hereafter. We ought to have told you about them, but as all the newspapers were making mention of the subject for many days before, I should have thought Mr. B. would have noticed the subject himself. The girls at Malvern were fully aware of it, and they all got up in the middle of the night and saw it very well.

Mamma and I sat up for the purpose last Tuesday night. It was a fine clear night, and very cold. I looked out two or three times before midnight, but saw nothing. But when I looked out at a quarter-past twelve, I saw three or four stars shooting through the sky, and leaving long trails of light behind them, in the space of a minute. As it was evident that the performance had begun, mamma and I wrapped up very well, and we went into the garden, where we saw many constantly flying across the sky. But as we wished to have an unobstructed view, we walked up to the Moor. We were on the Moor for a considerable time about one o'clock, and saw numberless shooting stars. They seemed chiefly to rise out of the north-east, and they shot across the sky in various directions, like a bright star sailing quickly along, and leaving a long streak of pale light behind, which remained visible for some seconds after the star had vanished. Some of the stars became more brilliant as they moved along, and some seemed to burst into a flame and change from a yellow to a green light before going out. They were a good deal like rockets at a great distance. They did not seem to fall to the ground, but rather to shoot *across* the sky, with some tendency downwards. They seemed suddenly to go out in the sky, not to disappear by falling to the earth.

After two o'clock the sky became overcast, and it began to rain heavily, when we could see neither shooting stars nor real stars, and we went into the house. I looked out again before getting into bed between three and four, and the sky was again clear, and the stars shooting as before, though they were not so numerous. I suppose after four they disappeared altogether.

You ask what falling stars are? I can only tell you what astronomers *conjecture*, for nothing is known certainly. It is supposed that there is a very large number of small solid bodies, forming a sort of ring or zone, constantly revolving round the sun as the earth and other planets do, and that sometimes the earth comes across the orbit of these bodies. When it does so, it draws some of them to it, and these, when they get into the atmosphere which surrounds the earth, become intensely heated by their friction with the air, in consequence of the immense rapidity with which they move, and so they become luminous. But the heat which they acquire is so intense that they are dissipated in vapour or broken up into dust, and then they disappear.

I say this is merely conjecture ; but it is certain that solid bodies do sometimes fall to the earth from the sky, and have been found very hot, and having the appearance of having been melted on the surface. These are supposed to have been larger bodies which have been attracted to the earth, and have been too large to be dispersed by heat as smaller bodies like the shooting stars are.

It has been observed that these appearances are seen most at particular times of the year, and November 14 is one of these times, when shooting stars may be seen every year. But once in thirty-three years they are to be seen at this time in remarkable profusion. This year is the thirty-third since they were so seen last. They are to be seen when the earth gets into the ring of these small bodies, and it is thought that some parts of this ring are much more crowded with these bodies than other parts, and that when the earth gets into the thickest part of the ring the falling stars are most abundant. Men believe that once in thirty-three years the earth *does* get into the thickest part, and then we see all these stars.

I have given this letter because of the light it throws upon the writer's anxiety to give not a mere general but a careful and accurate reply to the inquiries even of a schoolboy. Another letter, to a younger son, written in August 1875, during the meeting of the British Association at Bristol, gives the same impression of his interest in and sympathy with his children.

My dear Boy Berry,—I think it is now your turn to have a letter; so here goes, though I fear I have said nearly all that I have to say in writing already to mother and sisters. And besides all which, sirree! you have not written a single line to me since I left home, and perhaps not written a line to anybody else, though I have been writing long letters daily to ever so many people. Now I shall expect you to write me one of your cleverest letters, about all sorts of things, in reply to this, and you will have to begin at once, lest I should have come home before you get it finished and sent off. I scarcely know what to tell you of my doings here that will much interest you, as perhaps my proceedings would not amuse you even if you were here with me, which I should

like very well sometimes, I can tell you. When you
grow up I dare say you will like science and attend
meetings, and perhaps you may have something to
say yourself in them—of which I should be very
glad. Your friend Mr. D. L. (who gave you
a dinner at Rugby) is here with his brother S.
He was to have gone on an excursion with us yesterday afternoon, but somehow we missed him, and he
went to see a Reformatory instead, which perhaps
pleased him as well, as he is very much interested in
Reformatory Schools and such things. Perhaps we
may make another excursion before leaving here, and
get him to go with us then. You would have liked
it very much if you had been with us yesterday.
We had buns and pears and plums to eat as we drove
along the banks of the River Avon. The place which
we went to see is called Ashton Court. It is a fine
old house with very beautiful gardens. I never saw
a house so full of stuffed birds in glass cases. The
entrance hall, the staircases, dining and drawing-
rooms were all full of cases of birds. I did not see a
room anywhere, where Bobby could have played
safely for five minutes. It would be a very bad
place for boys inside that house. But out of doors
they would have fine times; beautiful gardens and a
park to play in, and great trees to climb, and no end
of rabbits to shoot ; and large cages like houses, with
great eagles in them which scream at us very queerly.

Great ships come up the River Avon to Bristol from the Bristol Channel. There are very large steamers coming and going, with crowds of passengers, and large sailing vessels which go off to foreign parts with cargoes of goods, or bring cargoes from abroad. So that there is a great deal of loading and unloading, and it is very busy all along the river from Bristol and down the river to Portishead, where there are great docks.

I hope your little dog is all right, and that it is properly grateful for all your attentions to it. I don't know what it is called. Sis Helen has sent me a picture of it which is very like a little pig. You know there is a great animal called a camelopard, because it is rather like a camel, and coloured like a leopard : so I shall call your little animal a pig-dog, because it is a dog rather like a pig.

How are you getting on with your Euclid? I hope you do a bit *well* each day. Can you do the Asses' Bridge?

To his youngest son, at school, he writes as follows :—

Claremont, Leeds : March 2, 1880.

My dear Bob,—I wish you to take notice in the first place, that you are a *great rascal*. I got a letter from you a week ago, with only a halfpenny stamp on it ; and now you have grown bolder, and sent me a letter without any stamp at all, for which I had to pay twopence. This was more than it was worth, as, I am sorry to say, it was very carelessly written, and had many words wrong or wrongly spelt. . . . I greatly admire the decorations on the first page, about which I think you have taken more pains than the writing. C. came here this afternoon, and I showed her your letter, which amused her. She thought that your handwriting improved, but she did not admire the blunders. Dear mother is very sorry that she forgot to answer your inquiry about going to lunch with a fellow on your way home. As you do not come home for some weeks, perhaps no time is lost. We have no objection to your doing as you propose, if you can still get home in good time in the evening.

Brief as are these extracts from a correspondence which was kept up with characteristic regularity with all his children, they will do something to indicate the character of his relationship with his family, and to dispel any idea which may have been formed in some quarters, that Dr. Heaton was of a cold and unsociable disposition, too much engrossed in the public work to which he had devoted himself to find time for the indulgence of the affections or the cultivation of the gentler graces of life.

I am permitted on this point, however, to print the testimony of one of his own children : ' It is very

difficult,' she says, ' to convey any true idea of my
dear father, because, though widely known, he was
known only from one point of view, except just
among ourselves. The rather stern and somewhat
unsociable aspect of which we were all aware was
curiously different from the sweetness and demon-
strative affection of his private home life. He was
himself painfully cognisant of the unsociable side of
his disposition, and he always acknowledged it as a
great drawback in his career. His inability to lay
himself out for popularity, or to gloss over with
indulgence qualities and traits of character of which
he disapproved, assumed at times quite morbid proportions in his mind and led almost to despondency.
I believe he considered himself an unpopular man,
but at the time of his death we had every reason
to think the contrary. Among young people he was
always liked. Our own young visitors always made a
friend for life in him, and Christmastide and his
birthdays used to bring an amount of remembrance
that was productive of much pleasure, and that bore
testimony to the extent to which he was loved. We
(his children) were always certain of his sympathy in
any pursuit, study, or accomplishment, or in any
undertaking of a charitable nature. He was fond of
teaching us as he had time and opportunity, and he
set his face firmly against our leading flippant and
desultory lives, always encouraging us in any endea-

vour to be useful to the people among whom we
lived. If he considered our work practical and not
merely impulsive, we were certain of his warmest
sympathy. We always looked to him for our indul-
gences; and though a request for a riding-horse or
a new grand piano would be received by some such
remark as, " It would be a white elephant in a fortnight," the desired object would surely appear within
a short time. He always encouraged us to make
visits from home, particularly if any instruction could
be combined with them. He not unfrequently took
us to meetings of the British Association, and he fell
in with our desire and schemes for foreign travel,
though he would always leave the plans and arrangements to our mother, making out in his humorous
way that, whether abroad or in England, he was a
victim to our designs. On any expedition of pleasure
he was the life of the party, the chief figure in every
excursion, the centre of all our jokes. We all agreed
that there would have been no fun without him.
When we lost him we did indeed feel that we had
lost our playfellow.

'I do not think any account of his life could
be complete without special notice of his peculiar affection for our youngest brother, for it was
a marked feature of his later years. From the time
when he could just run after him till he became a
schoolboy he was my father's constant companion.

After he escaped from his own dressing in the morning, he invariably found his way to his father's dressing-room. They went downstairs together, and from sitting on his knee at family prayers, to being extracted with difficulty from the library at bedtime, he could hardly be separated from my father. When the carriage came to the door for the morning professional round, it was always found to contain the little boy and his picture book which was to be his diversion when he was left alone. When indoors he was always curled up in the large library-chair while our father wrote or read. This quiet intercourse not unfrequently gave place to the wildest romps, when the house resounded with shrieks, and they were found chasing each other from room to room, to the great peril of the furniture.

'The same affection was equally, though of course in a different manner, displayed by my father towards each member of the family. I never remember his leaving the house without coming first into the room where we were sitting with our mother, working or reading aloud. After some humorous remarks (often of covert praise or otherwise) on our occupation, he would kiss each one of us before going out. Although thus affectionate and indulgent, however, it must not be supposed that he lightly regarded our faults. On the contrary, he strictly corrected them, and was most watchful against the formation of bad habits.'

It would be impossible to add anything to this
simply pathetic account of the character of Dr.
Heaton, traced by one who seems to have inherited
his own stern fidelity to the truth even in dealing
with those nearest and dearest to him, without in-
juring the sketch as a whole. It is pleasant to think
that the public man, whose time was so largely
at the service of the town and the community in
which his lot had been cast that he seemed to have
scarcely any object in life save this kind of work,
was able to wear so different an aspect among those
of his own household. When he died his fellow-
townsmen were quick to praise the good citizen who
had laid Leeds under such heavy obligations by his
consistent and laborious life of public effort, but
within the circle of his own family, among those who
really knew him as he was, it was the tenderest of
husbands, the gentlest and most kindly of fathers,
the most forbearing, generous, and sympathetic of
friends, whose loss was mourned as truly irreparable.

Something has been said already in these pages
of his love of order, and of the systematic as well as
faithful manner in which he discharged every duty
he undertook. His house bore testimony to this
feature of his character as well as to his love of
literature and of art. The library at Claremont contained many valuable books, and they have been
preserved and catalogued by Dr. Heaton himself

with a care and regularity that are strongly characteristic of his usual habits. The house too abounds with pictures, busts, statuary, china, metal-work, and other objects of a like nature, all bespeaking the man of taste, and most of them collected by himself during his repeated visits to the Continent. In another respect the house speaks of the character of the master. He was a great lover of mottoes, and at Claremont they abound. In dining-room, drawing-room, hall, and porch, Latin inscriptions are to be found conveying in the terse syllables of the olden tongue the admonitions, welcomes, or warnings specially appropriate to the spot where they are inscribed.

It has already been stated more than once that he had no great love for party politics. As a matter of fact he was blessed beyond most men with the power of seeing and discussing with fairness both sides of a question. His vote was given rather for the man than for the party, but he became more Conservative in his views in later years. He would never ask his men-servants for whom they had voted, and never avowed himself a member of either political party. His religious knowledge he had derived chiefly from the teaching of his mother, who was a woman of great personal piety, and who early instilled into her children an acquaintance with the Bible which they retained through life. Dr. Heaton could at all times furnish the required words of a text, though not its chapter and verse. The Bible which he used was marked carefully throughout by him. His own personal religion was deep and practical. It was impossible for those who lived with him not to be aware of the purity of the motives which influenced his conduct both in great things and in small, but he never spoke of his religious feelings. He was a man of prayer, and no hurry in travelling or professional work ever interfered with his morning and evening prayers. He was very decidedly a churchman. As soon as he left his father's roof, at sixteen years of age, he took for himself a sitting in St. Paul's Church, which he attended whilst he was with Dr. Braithwaite. He never failed to attend morning and evening service on Sunday, until his wife, after a severe illness, being unable to attend more than once a day, he made it a practice to spend the evening with her at home. Whilst a student in Paris he regularly attended the Marbœuf Chapel, where Mr. Lovett was the Chaplain. He and his wife arrived in Paris at five o'clock on Sunday morning at the end of their wedding tour. Though fatigued with the journey, he said, ' I must take you to my church,' and they went there accordingly to both morning and evening service. When in Paris he had lived almost entirely among French people in order to improve his knowledge of the language, but he had never attended French services, and he used to say that the

Marbœuf Chapel was the only place where he heard any English.

These scattered notes upon the personal character of Dr. Heaton may seem wanting in importance to some, but as a matter of fact it is by the narration of little traits of character and trifling habits of this kind that the only true conception of the man himself can be obtained. Grave, reserved, absorbed in work both public and private, Dr. Heaton was often misunderstood by those around him. His shyness was mistaken for pride, his reserved manner for the mask of cynicism. But those who knew him best knew that under that somewhat cold exterior beat one of the warmest of hearts, a heart in which a strong sense of justice and an unswerving loyalty to the claims of duty were mingled with a spirit of gentleness, kindness, and affection.

CONCLUSION.

The public feeling which the sudden death of Dr.
Heaton caused in his own town was deep and widespread.   His death, as has been mentioned, happened
in the midst of the general election of 1880, and
nowhere did popular excitement reach a higher point
in connection with that election than at Leeds.   Dr.
Heaton had gradually drawn away from that which
is in Leeds the popular side in these matters.   The
reader has seen him on his death-bed expressing a
wish to record his vote for the Conservative candidate for the University of London.   Everything
therefore seemed unfavourable to any demonstration
of popular feeling in connection with his death.   But
the people of Leeds did not regard him as a politician.
They knew him simply as the indefatigable worker
in a hundred different enterprises, each intended to
benefit their town or the district in which it is
situated ; and when on that Easter Monday morning
they heard of his death, a great wave of bewilderment
and incredulity seemed to sweep over them.   He had
filled so large a place in so many different departments of work, he had been so constantly with them,

so constantly at their service, that they could not
realise for the moment the fact that he was taken
from them, and that henceforth Infirmary and College,
School and Philosophical Society, must go on as best
they could without him.

Perhaps the best way of showing the estimation
in which he was held by those who knew him well
may be gathered from a few of the letters written at
this time to his widow.

The Archbishop of York wrote: 'I cannot tell
you with what deep regret I have read just now the
announcement of the sudden death of Dr. Heaton. It
is a great public loss; but it is also a blow to many
private persons, who will mourn the loss of a most
wise, trusty, and genial friend. Though my intercourse with Dr. Heaton began comparatively lately,
I must take leave to rank him among my friends.
Such was the feeling with which I regarded him from
the first: and at each opportunity it was strengthened.
I had a true regard for him, and shall always cherish
his memory with the same feeling. It is early to ask
you, in the first shock of your bereavement, to see
clear marks of God's great love in such a death. It
seemed that for many years you might hope for the
continuance of happy intercourse. But still I must
say that, in such an ending of a most honourable life,
there is love to be seen. Spared from protracted
suffering, surrounded by the respect of all, visited

with no preceding failure of the faculties, with a long
list of useful works behind him, he has been called to
rest.   His name will be held in love and honour not
alone in your house, where he leaves many sorrowing
hearts, but throughout your great town. As life must
end, an end more full of dignity, of general respect,
of ripe completeness, could hardly have been given.'

Dr. H. R. Reynolds, the principal of Cheshunt
College, and formerly of Leeds, bore testimony in the
following words to what Dr. Heaton had been and
had done in his earlier life : ' Please pardon my
intrusion on the sacredness of your great sorrow, but
allow Mrs. Reynolds and myself to say how keenly
we have felt with and for you in this terrible desolation of your home.   I cannot help remembering how
between twenty and thirty years ago your beloved
husband filled a large space in the horizon of our
Leeds life, how in many objects and places he and I
were working side by side, and how every day since he
has been growing in usefulness and power to benefit
all that came under his influence.   Surely he has been
training all the while for the nobler work to which
our dear Lord and God has now summoned him.'

Here again, from Professor E. C. Clark, of Cambridge, who had known Dr. Heaton well for many
years, is the testimony that more than any of the
commonplaces of consolation comforts the heart of
the mourner beside a newly made grave. ' We

received the paragraph from the " Leeds Mercury "
here yesterday, having seen the most deplorable news
to which it referred a day or two before in the
" Times." I feel scarcely able to appreciate the *fact* of
so great and good a nature being removed from us,
still less to attempt any ordinary expressions of condolence. Dr. Heaton had accustomed every one so
much to take his immense usefulness and untiring
activity in all good works as a matter of course, that
it needs something like the very able statement in the
" Mercury " to show what a gap he will leave. But of
his *private* character a notice in a public print can
say nothing that will do him any justice. For myself, apart from the pleasure of his society and his
charming hospitality, I esteem it a real privilege to
have known even for a short time a man of such
exalted character. For while all the world could see
what he got through, and how he worked—alas !
far beyond his strength—those who knew him alone
could tell the perfect unselfishness of his objects and
motives. I never yet met with a man who was so
purely disinterested in a great public life, or who,
doing so much, did so little, or rather *nothing*, for his
own personal advantage. He had another object
and a better reward. Or surely I may say, without
any presumption, he *has* now. If there ever was a
man in whom it seemed inconceivable that so much
vital power for good should perish, it was he. And

as, on a higher authority than these human inferences, *he* firmly believed in a future of still better life and greater usefulness, *we* may most confidently trust that he has attained it.'

There was another who had known Dr. Heaton all his life, who though separated from him on many matters of opinion had been his loyal co-worker in many a useful enterprise, whose words are worth recording, especially as the name of the writer recalls the memory of the days when the elder Edward Baines and the elder John Heaton were both working under the roof of Mr. Binns in the old shop and printing-office in Briggate.   Sir Edward Baines wrote : ' It was with great sadness of heart that I yesterday took *pro tem.* the chair which was so long and efficiently filled by your lamented husband ; and it is with the same feeling that I now, together with our honorary secretaries, transmit to you the resolution of condolence passed with deep and unanimous sympathy by the council of the Yorkshire College. We all felt that in him we have lost a personal friend, as well as an officer of our College whose services we cannot too highly estimate.   He was one of the most valued citizens of our borough, and he will long be remembered for the importance of the educational and benevolent institutions of which he was a chief founder and support.   The loss sustained by yourself and your family we cannot presume to measure ;

but as it has been ordained by Infinite Wisdom, we believe you will receive it with Christian submission, and that it will yield the fruits for which these heavy afflictions are designed. You will permit me to say that I sign the resolution of the council not merely as an official duty, but as your own and your husband's life-long and sorrowing friend.'

Lord Frederick Cavendish, who had worked so cheerfully and so zealously with Dr. Heaton in connection with the Yorkshire College, added his testimony to that of Sir Edward Baines as to the services which the chairman of the council of that institution had rendered. 'I was much grieved,' he wrote, 'not to be able to join in the tribute of respect which was so justly paid by the representatives of the Yorkshire College to the memory of Dr. Heaton on Friday. The loss of the College is indeed irreparable, and it is impossible to say how much of the success which it has attained has been due to his untiring exertions.'

From Dr. Chadwick, who had been during so many years the medical colleague of Dr. Heaton in work in Leeds, there came the same witness to his high character and public usefulness. 'I have known Dr. Heaton,' he wrote, ' for nearly fifty years, and during a large portion of that time we have been brought into close and intimate association. Occupied in the same pursuits, and striving for the attainment of the same great objects in the same profession—

which in its eager pursuit does not always, I am sorry to say, tend to produce harmony—I fail to charge my memory with a single, even trivial, instance approaching misunderstanding. This I attribute mainly to my good friend's uniform courtesy and forbearance. I assure you that this is no conviction of the moment. I have often in my own family and to many others expressed my deep sense of obligation to him on this account; and I have therefore been led through this, and my constant intercourse with him in the exercise of our common profession, to entertain the highest possible sense of his professional acquirements, his sound judgment and wisdom, and of his courteous, Christian, and gentlemanlike demeanour.'

The words of three of the medical men of Leeds who had begun practice long after Dr. Heaton was established in the town, and who could therefore regard his character from a different point of view from that of a veteran like Dr. Chadwick, may be appropriately added to the testimony borne above. Dr. Clifford Allbutt says: 'I must not speak of my regrets in the midst of your own terrible sorrow, but I cannot refrain from saying that Dr. Heaton's loss to me is one which I feel very deeply. As I returned hither feeling very sad, I remembered all his goodness and usefulness as I had seen them for twenty years past : his unswerving rectitude, his generous fairness and welcome to his juniors, his kindly hospitality and thorough sincerity; all of which I can never forget. He was a leader with whom one always felt *safe*, and there is no rarer quality than this. On public grounds his loss is simply irreparable.'

Dr. Eddison, who attended him throughout his last illness, after bearing witness to that singular unselfishness which led Dr. Heaton, up to the very last, to think of anybody else rather than of himself, and which was exhibited in a marked manner in his intercourse with the medical men who attended him on his death-bed, adds: 'You and your children may well be proud of him, and his sons may be well satisfied to follow in his steps. It is impossible to avoid wishing that he could have known what were the feelings of those who worked with him in so many ways. I trust that in some measure he did know; but he could never know the full extent of the feeling that drew so many men, of every shade of opinion and of almost every age, to gather round his grave to do him what honour there was left to do. I feel that I have in him lost a kind, firm, and trusted friend, whose place cannot be filled indeed, but whose friendship I shall gratefully remember as long as I live.'

Mr. Scattergood, after expressing the confidence and pleasure he had always felt when he found himself associated with Dr. Heaton in his professional work, says: 'I must add also that in his dealing

with the delicate questions of etiquette and propriety
which sometimes arise between practitioners and
patients, and between one practitioner and another, and
which may so easily lead to ill-feeling and dissensions,
I always observed that Dr. Heaton's judgment of
others was kind and charitable, while his own line of
action was transparently honest and straightforward.
It was indeed clear that the golden rule of duty regu-
lated his course of conduct.'

It would be an easy matter to multiply indefinitely
the testimonies that were thus borne to the character
of Dr. Heaton at his death.   But, precious though
such testimonials are, they do not gain by mere mul-
tiplication.   Enough has been said to show how those
who were his colleagues in public and professional
life esteemed one whose whole career had been based
upon that golden rule of conduct to which the writer
of the last letter quoted refers.   To these private expressions of opinion might be added those of many
public bodies with which Dr. Heaton had been connected.   There was scarcely a charitable or educational institution in Leeds which he had not served,
and from all sides there poured in expressions of the
recognition of his worth now he was gone.   Only one
of these resolutions, however, need be printed here.
It is that passed at a meeting of the council of the
Yorkshire College on April 14, 1880.

'That the council record its deep sorrow at the

removal by death of Dr. J. D. Heaton, F.R.C.P. &c. &c., who had held the office of its chairman from the time of its creation. During the past five years of the active existence of the College, as also in the more anxious period when public sympathy had to be aroused for its foundation, Dr. Heaton energetically performed the duties of the position of leading responsibility, always pleading the claims for donations, watching for opportunities of new developments, and giving an unflagging attention to multifarious routine duties. Besides these labours, Dr. Heaton greatly promoted the interests of the College and the pleasure of its friends by the exercise of many graceful hospitalities. Although fully aware that the services of the late Dr. Heaton were freely given to a large number of institutions intended to benefit his fellow-townsmen in various ways, the council believe that a common consent will associate the Yorkshire College with his name as the *magnum opus* of his life. It may not be too much to say of our late friend, in the words of Lord Bacon, that " he might rest secure that the care of those things which he had principally at heart would continue after him." '

The Leeds Infirmary has since been adorned with a bust of Dr. Heaton, by H. H. Armstead, R.A., purchased by public subscription as a mark of respect to his memory.

On Friday, April 3, as has already been said,

the remains of Dr. Heaton were laid in the family
vault adjoining St. George's Church, in which already reposed the bodies of his father and mother.
The funeral was conducted in the simplest manner,
as befitted the tastes of the deceased during life.
But not often have the people of Leeds witnessed
a more impressive scene than that which was then
offered to them. St. George's Church, in which
almost from boyhood Dr. Heaton had been a constant
worshipper, lies but a stone's throw from Claremont. No carriages were provided for the use of
the mourners, nor was even a hearse employed for
the conveyance of the dead. The simple coffin,
covered with the flowers that had poured in from
friends far and near, was borne along the street to the
church, followed by such a throng of mourners as are
seldom seen even at a public funeral. In addition to
the family and personal friends, there were gathered
around the grave nearly the whole of the leading inhabitants of Leeds and of the neighbouring districts.
The representatives of the medical profession, of
science, art, and literature, were there along with the
leading members of the greatest business community
of the West Riding. From numberless public bodies
with which Dr. Heaton had been connected during
his life there were deputations. The time of the
funeral was in the very midst of the great political
battle of that year. But the rival combatants formed

a truce for that day, and stood side by side in presence of the dead who had been the friend of all without distinction of sect or party. To those who knew anything of the character of that vast throng of mourners, the appearance of the crowd was most impressive, for it seemed as though all the life and energy, the best talent and the highest moral influence of the great town of which Dr. Heaton had proved himself one of the worthiest and most useful citizens, was gathered there. And so amid a solemn silence and universal sorrow he was laid in his last resting-place, in the very midst of 'the city of his love'; within full sound of the tumult of forge and mill; within sight of the noble infirmary in which he had worked so long, and under the shadow of the church in which he had prayed so often.

There is nothing beautiful in the situation of that tomb, close to the crowded street. One can imagine a hundred last-resting places where the sights and sounds would be more likely to soothe the hearts of the mourners than is the case here. Yet those who knew and loved Dr. Heaton could desire for him no better, no more appropriate place of burial than this, in the very heart of the town to which he gave the best years of his manhood and the best energies of his life.

Spottiswoode & Co., Printers, New-street Square, London.

39 PATERNOSTER ROW, E.C.
LONDON, *April* 1883.

GENERAL LISTS OF WORKS

PUBLISHED BY

MESSRS. LONGMANS, GREEN & CO.

———∘∘⦂⊙⦂∘∘———

HISTORY, POLITICS, HISTORICAL MEMOIRS, &c.

History of England from the Conclusion of the Great War in 1815 to the year 1841. By SPENCER WALPOLE. 3 vols. 8vo. £2. 14*s.*

History of England in the 18th Century. By W. E. H. LECKY, M.A. 4 vols. 8vo. 1700–1784, £3. 12*s.*

The History of England from the Accession of James II. By the Right Hon. Lord MACAULAY.
STUDENT'S EDITION, 2 vols. cr. 8vo. 12*s.*
PEOPLE'S EDITION, 4 vols. cr. 8vo. 16*s.*
CABINET EDITION, 8 vols. post 8vo. 48*s.*
LIBRARY EDITION, 5 vols. 8vo. £4.

The Complete Works of Lord Macaulay. Edited by Lady TREVELYAN.
CABINET EDITION, 16 vols. crown 8vo. price £4. 16*s.*
LIBRARY EDITION, 8 vols. 8vo. Portrait, price £5. 5*s.*

Lord Macaulay's Critical and Historical Essays.
CHEAP EDITION, crown 8vo. 2*s.* 6*d.*
STUDENT'S EDITION, crown 8vo. 6*s.*
PEOPLE'S EDITION, 2 vols. crown 8vo. 8*s.*
CABINET EDITION, 4 vols. 24*s.*
LIBRARY EDITION, 3 vols. 8vo. 36*s.*

The History of England from the Fall of Wolsey to the Defeat of the Spanish Armada. By J. A. FROUDE, M.A.
POPULAR EDITION, 12 vols. crown, £2. 2*s.*
CABINET EDITION, 12 vols. crown, £3. 12*s.*

The English in Ireland in the Eighteenth Century. By J. A. FROUDE, M.A. 3 vols. crown 8vo. 18*s.*

The English in America; Virginia, Maryland, and the Carolinas. By J. A. DOYLE, Fellow of All Souls' College, Oxford. 8vo. Map, 18*s.*

Journal of the Reigns of King George IV. and King William IV. By the late C. C. F. GREVILLE, Esq. Edited by H. REEVE, Esq. Fifth Edition. 3 vols. 8vo. price 36*s.*

The Life of Napoleon III. derived from State Records, Unpublished Family Correspondence, and Personal Testimony. By BLANCHARD JERROLD. With numerous Portraits and Facsimiles. 4 vols. 8vo. £3. 18*s.*

The Early History of Charles James Fox. By the Right Hon. G. O. TREVELYAN, M.P. Fourth Edition. 8vo. 6*s.*

Selected Speeches of the Earl of Beaconsfield, K.G. With Introduction and Notes, by T. E. KEBBEL, M.A. 2 vols. 8vo. Portrait, 32*s.*

The Constitutional His-tory of England since the Accession of George III. 1760–1870. By Sir THOMAS ERSKINE MAY, K.C.B. D.C.L. Seventh Edition. 3 vols. cr. 8vo. 18*s.*

Democracy in Europe; a History. By Sir THOMAS ERSKINE MAY, K.C.B. D.C.L. 2 vols. 8vo. 32*s.*

A

Introductory Lectures on

Modern History delivered in 1841 and 1842. By the late THOMAS ARNOLD, D.D. 8vo. 7s. 6d.

History of Civilisation in

England and France, Spain and Scotland. By HENRY THOMAS BUCKLE. 3 vols. crown 8vo. 24s.

Lectures on the History

of England from the Earliest Times to the Death of King Edward II. By W. LONGMAN, F.S.A. Maps and Illustrations. 8vo. 15s.

History of the Papacy

during the Reformation. By the Rev. Canon CREIGHTON, M.A. VOLS. I. & II. 1378–1464. 2 vols. 8vo. 32s.

History of the Life &

Times of Edward III. By W. LONGMAN, F.S.A. With 9 Maps, 8 Plates, and 16 Woodcuts. 2 vols. 8vo. 28s.

Historic Winchester;

England's First Capital. By A. R. BRAMSTON and A. C. LEROY. Crown 8vo. 6s.

The Historical Geogra-

phy of Europe. By E. A. FREEMAN, D.C.L. LL.D. Second Edition, with 65 Maps. 2 vols. 8vo. 31s. 6a.

History of England un-

der the Duke of Buckingham and Charles I. 1624–1628. By S. R. GARDINER, LL.D. 2 vols. 8vo. Maps, price 24s.

The Personal Govern-

ment of Charles I. from the Death of Buckingham to the Declaration in favour of Ship Money, 1628–1637. By S. R. GARDINER, LL.D. 2 vols. 8vo. 24s.

A Student's Manual of

the History of India from the Earliest Period to the Present. By Col. MEADOWS TAYLOR, M.R.A.S. Third Thousand. Crown 8vo. Maps, 7s. 6d.

Outline of English His-

tory, B.C. 55–A.D. 1880. By S. R. GARDINER, LL.D. With 96 Woodcuts Fcp. 8vo. 2s. 6d.

Waterloo Lectures; a

Study of the Campaign of 1815. By Col. C. C. CHESNEY, R.E. 8vo. 10s. 6d.

The Oxford Reformers—

John Colet, Erasmus, and Thomas More; a History of their Fellow-Work. By F. SEEBOHM. 8vo. 14s.

History of the Romans

under the Empire. By Dean MERIVALE, D.D. 8 vols. post 8vo. 48s.

General History of Rome

from B.C. 753 to A.D. 476. By Dean MERIVALE, D.D. Crown 8vo. Maps, price 7s. 6d.

The Fall of the Roman

Republic; a Short History of the Last Century of the Commonwealth. By Dean MERIVALE, D.D. 12mo. 7s. 6d.

The History of Rome.

By WILHELM IHNE. 5 vols. 8vo. price £3. 17s.

Carthage and the Cartha-

ginians. By R. BOSWORTH SMITH, M.A. Second Edition; Maps, Plans, &c. Crown 8vo. 10s. 6d.

History of Ancient Egypt.

By G. RAWLINSON, M.A. With Map and Illustrations. 2 vols. 8vo. 63s.

The Seventh Great Ori-

ental Monarchy; or, a History of the Sassanians. By G. RAWLINSON, M.A. With Map and 95 Illustrations. 8vo. 28s.

The History of European

Morals from Augustus to Charlemagne. By W. E. H. LECKY, M.A. 2 vols. crown 8vo. 16s.

History of the Rise and

Influence of the Spirit of Rationalism in Europe. By W. E. H. LECKY, M.A. 2 vols. crown 8vo. 16s.

The History of Philo-

sophy, from Thales to Comte. By GEORGE HENRY LEWES. Fifth Edition. 2 vols. 8vo. 32s.

A History of Latin

Literature. By G. A. SIMCOX, M.A. Fellow of Queen's College, Oxford. 2 vols. 8vo. 32s.

A History of Classical

Greek Literature. By the Rev. J. P. MAHAFFY, M.A. Crown 8vo. VOL. I. Poets, 7s. 6d. VOL. II. Prose Writers, 7s. 6d.

Witt's Myths of Hellas,

or Greek Tales Told in German. Translated into English by F. M. YOUNGHUSBAND. With a Preface by A. SIDGWICK, M.A. C.C. Coll. Oxon. Crown 8vo. 3s. 6d.

Zeller's Stoics, Epicureans, and Sceptics.

Translated by the Rev. O. J. REICHEL, M.A. New Edition revised. Crown 8vo. 15s.

Zeller's Socrates & the Socratic Schools.

Translated by the Rev. O. J. REICHEL, M.A. Second Edition. Crown 8vo. 10s. 6d.

Zeller's Plato & the Older Academy.

Translated by S. FRANCES ALLEYNE and ALFRED GOODWIN, B.A. Crown 8vo. 18s.

Zeller's Pre-Socratic Schools;

a History of Greek Philosophy from the Earliest Period to the time of Socrates. Translated by SARAH F. ALLEYNE. 2 vols. crown 8vo. 30s.

Epochs of Modern History.

Edited by C. COLBECK, M.A.

Church's Beginning of the Middle Ages. price 2s. 6d.
Cox's Crusades, 2s. 6d.
Creighton's Age of Elizabeth, 2s. 6d.
Gairdner's Lancaster and York, 2s. 6d.
Gardiner's Puritan Revolution, 2s. 6d.
——————— Thirty Years' War, 2s. 6d.
——————— (Mrs.) French Revolution, 2s. 6d.
Hale's Fall of the Stuarts, 2s. 6d.
Johnson's Normans in Europe, 2s. 6d.
Longman's Frederic the Great, 2s. 6d.
Ludlow's War of American Independence, price 2s. 6d.

M'Carthy's Epoch of Reform, 1830–1850. price 2s. 6d.
Morris's Age of Anne, 2s. 6d.
Seebohm's Protestant Revolution, 2s. 6d.
Stubbs' Early Plantagenets, 2s. 6d.
Warburton's Edward III. 2s. 6d.

Epochs of Ancient History.

Edited by the Rev. Sir G. W. COX, Bart. M.A. & C. SANKEY, M.A.

Beesly's Gracchi, Marius and Sulla, 2s. 6d.
Capes's Age of the Antonines, 2s. 6d.
——————— Early Roman Empire, 2s. 6d.
Cox's Athenian Empire, 2s. 6d.
——————— Greeks & Persians, 2s. 6d.
Curteis's Macedonian Empire, 2s. 6d.
Ihne's Rome to its Capture by the Gauls, price 2s. 6d.
Merivale's Roman Triumvirates, 2s. 6d.
Sankey's Spartan & Theban Supremacies, price 2s. 6d.
Smith's Rome and Carthage, 2s. 6d.

Creighton's Shilling History

of England, introductory to 'Epochs of English History.' Fcp. 1s.

Epochs of English History.

Edited by the Rev. MANDELL CREIGHTON, M.A. In One Volume. Fcp. 8vo. 5s.

The Student's Manual of

Ancient History; the Political History, Geography and Social State of the Principal Nations of Antiquity. By W. COOKE TAYLOR, LL.D. Cr. 8vo. 7s. 6d.

The Student's Manual of

Modern History; the Rise and Progress of the Principal European Nations. By W. COOKE TAYLOR, LL.D. Crown 8vo. 7s. 6d.

BIOGRAPHICAL WORKS.

Reminiscences chiefly of

Oriel College and the Oxford Movement. By the Rev. THOMAS MOZLEY, M.A. 2 vols. crown 8vo. 18s.

Apologia pro Vitâ Suâ;

Being a History of his Religious Opinions by Cardinal NEWMAN. Crown 8vo. 6s.

Reminiscences. By

THOMAS CARLYLE. Edited by J. A. FROUDE, M.A. 2 vols. crown 8vo. 18s.

Thomas Carlyle, a History

of the first Forty Years of his Life, 1795 to 1835. By J. A. FROUDE. M.A. With 2 Portraits and 4 Illustrations. 2 vols. 8vo. 32s.

Letters and Memorials
of Jane Welsh Carlyle. Prepared for publication by THOMAS CARLYLE, and edited by J. A. FROUDE, M.A. 3 vols. 8vo. 36*s*.

Life of Sir William
Rowan Hamilton, Kt. LL.D. D.C.L. M.R.I.A. &c. Including Selections from his Poems, Correspondence, and Miscellaneous Writings. By the Rev. R. P. GRAVES, M.A. VOL. I. 8vo. 15*s*.

Skobeleff and the Sla-
vonic Cause. By O. K., Honorary Member of the Benevolent Slavonic Society. 8vo. with Portrait, 14*s*.

The Marriages of the
Bonapartes. By the Hon. D. A. BINGHAM. 2 vols. crown 8vo. 21*s*.

Recollections of the Last
Half-Century. By COUNT ORSI. With a Portrait of Napoleon III. and 4 Woodcuts. Crown 8vo. 7*s*. 6*d*.

Autobiography. By JOHN
STUART MILL. 8vo. 7*s*. 6*d*.

Felix Mendelssohn's Let-
ters, translated by Lady WALLACE. 2 vols. crown 8vo. 5*s*. each.

The Correspondence of
Robert Southey with Caroline Bowles. Edited by EDWARD DOWDEN, LL.D. 8vo. Portrait, 14*s*.

The Life and Letters of
Lord Macaulay. By the Right Hon. G. O. TREVELYAN, M.P.

LIBRARY EDITION, 2 vols. 8vo. 36*s*.
CABINET EDITION, 2 vols. crown 8vo. 12*s*.
POPULAR EDITION, 1 vol. crown 8vo. 6*s*.

William Law, Nonjuror
and Mystic. By the Rev. J. H. OVER-TON, M.A. 8vo. 15*s*.

James Mill; a Biography.
By A. BAIN, LL.D. Crown 8vo. 5*s*.

John Stuart Mill; a Cri-
ticism, with Personal Recollections. By A. BAIN, LL.D. Crown 8vo. 2*s*. 6*d*.

A Dictionary of General
Biography. By W. L. R. CATES. Third Edition. 8vo. 28*s*.

Outlines of the Life of
Shakespeare. By J. O. HALLIWELL-PHILLIPPS, F.R.S. 8vo. 7*s*. 6*d*.

Biographical Studies. By
the late WALTER BAGEHOT, M.A. 8vo. 12*s*.

Essays in Ecclesiastical
Biography. By the Right Hon. Sir J. STEPHEN, LL.D. Crown 8vo. 7*s*. 6*d*.

Cæsar; a Sketch. By J. A.
FROUDE, M.A. With Portrait and Map. 8vo. 16*s*.

Life of the Duke of Wel-
lington. By the Rev. G. R. GLEIG, M.A. Crown 8vo. Portrait, 6*s*.

Memoirs of Sir Henry
Havelock, K.C.B. By JOHN CLARK MARSHMAN. Crown 8vo. 3*s*. 6*d*.

Leaders of Public Opi-
nion in Ireland. By W. E. H. LECKY, M.A. Crown 8vo. 7*s*. 6*d*.

Memoir of Augustus De
Morgan, with Selections from his Letters. By his Wife, SOPHIA ELIZABETH DE MORGAN. 8vo. with Portrait, 14*s*.

MENTAL and POLITICAL PHILOSOPHY.

De Tocqueville's Demo-
cracy in America, translated by H. REEVE. 2 vols. crown 8vo. 16*s*.

Principles of Economical
Philosophy. By H. D. MACLEOD M.A. Second Edition, in 2 vols. VOL. I. 8vo. 15*s*. VOL. II. PART I. 12*s*.

Analysis of the Pheno-
mena of the Human Mind. By JAMES MILL. With Notes, Illustrative and Critical. 2 vols. 8vo. 28*s*.

On Representative Go-
vernment. By JOHN STUART MILL. Crown 8vo. 2*s*.

On Liberty. By JOHN STUART MILL. Crown 8vo. 1s. 4d.

Principles of Political Economy. By JOHN STUART MILL. 2 vols. 8vo. 30s. or 1 vol. crown 8vo. 5s.

Essays on some Unset- tled Questions of Political Economy. By JOHN STUART MILL. 8vo. 6s. 6d.

Utilitarianism. By JOHN STUART MILL. 8vo. 5s.

The Subjection of Wo- men. By JOHN STUART MILL. Fourth Edition. Crown 8vo. 6s.

Examination of Sir Wil- liam Hamilton's Philosophy. By JOHN STUART MILL. 8vo. 16s.

A System of Logic, Ratiocinative and Inductive. By JOHN STUART MILL. 2 vols. 8vo. 25s.

Dissertations and Dis- cussions. By JOHN STUART MILL. 4 vols. 8vo. £2. 6s. 6d.

A Systematic View of the Science of Jurisprudence. By SHELDON AMOS, M.A. 8vo. 18s.

Path and Goal; a Discussion on the Elements of Civilisation and the Conditions of Happiness. By M. M. KALISCH, Ph.D. M.A. 8vo. price 12s. 6d.

Sir Travers Twiss on the Rights and Duties of Nations, considered as Independent Communities, in Time of War. 8vo. 21s.

A Primer of the English Constitution and Government. By S. AMOS, M.A. Crown 8vo. 6s.

Fifty Years of the English Constitution, 1830-1880. By SHELDON AMOS, M.A. Crown 8vo. 10s. 6d.

Francis Bacon's Promus of Formularies and Elegancies, illustrated by Passages from SHAKESPEARE. By Mrs. H. POTT. Preface by E. A. ABBOTT, D.D. 8vo. 16s.

Selections from the Wri- tings of Lord Macaulay. Edited, with Notes, by the Right Hon. G. O. TREVELYAN, M.P. Crown 8vo. 6s.

Lord Bacon's Works, collected & edited by R. L. ELLIS, M.A. J. SPEDDING, M.A. and D. D. HEATH. 7 vols. 8vo. £3. 13s. 6d.

Letters and Life of Fran- cis Bacon, including all his Occasional Works. Collected and edited, with a Commentary, by J. SPEDDING. 7 vols. 8vo. £4. 4s.

The Institutes of Jus- tinian; with English Introduction, Translation, and Notes. By T. C. SANDARS, M.A. 8vo. 18s.

The Nicomachean Ethics of Aristotle, translated by R. WILLIAMS, B.A. Crown 8vo. 7s. 6d.

Aristotle's Politics, Books I. III. IV. (VII.) Greek Text, with an English Translation by W. E. BOLLAND, M.A. and Short Essays by A. LANG, M.A. Crown 8vo. 7s. 6d.

The Ethics of Aristotle; with Essays and Notes. By Sir A. GRANT, Bart. LL.D. 2 vols. 8vo. 32s.

Bacon's Essays, with Annotations. By R. WHATELY, D.D. 8vo. 10s. 6d.

An Introduction to Logic. By WILLIAM H. STANLEY MONCK, M.A. Prof. of Moral Philos. Univ. of Dublin. Crown 8vo. 5s.

Picture Logic; an Attempt to Popularise the Science of Reasoning. By A. J. SWINBURNE, B.A. Post 8vo. 5s.

Elements of Logic. By R. WHATELY, D.D. 8vo. 10s. 6d. Crown 8vo. 4s. 6d.

Elements of Rhetoric. By R. WHATELY, D.D. 8vo. 10s. 6d. Crown 8vo. 4s. 6d.

The Senses and the In- tellect. By A. BAIN, LL.D. 8vo. 15s.

The Emotions and the Will. By A. BAIN, LL.D. 8vo. 15s.

Mental and Moral Sci- ence; a Compendium of Psychology and Ethics. By A. BAIN, LL.D. Crown 8vo. 10s. 6d.

An Outline of the Necessary Laws of Thought ; a Treatise on Pure and Applied Logic. By W. THOMSON, D.D. Crown 8vo. 6s.

Essays in Political and Moral Philosophy. By T. E. CLIFFE LESLIE, Barrister-at-Law. 8vo. 10s. 6d.

On the Influence of Authority in Matters of Opinion. By Sir G. C. LEWIS, Bart. 8vo. 14s.

Hume's Philosophical Works. Edited by T. H. GREEN, M.A. and the Rev. T. H. GROSE, M.A. 4 vols. 8vo. 56s. Or separately, Essays, 2 vols. 28s. Treatise on Human Nature, 2 vols. 28s.

Essays in Philosophical Criticism. Edited by A. SETH and R. B. HALDANE, M.A. Preface by Prof. E. CAIRD, LL.D. 8vo. 9s.

MISCELLANEOUS & CRITICAL WORKS.

Studies of Modern Mind and Character at Several European Epochs. By JOHN WILSON. 8vo. 12s.

Short Studies on Great Subjects. By J. A. FROUDE, M.A. 4 vols. crown 8vo. 24s.

Literary Studies. By the late WALTER BAGEHOT, M.A. Second Edition. 2 vols. 8vo. Portrait, 28s.

Manual of English Literature, Historical and Critical. By THOMAS ARNOLD, M.A. Univ. Coll. Oxon. Crown 8vo. 7s. 6d.

Poetry and Prose ; Illustrative Passages from English Authors from the Anglo-Saxon Period to the Present Time. Edited by T. ARNOLD, M.A. Crown 8vo. 6s.

Supernatural Religion ; an Inquiry into the Reality of Divine Revelation. Complete Edition, thoroughly revised. 3 vols. 8vo. 36s.

The Wit and Wisdom of Benjamin Disraeli, Earl of Beaconsfield, collected from his Writings and Speeches. Crown 8vo. 6s.

The Wit and Wisdom of the Rev. Sydney Smith. Crown 8vo. 3s. 6d.

Lord Macaulay's Miscellaneous Writings :—
LIBRARY EDITION, 2 vols. 8vo. 21s.
PEOPLE'S EDITION, 1 vol. cr. 8vo. 4s. 6d.

Lord Macaulay's Miscellaneous Writings and Speeches. Student's Edition. Crown 8vo. 6s. Cabinet Edition, including Indian Penal Code, Lays of Ancient Rome, and other Poems. 4 vols. post 8vo. 24s.

Speeches of Lord Macaulay, corrected by Himself. Crown 8vo. 3s. 6d.

Selections from the Writings of Lord Macaulay. Edited, with Notes, by the Right Hon. G. O. TREVELYAN, M.P. Crown. 8vo. 6s.

The Medical Language of St. Luke : a Proof from Internal Evidence that St. Luke's Gospel and the Acts were written by the same person, and that the writer was a Medical Man. By the Rev. W. K. HOBART, LL.D. 8vo. 16s.

Evenings with the Skeptics ; or, Free Discussion on Free Thinkers. By JOHN OWEN, Rector of East Anstey, Devon. 2 vols. 8vo. 32s.

Outlines of Primitive Belief among the Indo-European Races. By CHARLES F. KEARY, M.A. 8vo. 18s.

Language & Languages.

A Revised Edition of Chapters on Language and Families of Speech. By F. W. FARRAR, D.D. F.R.S. Crown 8vo. 6s.

Grammar of Elocution.

By JOHN MILLARD, Elocution Master in the City of London School. Second Edition. Fcp. 8vo. 3s. 6d.

Selected Essays on Language, Mythology, and Religion.

By F. MAX MÜLLER, M.A. K.M. 2 vols. crown 8vo. 16s.

Lectures on the Science of Language.

By F. MAX MÜLLER, M.A. K.M. 2 vols. crown 8vo. 16s.

Chips from a German Workshop;

Essays on the Science of Religion, and on Mythology, Traditions & Customs. By F. MAX MÜLLER, M.A. K.M. 4 vols. 8vo. £1. 16s.

India, What Can it Teach Us?

A Course of Lectures delivered before the University of Cambridge. By F. MAX MÜLLER, M.A. K.M. 8vo. 12s. 6d.

The Essays and Contributions of A. K. H. B.

Uniform Cabinet Editions in crown 8vo.

Autumn Holidays, 3s. 6d.
Changed Aspects of Unchanged Truths, price 3s. 6d.
Commonplace Philosopher, 3s. 6d.
Counsel and Comfort, 3s. 6d.
Critical Essays, 3s. 6d.
Graver Thoughts. Three Series, 3s. 6d. each.
Landscapes, Churches, and Moralities, 3s. 6d.
Leisure Hours in Town, 3s. 6d.
Lessons of Middle Age, 3s. 6d.
Our Little Life, 3s. 6d.
Present Day Thoughts, 3s. 6d.
Recreations of a Country Parson, Three Series, 3s. 6d. each.
Seaside Musings, 3s. 6d.
Sunday Afternoons, 3s. 6d.

DICTIONARIES and OTHER BOOKS of REFERENCE.

English Synonymes.

By E. J. WHATELY. Edited by R. WHATELY, D.D. Fcp. 8vo. 3s.

Roget's Thesaurus of English Words and Phrases,

classified and arranged so as to facilitate the expression of Ideas, and assist in Literary Composition. Re-edited by the Author's Son, J. L. ROGET. Crown 8vo. 10s. 6d.

Handbook of the English Language.

By R. G. LATHAM, M.A. M.D. Crown 8vo. 6s.

Contanseau's Practical Dictionary

of the French and English Languages. Post 8vo. price 7s. 6d.

Contanseau's Pocket Dictionary,

French and English, abridged from the Practical Dictionary by the Author. Square 18mo. 3s. 6d.

A Practical Dictionary of the German and English Languages.

By Rev. W. L. BLACKLEY, M.A. & Dr. C. M. FRIEDLÄNDER. Post 8vo. 7s. 6d.

A New Pocket Dictionary of the German and English Languages.

By F. W. LONGMAN, Ball. Coll. Oxford. Square 18mo. 5s.

Becker's Gallus; Roman Scenes of the Time of Augustus.

Translated by the Rev. F. METCALFE, M.A. Post 8vo. 7s. 6d.

Becker's Charicles;

Illustrations of the Private Life of the Ancient Greeks. Translated by the Rev. F. METCALFE, M.A. Post 8vo. 7s. 6d.

A Dictionary of Roman and Greek Antiquities.

With 2,000 Woodcuts illustrative of the Arts and Life of the Greeks and Romans. By A. RICH, B.A. Crown 8vo. 7s. 6d.

A Greek-English Lexicon. By H. G. LIDDELL, D.D. Dean of Christchurch, and R. SCOTT, D.D. Dean of Rochester. 4to. 36*s*.

Liddell & Scott's Lexicon, Greek and English, abridged for Schools. Square 12mo. 7*s*. 6*d*.

An English-Greek Lexicon, containing all the Greek Words used by Writers of good authority. By C. D. YONGE, M.A. 4to. 21*s*. School Abridgment, square 12mo. 8*s*. 6*d*.

A Latin-English Dictionary. By JOHN T. WHITE, D.D. Oxon. and J. E. RIDDLE, M.A. Oxon. Sixth Edition, revised. Quarto 21*s*.

White's Concise Latin-English Dictionary, for the use of University Students. Royal 8vo. 12*s*.

M'Culloch's Dictionary of Commerce and Commercial Navigation. Re-edited (1882), with a Supplement containing the most recent Information, by A. J. WILSON. With 48 Maps, Charts, and Plans. Medium 8vo. 63*s*.

Keith Johnston's General Dictionary of Geography, Descriptive, Physical, Statistical, and Historical; a complete Gazetteer of the World. Medium 8vo. 42*s*.

The Public Schools Atlas of Ancient Geography, in 28 entirely new Coloured Maps. Edited by the Rev. G. BUTLER, M.A. Imperial 8vo. or imperial 4to. 7*s*. 6*d*.

The Public Schools Atlas of Modern Geography, in 31 entirely new Coloured Maps. Edited by the Rev. G. BUTLER, M.A. Uniform, 5*s*.

ASTRONOMY and METEOROLOGY.

Outlines of Astronomy. By Sir J. F. W. HERSCHEL, Bart. M.A. Latest Edition, with Plates and Diagrams. Square crown 8vo. 12*s*.

The Moon, and the Condition and Configurations of its Surface. By E. NEISON, F.R.A.S. With 26 Maps and 5 Plates. Medium 8vo. price 31*s*. 6*d*.

Air and Rain; the Beginnings of a Chemical Climatology. By R. A. SMITH, F.R.S. 8vo. 24*s*.

Celestial Objects for Common Telescopes. By the Rev. T. W. WEBB, M.A. Fourth Edition, adapted to the Present State of Sidereal Science; Map, Plate, Woodcuts. Crown 8vo. 9*s*.

The Sun; Ruler, Light, Fire, and Life of the Planetary System. By R. A. PROCTOR, B.A. With Plates & Woodcuts. Crown 8vo. 14*s*.

Proctor's Orbs Around Us; a Series of Essays on the Moon & Planets, Meteors & Comets, the Sun & Coloured Pairs of Suns. With Chart and Diagrams. Crown 8vo. 7*s*. 6*d*.

Proctor's Other Worlds than Ours; The Plurality of Worlds Studied under the Light of Recent Scientific Researches. With 14 Illustrations. Crown 8vo. 10*s*. 6*d*.

Proctor on the Moon; her Motions, Aspects, Scenery, and Physical Condition. With Plates, Charts, Woodcuts, and Lunar Photographs. Crown 8vo. 10*s*.6*d*.

Proctor's Universe of Stars; Presenting Researches into and New Views respecting the Constitution of the Heavens. Second Edition, with 22 Charts and 22 Diagrams. 8vo. 10*s*. 6*d*.

Proctor's New Star Atlas, for the Library, the School, and the Observatory, in 12 Circular Maps (with 2 Index Plates). Crown 8vo. 5*s.*

Proctor's Larger Star Atlas, for the Library, in Twelve Circular Maps, with Introduction and 2 Index Plates. Folio, 15*s.* or Maps only, 12*s.* 6*d.*

Proctor's Essays on Astronomy. A Series of Papers on Planets and Meteors, the Sun and Sun-surrounding Space, Stars and Star Cloudlets. With 10 Plates and 24 Woodcuts. 8vo. price 12*s.*

Proctor's Transits of Venus; a Popular Account of Past and Coming Transits from the First Observed by Horrocks in 1639 to the Transit of 2012. Fourth Edition, with 20 Lithographic Plates (12 Coloured) and 38 Illustrations engraved on Wood. 8vo. 8*s.* 6*d.*

Proctor's Studies of Venus-Transits; an Investigation of the Circumstances of the Transits of Venus in 1874 and 1882. With 7 Diagrams and 10 Plates. 8vo. 5*s.*

NATURAL HISTORY and PHYSICAL SCIENCE.

Ganot's Elementary Treatise on Physics, for the use of Colleges and Schools. Translated by E. ATKINSON, Ph.D. F.C.S. Tenth Edition. With 4 Coloured Plates and 844 Woodcuts. Large crown 8vo. 15*s.*

Ganot's Natural Philosophy for General Readers and Young Persons. Translated by E. ATKINSON, Ph.D. F.C.S. Fourth Edition; with 2 Plates and 471 Woodcuts. Crown 8vo. 7*s.* 6*d.*

Professor Helmholtz' Popular Lectures on Scientific Subjects. Translated and edited by EDMUND ATKINSON, Ph.D. F.C.S. With a Preface by Prof. TYNDALL, F.R.S. and 68 Woodcuts. 2 vols. crown 8vo. 15*s.* or separately, 7*s.* 6*d.* each.

Arnott's Elements of Physics or Natural Philosophy. Seventh Edition, edited by A. BAIN, LL.D. and A. S. TAYLOR, M.D. F.R.S. Crown 8vo. Woodcuts, 12*s.* 6*d.*

The Correlation of Physical Forces. By the Hon. Sir W. R. GROVE, F.R.S. &c. Sixth Edition revised and augmented. 8vo. 15*s.*

A Treatise on Magnetism, General and Terrestrial. By H. LLOYD, D.D. D.C.L. 8vo. 10*s.* 6*d.*

The Mathematical and other Tracts of the late James M'Cullagh, F.T.C.D. Prof. of Nat. Philos. in the Univ. of Dublin. Edited by the Rev. J. H. JELLETT, B.D. and the Rev. S. HAUGHTON, M.D. 8vo. 15*s.*

Elementary Treatise on the Wave-Theory of Light. By H. LLOYD, D.D. D.C.L. 8vo. 10*s.* 6*d.*

Fragments of Science. By JOHN TYNDALL, F.R.S. Sixth Edition. 2 vols. crown 8vo. 16*s.*

Heat a Mode of Motion. By JOHN TYNDALL, F.R.S. Sixth Edition. Crown 8vo. 12*s.*

Sound. By JOHN TYNDALL, F.R.S. Fourth Edition, including Recent Researches.

Essays on the Floating-Matter of the Air in relation to Putrefaction and Infection. By JOHN TYNDALL, F.R.S. With 24 Woodcuts. Crown 8vo. 7*s.* 6*d.*

Professor Tyndall's Lectures on Light, delivered in America in 1872 and 1873. With Portrait. Plate & Diagrams. Crown 8vo. 7*s.* 6*d.*

Professor Tyndall's Lessons in Electricity at the Royal Institution, 1875-6. With 58 Woodcuts. Crown 8vo. 2*s*. 6*d*.

Professor Tyndall's Notes of a Course of Seven Lectures on Electrical Phenomena and Theories, delivered at the Royal Institution. Crown 8vo. 1*s*. sewed, 1*s*. 6*d*. cloth.

Professor Tyndall's Notes of a Course of Nine Lectures on Light, delivered at the Royal Institution. Crown 8vo. 1*s*. swd., 1*s*. 6*d*. cloth.

Six Lectures on Physical Geography, delivered in 1876, with some Additions. By the Rev. SAMUEL HAUGHTON, F.R.S. M.D. D.C.L. With 23 Diagrams. 8vo. 15*s*.

An Introduction to the Systematic Zoology and Morphology of Vertebrate Animals. By A. MACALISTER, M.D. With 28 Diagrams. 8vo. 10*s*. 6*d*.

Text-Books of Science, Mechanical and Physical, adapted for the use of Artisans and of Students in Public and Science Schools. Small 8vo. with Woodcuts, &c.

Abney's Photography, 3*s*. 6*d*.
Anderson's (Sir John) Strength of Materials, price 3*s*. 6*d*.
Armstrong's Organic Chemistry, 3*s*. 6*d*.
Ball's Elements of Astronomy, 6*s*.
Barry's Railway Appliances, 3*s*. 6*d*.
Bauerman's Systematic Mineralogy, 6*s*.
Bloxam & Huntington's Metals, 5*s*.
Glazebrook's Physical Optics, 6*s*.
Gore's Electro-Metallurgy, 6*s*.
Griffin's Algebra and Trigonometry, 3*s*. 6*d*.
Jenkin's Electricity and Magnetism, 3*s*. 6*d*.
Maxwell's Theory of Heat, 3*s*. 6*d*.
Merrifield's Technical Arithmetic, 3*s*. 6*d*.
Miller's Inorganic Chemistry, 3*s*. 6*d*.
Preece & Sivewright's Telegraphy, 3*s*. 6*d*.
Rutley's Study of Rocks, 4*s*. 6*d*.
Shelley's Workshop Appliances, 3*s*. 6*d*.
Thomé's Structural and Physical Botany, 6*s*.
Thorpe's Quantitative Analysis, 4*s*. 6*d*.
Thorpe & Muir's Qualitative Analysis, 3*s*. 6*d*.
Tilden's Chemical Philosophy, 3*s*. 6*d*.
Unwin's Machine Design, 6*s*.
Watson's Plane and Solid Geometry, 3*s*. 6*d*.

Experimental Physiology, its Benefits to Mankind; with an Address on Unveiling the Statue of William Harvey at Folkestone August 1881. By RICHARD OWEN, F.R.S. &c. Crown 8vo. 5*s*.

The Comparative Anatomy and Physiology of the Vertebrate Animals. By RICHARD OWEN, F.R.S. With 1,472 Woodcuts. 3 vols. 8vo. £3. 13*s*. 6*d*.

Homes without Hands; a Description of the Habitations of Animals, classed according to their Principle of Construction. By the Rev. J. G. WOOD, M.A. With about 140 Vignettes on Wood. 8vo. 14*s*.

Wood's Strange Dwellings; a Description of the Habitations of Animals, abridged from 'Homes without Hands.' With Frontispiece and 60 Woodcuts. Crown 8vo. 5*s*. Sunbeam Edition, 4to. 6*d*.

Wood's Insects at Home; a Popular Account of British Insects, their Structure, Habits, and Transformations. 8vo. Woodcuts, 14*s*.

Common British Insects, Beetles, Moths, and Butterflies. By the Rev. J. G. WOOD, M.A. F.L.S. Crown 8vo. with 130 Woodcuts, 3*s*. 6*d*.

Wood's Insects Abroad; a Popular Account of Foreign Insects, their Structure, Habits, and Transformations. 8vo. Woodcuts, 14*s*.

Wood's Out of Doors; a Selection of Original Articles on Practical Natural History. With 6 Illustrations. Crown 8vo. 5*s*.

Wood's Bible Animals; a description of every Living Creature mentioned in the Scriptures. With 112 Vignettes. 8vo. 14*s*.

The Sea and its Living Wonders. By Dr. G. HARTWIG. 8vo. with many Illustrations, 10*s*. 6*d*.

Hartwig's Tropical World. With about 200 Illustrations. 8vo. 10*s*. 6*d*.

Hartwig's Polar World;

a Description of Man and Nature in the Arctic and Antarctic Regions of the Globe. Maps, Plates & Woodcuts. 8vo. 10s. 6d. Sunbeam Edition, 6d.

Hartwig's Subterranean World.

With Maps and Woodcuts. 8vo. 10s. 6d.

Hartwig's Aerial World;

a Popular Account of the Phenomena and Life of the Atmosphere. Map, Plates, Woodcuts. 8vo. 10s. 6d.

A Familiar History of Birds.

By E. STANLEY, D.D. Revised and enlarged, with 160 Woodcuts. Crown 8vo. 6s.

Rural Bird Life; Essays

on Ornithology, with Instructions for Preserving Objects relating to that Science. By C. DIXON. With Frontispiece and 44 Woodcuts. Crown 8vo. 5s.

Country Pleasures; the

Chronicle of a Year, chiefly in a Garden. By GEORGE MILNER. Second Edition, with Vignette. Crown 8vo. 6s.

Rocks Classified and Described.

By BERNHARD VON COTTA. An English Translation, by P. H. LAWRENCE, with English, German, and French Synonymes. Post 8vo. 14s.

The Study of Rocks; an

Elementary Text-Book of Petrology. By F. RUTLEY, F.G.S. of H.M. Geolog. Survey. With 6 Plates and 88 Woodcuts. Fcp. 8vo. 4s. 6d.

Systematic Mineralogy.

By H. BAUERMAN, F.G.S. Assoc. Royal School of Mines. With 372 Woodcuts. Fcp. 8vo. 6s.

Keller's Lake Dwellings

of Switzerland, and other Parts of Europe. Translated by JOHN E. LEE, F.S.A. F.G.S. With 206 Illustrations. 2 vols. royal 8vo. 42s.

Heer's Primæval World

of Switzerland. Edited by JAMES HEYWOOD, M.A. F.R.S. With Map, Plates & Woodcuts. 2 vols. 8vo. 12s.

The Puzzle of Life; a

Short History of Praehistoric Vegetable and Animal Life on the Earth. By A. NICOLS, F.R.G.S. With 12 Illustrations. Crown 8vo. 3s. 6d.

The Bronze Implements,

Arms, and Ornaments of Great Britain and Ireland. By JOHN EVANS, D.C.L. LL.D. F.R.S. With 540 Illustrations. 8vo. 25s.

The Origin of Civilisation,

and the Primitive Condition of Man. By Sir J. LUBBOCK, Bart. M.P. F.R.S. Fourth Edition, enlarged. 8vo. Woodcuts, 18s.

Proctor's Light Science

for Leisure Hours; Familiar Essays on Scientific Subjects, Natural Phenomena, &c. 3 vols. cr. 8vo. 7s. 6d. ea.

Brande's Dictionary of

Science, Literature, and Art. Re-edited by the Rev. Sir G. W. COX, Bart. M.A. 3 vols. medium 8vo. 63s.

Hullah's Course of Lectures

on the History of Modern Music. 8vo. 8s. 6d.

Hullah's Second Course

of Lectures on the Transition Period of Musical History. 8vo. 10s. 6d.

Loudon's Encyclopædia

of Plants; the Specific Character, Description, Culture, History, &c. of all Plants found in Great Britain. With 12,000 Woodcuts. 8vo. 42s.

Loudon's Encyclopædia

of Gardening; the Theory and Practice of Horticulture, Floriculture, Arboriculture & Landscape Gardening. With 1,000 Woodcuts. 8vo. 21s.

De Caisne & Le Maout's

Descriptive and Analytical Botany. Translated by Mrs. HOOKER; edited and arranged by J. D. HOOKER, M.D. With 5,500 Woodcuts. Imperial 8vo. price 31s. 6d.

Rivers's Orchard-House;

or, the Cultivation of Fruit Trees under Glass. Sixteenth Edition. Crown 8vo. with 25 Woodcuts, 5s.

The Rose Amateur's

Guide. By THOMAS RIVERS. Latest Edition. Fcp. 8vo. 4s. 6d.

Elementary Botany,

Theoretical and Practical; a Text-Book for Students. By H. EDMONDS, B.Sc. With 312 Woodcuts. Fcp. 8vo. 2s.

CHEMISTRY and PHYSIOLOGY.

Experimental Chemistry for Junior Students. By J. E. REYNOLDS, M.D. F.R.S. Prof. of Chemistry, Univ. of Dublin. Fcp. 8vo. PART I. 1s. 6d. PART II. 2s. 6d.

Practical Chemistry; the Principles of Qualitative Analysis. By W. A. TILDEN, F.C.S. Fcp. 8vo. 1s. 6d.

Miller's Elements of Chemistry, Theoretical and Practical. Re-edited, with Additions, by H. MACLEOD, F.C.S. 3 vols. 8vo.

PART I. CHEMICAL PHYSICS. 16s.
PART II. INORGANIC CHEMISTRY, 24s.
PART III. ORGANIC CHEMISTRY, 31s. 6d.

An Introduction to the Study of Inorganic Chemistry. By W. ALLEN MILLER, M.D. LL.D. late Professor of Chemistry, King's College, London. With 71 Woodcuts. Fcp. 8vo. 3s. 6d.

Annals of Chemical Medicine; including the Application of Chemistry to Physiology, Pathology, Therapeutics, Pharmacy, Toxicology & Hygiene. Edited by J. L. W. THUDICHUM, M.D. 2 vols. 8vo. 14s. each.

A Dictionary of Chemistry and the Allied Branches of other Sciences. Edited by HENRY WATTS, F.R.S. 9 vols. medium 8vo. £15. 2s. 6d.

Inorganic Chemistry, Theoretical and Practical; an Elementary Text-Book. By W. JAGO, F.C.S. Third Edition, revised, with 37 Woodcuts. Fcp. 8vo. 2s.

Health in the House; Lectures on Elementary Physiology in its Application to the Daily Wants of Man and Animals. By Mrs. BUCKTON. Crown 8vo. Woodcuts, 2s.

The FINE ARTS and ILLUSTRATED EDITIONS.

The New Testament of Our Lord and Saviour Jesus Christ, Illustrated with Engravings on Wood after Paintings by the Early Masters chiefly of the Italian School. New Edition in course of publication in 18 Monthly Parts, 1s. each. 4to.

A Popular Introduction to the History of Greek and Roman Sculpture, designed to Promote the Knowledge and Appreciation of the Remains of Ancient Art. By WALTER C. PERRY. With 268 Illustrations. Square crown 8vo. 31s. 6d.

Japan; its Architecture, Art, and Art-Manufactures. By CHRISTOPHER DRESSER, Ph.D. F.L.S. &c. With 202 Graphic Illustrations engraved on Wood for the most part by Native Artists in Japan, the rest by G. Pearson, after Photographs and Drawings made on the spot. Square crown 8vo. 31s. 6d.

Lord Macaulay's Lays of Ancient Rome. With Ninety Illustrations engraved on Wood from Drawings by G. Scharf. Fcp. 4to. 21s.

Lord Macaulay's Lays of Ancient Rome, with Ivry and the Armada. With 41 Wood Engravings by G. Pearson from Original Drawings by J. R. Weguelin. Crown 8vo. 6s.

The Three Cathedrals dedicated to St. Paul in London. By W. LONGMAN, F.S.A. With Illustrations. Square crown 8vo. 21s.

Moore's Lalla Rookh, TENNIEL'S Edition, with 68 Woodcut Illustrations. Crown 8vo. 10s. 6d.

Moore's Irish Melodies, MACLISE'S Edition, with 161 Steel Plates. Super-royal 8vo. 21s.

Lectures on Harmony,
delivered at the Royal Institution. By G. A. MACFARREN. 8vo. 12s.

Jameson's Legends of the
Saints and Martyrs. With 19 Etchings and 187 Woodcuts. 2 vols. 31s. 6d.

Jameson's Legends of the
Madonna, the Virgin Mary as represented in Sacred and Legendary Art. With 27 Etchings and 165 Woodcuts. 1 vol. 21s.

Jameson's Legends of the
Monastic Orders. With 11 Etchings and 88 Woodcuts. 1 vol. 21s.

Jameson's History of the
Saviour, His Types and Precursors. Completed by Lady EASTLAKE. With 13 Etchings and 281 Woodcuts. 2 vols. 42s.

Art-Instruction in England.
By F. E. HULME, F.L.S. F.S.A. Fcp. 8vo. 3s. 6d.

Notes on Foreign Picture Galleries.
By C. L. EASTLAKE, F.R.I.B.A. Keeper of the National Gallery, London. Crown 8vo.

The Louvre Gallery, *Paris*, with 114 Illustrations, 7s. 6d.

The Brera Gallery, *Milan*, with 55 Illustrations, 5s.

The USEFUL ARTS, MANUFACTURES, &c.

The Elements of Mechanism.
By T. M. GOODEVE, M.A. Barrister-at-Law. New Edition, re-written and enlarged, with 342 Woodcuts. Crown 8vo. 6s.

Railways and Locomotives;
a Series of Lectures delivered at the School of Military Engineering, Chatham. *Railways*, by J. W. BARRY, M. Inst. C.E. *Locomotives*, by Sir F. J. BRAMWELL, F.R.S. M. Inst. C.E. With 228 Woodcuts. 8vo. 21s.

Gwilt's Encyclopædia of
Architecture, with above 1,600 Woodcuts. Revised and extended by W. PAPWORTH. 8vo. 52s. 6d.

Lathes and Turning, Simple, Mechanical, and Ornamental.
By W. H. NORTHCOTT. Second Edition, with 338 Illustrations. 8vo. 18s.

Industrial Chemistry;
a Manual for Manufacturers and for Colleges or Technical Schools; a Translation of PAYEN's *Précis de Chimie Industrielle*. Edited by B. H. PAUL. With 698 Woodcuts. Medium 8vo. 42s.

The British Navy: its
Strength, Resources, and Administration. By Sir T. BRASSEY, K.C.B. M.P. M.A. In 6 vols. 8vo. with numerous Illustrations. VOL. I. 10s. 6d. VOLS. II. & III. 3s. 6d. each.

A Treatise on Mills and
Millwork. By the late Sir W. FAIRBAIRN, Bart. C.E. Fourth Edition, with 18 Plates and 333 Woodcuts. 1 vol. 8vo. 25s.

Useful Information for
Engineers. By the late Sir W. FAIRBAIRN, Bart. C.E. With many Plates and Woodcuts. 3 vols. crown 8vo. 31s. 6d.

Hints on Household
Taste in Furniture, Upholstery, and other Details. By C. L. EASTLAKE. Fourth Edition, with 100 Illustrations. Square crown 8vo. 14s.

Handbook of Practical
Telegraphy. By R. S. CULLEY, Memb. Inst. C.E. Seventh Edition. Plates & Woodcuts. 8vo. 16s.

The Marine Steam Engine;
a Treatise for the use of Engineering Students and Officers of the Royal Navy. By RICHARD SENNETT, Chief Engineer, Royal Navy. With 244 Illustrations. 8vo. 21s.

A Treatise on the Steam
Engine, in its various applications to Mines, Mills, Steam Navigation, Railways and Agriculture. By J. BOURNE, C.E. With Portrait, 37 Plates, and 546 Woodcuts. 4to. 42s.

Bourne's Catechism of the Steam Engine, in its various Applications. Fcp. 8vo. Woodcuts, 6s.

Bourne's Recent Improvements in the Steam Engine. Fcp. 8vo. Woodcuts, 6s.

Bourne's Handbook of the Steam Engine, a Key to the Author's Catechism of the Steam Engine. Fcp. 8vo. Woodcuts, 9s.

Bourne's Examples of Steam and Gas Engines of the most recent Approved Types as employed in Mines, Factories, Steam Navigation, Railways and Agriculture. With 54 Plates & 356 Woodcuts. 4to. 70s.

Ure's Dictionary of Arts, Manufactures, and Mines. Seventh Edition, re-written and enlarged by R. HUNT, F.R.S. With 2,604 Woodcuts. 4 vols. medium 8vo. £7. 7s.

Kerl's Practical Treatise on Metallurgy. Adapted from the last German Edition by W. CROOKES, F.R.S. &c. and E. RÖHRIG, Ph.D. 3 vols. 8vo. with 625 Woodcuts, £4. 19s.

Cresy's Encyclopædia of Civil Engineering, Historical, Theoretical, and Practical. With above 3,000 Woodcuts, 8vo. 25s.

Ville on Artificial Manures, their Chemical Selection and Scientific Application to Agriculture. Translated and edited by W. CROOKES, F.R.S. With 31 Plates. 8vo. 21s.

Mitchell's Manual of Practical Assaying. Fifth Edition, revised, with the Recent Discoveries incorporated, by W. CROOKES, F.R.S. Crown 8vo. Woodcuts, 31s. 6d.

The Art of Perfumery, and the Methods of Obtaining the Odours of Plants; with Instructions for the Manufacture of Perfumes &c. By G. W. S. PIESSE, Ph.D. F.C.S. Fourth Edition, with 96 Woodcuts. Square crown 8vo. 21s.

Loudon's Encyclopædia of Gardening; the Theory and Practice of Horticulture, Floriculture, Arboriculture & Landscape Gardening. With 1,000 Woodcuts. 8vo. 21s.

Loudon's Encyclopædia of Agriculture; the Laying-out, Improvement, and Management of Landed Property; the Cultivation and Economy of the Productions of Agriculture. With 1,100 Woodcuts. 8vo. 21s.

RELIGIOUS and MORAL WORKS.

An Introduction to the Study of the New Testament, Critical, Exegetical, and Theological. By the Rev. S. DAVIDSON, D.D. LL.D. Revised Edition. 2 vols. 8vo. 30s.

History of the Papacy During the Reformation. By M. CREIGHTON, M.A. VOL. I. the Great Schism—the Council of Constance, 1378-1418. VOL. II. the Council of Basel—the Papal Restoration, 1418-1464. 2 vols. 8vo. 32s.

A History of the Church of England; Pre-Reformation Period. By the Rev. T. P. BOULTBEE. LL.D. 8vo. 15s.

Sketch of the History of the Church of England to the Revolution of 1688. By T. V. SHORT, D.D. Crown 8vo. 7s. 6d.

The English Church in the Eighteenth Century. By the Rev. C. J. ABBEY, and the Rev. J. H. OVERTON. 2 vols. 8vo. 36s.

An Exposition of the 39 Articles, Historical and Doctrinal. By E. H. BROWNE, D.D. Bishop of Winchester. Twelfth Edition. 8vo. 16s.

A Commentary on the 39 Articles, forming an Introduction to the Theology of the Church of England. By the Rev. T. P. BOULTBEE, LL.D. New Edition. Crown 8vo. 6s.

Sermons preached most-ly in the Chapel of Rugby School by the late T. ARNOLD, D.D. 6 vols. crown 8vo. 30s. or separately, 5s. each.

Dr. Arnold's Miscellaneous Works, 8vo. 7s. 6d.

Historical Lectures on the Life of Our Lord Jesus Christ. By C. J. ELLICOTT, D.D. 8vo. 12s.

The Eclipse of Faith ; or a Visit to a Religious Sceptic. By HENRY ROGERS. Fcp. 8vo. 5s.

Defence of the Eclipse of Faith. By H. ROGERS. Fcp. 8vo. 3s. 6d.

Nature, the Utility of Religion, and Theism. Three Essays by JOHN STUART MILL. 8vo. 10s. 6d.

A Critical and Grammatical Commentary on St. Paul's Epistles. By C. J. ELLICOTT, D.D. 8vo. Galatians, 8s. 6d. Ephesians, 8s. 6d. Pastoral Epistles, 10s. 6d. Philippians, Colossians, & Philemon, 10s. 6d. Thessalonians, 7s. 6d.

The Life and Letters of St. Paul. By ALFRED DEWES, M.A. LL.D. D.D. Vicar of St. Augustine's Pendlebury. With 4 Maps. 8vo. 7s. 6d.

Conybeare & Howson's Life and Epistles of St. Paul. Three Editions, copiously illustrated.

Library Edition, with all the Original Illustrations, Maps, Landscapes on Steel, Woodcuts, &c. 2 vols. 4to. 42s.

Intermediate Edition, with a Selection of Maps, Plates, and Woodcuts. 2 vols. square crown 8vo. 21s.

Student's Edition, revised and condensed, with 46 Illustrations and Maps. 1 vol. crown 8vo. 7s. 6d.

Smith's Voyage & Shipwreck of St. Paul ; with Dissertations on the Life and Writings of St. Luke, and the Ships and Navigation of the Ancients. Fourth Edition, with numerous Illustrations. Crown 8vo. 7s. 6d.

A Handbook to the Bible, or, Guide to the Study of the Holy Scriptures derived from Ancient Monuments and Modern Exploration. By F. R. CONDER, and Lieut. C. R. CONDER, R.E. Third Edition, Maps. Post 8vo. 7s. 6d.

Bible Studies. By M. M. KALISCH, Ph.D. PART I. *The Prophecies of Balaam.* 8vo. 10s. 6d. PART II. *The Book of Jonah.* 8vo. price 10s. 6d.

Historical and Critical Commentary on the Old Testament ; with a New Translation. By M. M. KALISCH, Ph.D. Vol. I. Genesis, 8vo. 18s. or adapted for the General Reader, 12s. Vol. II. Exodus, 15s. or adapted for the General Reader, 12s. Vol. III. Leviticus, Part I. 15s. or adapted for the General Reader, 8s. Vol. IV. Leviticus, Part II. 15s. or adapted for the General Reader, 8s.

The Four Gospels in Greek, with Greek-English Lexicon. By JOHN T. WHITE, D.D. Oxon. Square 32mo. 5s.

Ewald's History of Israel. Translated from the German by J. E. CARPENTER, M.A. with Preface by R. MARTINEAU, M.A. 5 vols. 8vo. 63s. VOL. VI. *Christ and His Time,* price 16s. and VOL. VII. *The Apostolic Age,* in the press, translated by J. F. SMITH.

Ewald's Antiquities of Israel. Translated from the German by H. S. SOLLY, M.A. 8vo. 12s. 6d.

The New Man and the Eternal Life ; Notes on the Reiterated Amens of the Son of God. By A. JUKES. Crown 8vo. 6s.

The Types of Genesis, briefly considered as revealing the Development of Human Nature. By A. JUKES. Crown 8vo. 7s. 6d.

The Second Death and the Restitution of all Things ; with some Preliminary Remarks on the Nature and Inspiration of Holy Scripture By A. JUKES. Crown 8vo. 3s. 6d.

Supernatural Religion ; an Inquiry into the Reality of Divine Revelation. Complete Edition, thoroughly revised. 3 vols. 8vo. 36s.

Lectures on the Origin and Growth of Religion, as illustrated by the Religions of India. By F. MAX MÜLLER, M.A. Crown 8vo. price 7s. 6d.

Introduction to the Science of Religion, Four Lectures delivered at the Royal Institution; with Notes and Illustrations on Vedic Literature, Polynesian Mythology, the Sacred Books of the East, &c. By F. MAX MÜLLER, M.A. Cr. 8vo. 7s. 6d.

The Gospel for the Nineteenth Century. Fourth Edition. 8vo. price 10s. 6d.

Christ our Ideal, an Argument from Analogy. By the same Author. 8vo. 8s. 6d.

The Temporal Mission of the Holy Ghost; or, Reason and Revelation. By H. E. MANNING, D.D. Cardinal-Archbishop. Third Edition. Crown 8vo. 8s. 6d.

Passing Thoughts on Religion. By Miss SEWELL. Fcp. 8vo. price 3s. 6d.

Preparation for the Holy Communion; the Devotions chiefly from the works of Jeremy Taylor. By Miss SEWELL. 32mo. 3s.

Private Devotions for Young Persons. Compiled by Miss SEWELL. 18mo. 2s.

Bishop Jeremy Taylor's Entire Works; with Life by Bishop Heber. Revised and corrected by the Rev. C. P. EDEN. 10 vols. £5. 5s.

The Psalms of David; a new Metrical English Translation of the Hebrew Psalter or Book of Praises. By WILLIAM DIGBY SEYMOUR, Q.C. LL.D. Crown 8vo. 7s. 6d.

The Wife's Manual; or Prayers, Thoughts, and Songs on Several Occasions of a Matron's Life. By the late W. CALVERT, Minor Canon of St. Paul's. Printed and ornamented in the style of *Queen Elizabeth's Prayer Book.* Crown 8vo. 6s.

Hymns of Praise and Prayer. Corrected and edited by Rev. JOHN MARTINEAU, LL.D. Crown 8vo. 4s. 6d. 32mo. 1s. 6d.

Spiritual Songs for the Sundays and Holidays throughout the Year. By J. S. B. MONSELL, LL.D. Fcp. 8vo. 5s. 18mo. 2s.

Christ the Consoler; a Book of Comfort for the Sick. By ELLICE HOPKINS. Second Edition. Fcp. 8vo. 2s. 6d.

Lyra Germanica; Hymns translated from the German by Miss C. WINKWORTH. Fcp. 8vo. 5s.

Hours of Thought on Sacred Things; Two Volumes of Sermons. By JAMES MARTINEAU, D.D. LL.D. 2 vols. crown 8vo. 7s. 6d. each.

Endeavours after the Christian Life; Discourses. By JAMES MARTINEAU, D.D. LL.D. Fifth Edition. Crown 8vo. 7s. 6d.

The Pentateuch & Book of Joshua Critically Examined. By J. W. COLENSO, D.D. Bishop of Natal. Crown 8vo. 6s.

Elements of Morality, In Easy Lessons for Home and School Teaching. By Mrs. CHARLES BRAY. Crown 8vo. 2s. 6d.

TRAVELS, VOYAGES, &c.

Three in Norway. By TWO of THEM. With a Map and 59 Illustrations on Wood from Sketches by the Authors. Crown 8vo. 6s.

Some Impressions of the United States. By E. A. FREEMAN, D.C.L. LL.D. Crown 8vo. price 6s.

Sunshine and Storm in
the East, or Cruises to Cyprus and Constantinople. By Lady BRASSEY. Cheaper Edition, with 2 Maps and 114 Illustrations engraved on Wood. Cr. 8vo. 7s. 6d.

A Voyage in the 'Sun-
beam,' our Home on the Ocean for Eleven Months. By Lady BRASSEY. Cheaper Edition, with Map and 65 Wood Engravings. Crown 8vo. 7s. 6d. School Edition, fcp. 2s. Popular Edition, 4to. 6d.

Eight Years in Ceylon.
By Sir SAMUEL W. BAKER, M.A. Crown 8vo. Woodcuts, 7s. 6d.

The Rifle and the Hound
in Ceylon. By Sir SAMUEL W. BAKER, M.A. Crown 8vo. Woodcuts, 7s. 6d.

Sacred Palmlands ; or,
the Journal of a Spring Tour in Egypt and the Holy Land. By A. G. WELD. Crown 8vo. 7s. 6d.

Wintering in the Ri-
viera ; with Notes of Travel in Italy and France, and Practical Hints to Travellers. By W. MILLER. With 12 Illustrations. Post 8vo. 7s. 6d.

San Remo and the Wes-
tern Riviera, climatically and medically considered. By A. HILL HASSALL, M.D. Map and Woodcuts. Crown 8vo. 10s. 6d.

Himalayan and Sub-
Himalayan Districts of British India, their Climate, Medical Topography, and Disease Distribution. By F. N. MACNAMARA, M.D. With Map and Fever Chart. 8vo. 21s.

The Alpine Club Map of
Switzerland, with parts of the Neighbouring Countries, on the scale of Four Miles to an Inch. Edited by R. C. NICHOLS, F.R.G.S. 4 Sheets in Portfolio, 42s. coloured, or 34s. uncoloured.

Enlarged Alpine Club Map of
the Swiss and Italian Alps, on the Scale of 3 English Statute Miles to 1 Inch, in 8 Sheets, price 1s. 6d. each.

The Alpine Guide. By
JOHN BALL, M.R.I.A. Post 8vo. with Maps and other Illustrations :—

The Eastern Alps, 10s. 6d.

Central Alps, including all
the Oberland District, 7s. 6d.

Western Alps, including
Mont Blanc, Monte Rosa, Zermatt, &c. Price 6s. 6d.

On Alpine Travelling and
the Geology of the Alps. Price 1s. Either of the Three Volumes or Parts of the 'Alpine Guide' may be had with this Introduction prefixed, 1s. extra.

WORKS of FICTION.

Arden, a Novel. By A.
MARY F. ROBINSON. 2 vols. crown 8vo. 12s.

Hester, a Novel. By Mrs.
HOPE. 2 vols. crown 8vo.
[*In the press.*

In the Olden Time. By
the Author of 'Mademoiselle Mori.' 2 vols. crown 8vo. 12s.

In Trust ; the Story of a
Lady and her Lover. By Mrs. OLIPHANT. Crown 8vo. 6s.

Novels and Tales. By the
EARL of BEACONSFIELD, K.G. The Cabinet Edition. Eleven Volumes, crown 8vo. 6s. each.

The Hughenden Edition
of the Novels and Tales of the Earl of Beaconsfield, K.G. from Vivian Grey to Endymion. With 2 Portraits & 11 Vignettes. Eleven Volumes, crown 8vo. 42s.

The Novels and Tales of
the Earl of Beaconsfield, K.G. Modern Novelist's Library Edition, complete in 11 vols. crown 8vo. 22s. boards, or 27s. 6d. cloth.

Novels and Tales by the

Earl of Beaconsfield, K.G. Modern Novelist's Library Edition, complete in Eleven Volumes, crown 8vo. cloth extra, with gilt edges, 33*s*.

Messer Agnolo's House-

hold, a Cinque-Cento Florentine Story. By LEADER SCOTT. Crown 8vo. 6*s*.

Whispers from Fairy-

land. By Lord BRABOURNE. With 9 Illustrations. Crown 8vo. 3*s*. 6*d*.

Higgledy-Piggledy. By

Lord BRABOURNE. With 9 Illustrations. Crown 8vo. 3*s*. 6*d*.

Stories and Tales. By

ELIZABETH M. SEWELL. Cabinet Edition, in Eleven Volumes, crown 8vo. 3*s*. 6*d*. each, in cloth extra, with gilt edges:—

    Amy Herbert. Gertrude.
    The Earl's Daughter.
    The Experience of Life.
    A Glimpse of the World.
    Cleve Hall. Ivors.
    Katharine Ashton.
    Margaret Percival.
Lancton Parsonage. Ursula.

The Modern Novelist's

Library. Each work complete in itself, price 2*s*. boards, or 2*s*. 6*d*. cloth :—

By the Earl of BEACONSFIELD, K.G.

Endymion.

Lothair.	Henrietta Temple.
Coningsby.	Contarini Fleming, &c.
Sybil.	Alroy, Ixion, &c.
Tancred.	The Young Duke, &c.
Venetia.	Vivian Grey, &c.

By ANTHONY TROLLOPE.

Barchester Towers.
The Warden.

By Major WHYTE-MELVILLE.

Digby Grand.	Good for Nothing.
General Bounce.	Holmby House.
Kate Coventry.	The Interpreter.
The Gladiators.	Queen's Maries.

By Various Writers.

The Atelier du Lys.
Atherston Priory.
The Burgomaster's Family.
Elsa and her Vulture.
Mademoiselle Mori.
The Six Sisters of the Valleys.
Unawares.

POETRY and THE DRAMA.

Poetical Works of Jean

Ingelow. New Edition, reprinted, with Additional Matter, from the 23rd and 6th Editions of the two volumes respectively; with 2 Vignettes. 2 vols. fcp. 8vo. 12*s*.

Faust. From the German

of GOETHE. By T. E. WEBB, LL.D. Reg. Prof. of Laws & Public Orator in the Univ. of Dublin. 8vo. 12*s*. 6*d*.

Goethe's Faust. A New

Translation, chiefly in Blank Verse; with a complete Introduction and copious Notes. By JAMES ADEY BIRDS, B.A. F.G.S. Large crown 8vo. 12*s*. 6*d*.

Goethe's Faust. The Ger-

man Text, with an English Introduction and Notes for Students. By ALBERT M. SELSS, M.A. Ph.D. Crown 8vo. 5*s*.

Lays of Ancient Rome;

with Ivry and the Armada. By LORD MACAULAY.

CABINET EDITION, post 8vo. 3*s*. 6*d*.
CHEAP EDITION, fcp. 8vo. 1*s*. sewed; 1*s*. 6*d*. cloth; 2*s*. 6*d*. cloth extra with gilt edges.

Lord Macaulay's Lays of

Ancient Rome, with Ivry and the Armada. With 41 Wood Engravings by G. Pearson from Original Drawings by J. R. Weguelin. Crown 8vo. 6*s*.

Festus, a Poem. By

PHILIP JAMES BAILEY. 10th Edition, enlarged & revised. Crown 8vo. 12*s*. 6*d*.

The Poems of Virgil trans-

lated into English Prose. By JOHN CONINGTON, M.A. Crown 8vo. 9*s*.

The Iliad of Homer, Homometrically translated by C. B. CAYLEY. 8vo. 12s. 6d.

Bowdler's Family Shakspeare. Genuine Edition, in 1 vol. medium 8vo. large type, with 36 Woodcuts, 14s. or in 6 vols. fcp. 8vo. 21s.

The Æneid of Virgil. Translated into English Verse. By J. CONINGTON, M.A. Crown 8vo. 9s.

Southey's Poetical Works, with the Author's last Corrections and Additions. Medium 8vo. with Portrait, 14s.

RURAL SPORTS, HORSE and CATTLE MANAGEMENT, &c.

William Howitt's Visits to Remarkable Places, Old Halls, Battle-Fields, Scenes illustrative of Striking Passages in English History and Poetry. New Edition, with 80 Illustrations engraved on Wood. Crown 8vo. 7s. 6d.

Dixon's Rural Bird Life; Essays on Ornithology, with Instructions for Preserving Objects relating to that Science. With 44 Woodcuts. Crown 8vo. 5s.

A Book on Angling; or, Treatise on the Art of Fishing in every branch; including full Illustrated Lists of Salmon Flies. By FRANCIS FRANCIS. Post 8vo. Portrait and Plates, 15s.

Wilcocks's Sea-Fisherman: comprising the Chief Methods of Hook and Line Fishing, a glance at Nets, and remarks on Boats and Boating. Post 8vo. Woodcuts, 12s. 6d.

The Fly-Fisher's Entomology. By ALFRED RONALDS. With 20 Coloured Plates. 8vo. 14s.

The Dead Shot, or Sportsman's Complete Guide; a Treatise on the Use of the Gun, with Lessons in the Art of Shooting Game of All Kinds, and Wild-Fowl, also Pigeon-Shooting, and Dog-Breaking. By MARKSMAN. Fifth Edition, with 13 Illustrations. Crown 8vo. 10s. 6d.

Horses and Roads; or, How to Keep a Horse Sound on his Legs. By FREE-LANCE. Second Edition. Crown 8vo. 6s.

Horses and Riding. By GEORGE NEVILE, M.A. With 31 Illustrations. Crown 8vo. 6s.

Horses and Stables. By Major-General Sir F. FITZWYGRAM, Bart. Second Edition, revised and enlarged; with 39 pages of Illustrations containing very numerous Figures. 8vo. 10s. 6d.

Youatt on the Horse. Revised and enlarged by W. WATSON, M.R.C.V.S. 8vo. Woodcuts, 7s. 6d.

Youatt's Work on the Dog. Revised and enlarged. 8vo. Woodcuts, 6s.

The Dog in Health and Disease. By STONEHENGE. Third Edition, with 78 Wood Engravings. Square crown 8vo. 7s. 6d.

The Greyhound. By STONEHENGE. Revised Edition, with 25 Portraits of Greyhounds, &c. Square crown 8vo. 15s.

A Treatise on the Diseases of the Ox; being a Manual of Bovine Pathology specially adapted for the use of Veterinary Practitioners and Students. By J. H. STEEL, M.R.C.V.S. F.Z.S. With 2 Plates and 116 Woodcuts. 8vo. 15s.

Stables and Stable Fittings. By W. MILES. Imp. 8vo. with 13 Plates, 15*s.*

The Horse's Foot, and How to keep it Sound. By W. MILES. Imp. 8vo. Woodcuts, 12*s. 6d.*

A Plain Treatise on Horse-shoeing. By W. MILES. Post 8vo. Woodcuts, 2*s. 6d.*

Remarks on Horses' Teeth, addressed to Purchasers. By W. MILES. Post 8vo. 1*s. 6d.*

WORKS of UTILITY and GENERAL INFORMATION.

Maunder's Biographical Treasury. Reconstructed, revised, and brought down to the year 1882, by W. L. R. CATES. Fcp. 8vo. 6*s.*

Maunder's Treasury of Natural History; or, Popular Dictionary of Zoology. Fcp. 8vo. with 900 Woodcuts, 6*s.*

Maunder's Treasury of Geography, Physical, Historical, Descriptive, and Political. With 7 Maps and 16 Plates. Fcp. 8vo. 6*s.*

Maunder's Historical Treasury; Outlines of Universal History, Separate Histories of all Nations. Revised by the Rev. Sir G. W. Cox, Bart. M.A. Fcp. 8vo. 6*s.*

Maunder's Treasury of Knowledge and Library of Reference; comprising an English Dictionary and Grammar, Universal Gazetteer, Classical Dictionary, Chronology, Law Dictionary, &c. Fcp. 8vo. 6*s.*

Maunder's Scientific and Literary Treasury; a Popular Encyclopædia of Science, Literature, and Art. Fcp. 8vo. 6*s.*

The Treasury of Botany, or Popular Dictionary of the Vegetable Kingdom. Edited by J. LINDLEY, F.R.S. and T. MOORE, F.L.S. With 274 Woodcuts and 20 Steel Plates. Two Parts, fcp. 8vo. 12*s.*

The Treasury of Bible Knowledge; a Dictionary of the Books, Persons, Places, and Events, of which mention is made in Holy Scripture. By Rev. J. AYRE, M.A. Maps, Plates, and Woodcuts. Fcp. 8vo. 6*s.*

Black's Practical Treatise on Brewing; with Formulæ for Public Brewers and Instructions for Private Families. 8vo. 10*s. 6d.*

The Theory of the Modern Scientific Game of Whist. By W. POLE, F.R.S. Thirteenth Edition. Fcp. 8vo. 2*s. 6d.*

The Correct Card; or, How to Play at Whist; a Whist Catechism. By Major A. CAMPBELL-WALKER, F.R.G.S. Seventh Thousand. Fcp. 8vo. 2*s. 6d.*

The Cabinet Lawyer; a Popular Digest of the Laws of England, Civil, Criminal, and Constitutional. Twenty-Fifth Edition. Fcp. 8vo. 9*s.*

Chess Openings. By F. W. LONGMAN, Balliol College, Oxford. New Edition. Fcp. 8vo. 2*s. 6d.*

Pewtner's Comprehensive Specifier; a Guide to the Practical Specification of every kind of Building-Artificer's Work. Edited by W. YOUNG. Crown 8vo. 6*s.*

Cookery and Housekeeping; a Manual of Domestic Economy for Large and Small Families. By Mrs. HENRY REEVE. Third Edition, with 8 Coloured Plates and 37 Woodcuts. Crown 8vo. 7*s. 6d.*

Modern Cookery for Private Families, reduced to a System of Easy Practice in a Series of carefully-tested Receipts. By ELIZA ACTON. With upwards of 150 Woodcuts. Fcp. 8vo. 4*s. 6d.*

Food and Home Cookery.

A Course of Instruction in Practical Cookery and Cleaning, for Children in Elementary Schools. By Mrs. BUCKTON. Crown 8vo. Woodcuts, 2s. 6d.

A Dictionary of Medicine.

Including General Pathology, General Therapeutics, Hygiene, and the Diseases peculiar to Women and Children. By Various Writers. Edited by R. QUAIN, M.D. F.R.S. &c. With 138 Woodcuts. Medium 8vo. 31s. 6d. cloth, or 40s. half-russia ; to be had also in 2 vols. 34s. cloth.

Bull's Hints to Mothers

on the Management of their Health during the Period of Pregnancy and in the Lying-in Room. Fcp. 8vo. 1s. 6d.

Bull on the Maternal

Management of Children in Health and Disease. Fcp. 8vo. 1s. 6d.

American Farming and

Food. By FINLAY DUN. Crown 8vo. 10s. 6d.

The Farm Valuer. By

JOHN SCOTT. Crown 8vo. 5s.

Rents and Purchases; or,

the Valuation of Landed Property, Woods, Minerals, Buildings, &c. By JOHN SCOTT. Crown 8vo. 6s.

Economic Studies. By

the late WALTER BAGEHOT, M.A. Edited by R. H. HUTTON. 8vo. 10s. 6d.

Health in the House;

Lectures on Elementary Physiology in its Application to the Daily Wants of Man and Animals. By Mrs. BUCKTON. Crown 8vo. Woodcuts, 2s.

Economics for Beginners

By H. D. MACLEOD, M.A. Small crown 8vo. 2s. 6d.

The Elements of Economics.

By H. D. MACLEOD, M.A. In 2 vols. VOL. I. crown 8vo. 7s. 6d.

The Elements of Banking.

By H. D. MACLEOD, M.A. Fourth Edition. Crown 8vo. 5s.

The Theory and Practice

of Banking. By H. D. MACLEOD, M.A. 2 vols. 8vo. 26s.

The Patentee's Manual;

a Treatise on the Law and Practice of Letters Patent, for the use of Patentees and Inventors. By J. JOHNSON and J. H. JOHNSON. Fourth Edition, enlarged. 8vo. price 10s. 6d.

Willich's Popular Tables

Arranged in a New Form, giving Information &c. equally adapted for the Office and the Library. 9th Edition, edited by M. MARRIOTT. Crown 8vo. 10s.

INDEX.